Lionel Zetter has been in
for more than forty years
childhood was spent trave
and then Strategic Studies at Sussex University, where, like
many before and since, he was approached to join MI6.

Lionel has been a special adviser and a policy fellow at
the Cabinet Office. His political life has included being
an election agent and an elected local councillor. As a
parliamentary candidate in the 2005 general election he
fought Edmonton, but Edmonton fought back…

He has won multiple professional awards and has headed
up three communications industry trade bodies. He has
written books on political campaigning and lobbying, but
this is his first novel.

He is a martial artist, and a failed restaurateur. Lionel is
married with three children and lives in north London.

For Claire

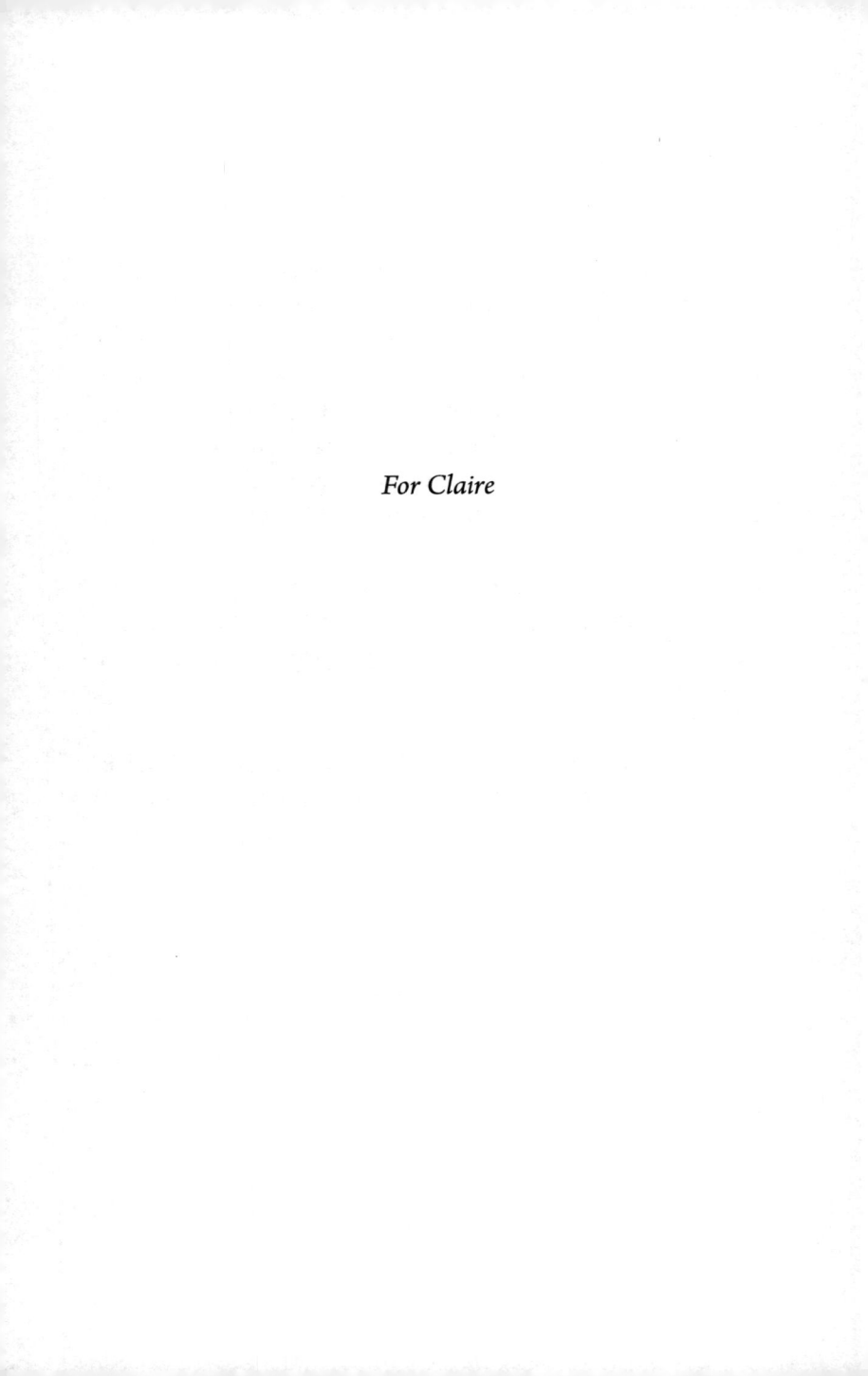

THE LOBBYIST

LIONEL ZETTER

NINE
ELMS
BOOKS

The Lobbyist
First published in 2025 by
Nine Elms Books
Unit 1g, Clapham North Arts Centre
26–32 Voltaire Road
London SW4 6DH

Email: info@nineelmsbooks.co.uk
www.nineelmsbooks.co.uk

Hardback ISBN: 978-1-910533-82-6
Paperback ISBN: 978-1-910533-83-3
eBook ISBN: 978-1-910533-84-0

Copyright © Lionel Zetter
Protected by copyright under the terms of the International Copyright Union. The rights of Lionel Zetter to be identified as the author of this work have been asserted by him in accordance with the Copyright, Designs and Patents Act, 1988. All rights reserved.

This book is sold under the condition that no part of it may be reproduced, copied, stored in a retrieval system or transmitted in any form or by any means, electronic, mechanical, photocopying, recording or otherwise without prior permission of the author.

This is a work of fiction. The names, characters, places, events, and incidents are fictional or used in a fictitious manner. Any resemblance to real people or events is coincidental.

Page design and typesetting: Alan Cooper Design
Cover design: Blacksheep Design
Cover photo reference: © Shutterstock & Depositphotos
Author photo: Panikos Hajistilly
Printed in the UK by CPI Antony Rowe

ACKNOWLEDGEMENTS

Many people helped me with this book, and some will have to remain unacknowledged.

My first thanks have to go to my publisher, Anthony Weldon, for taking a chance on a first-time novelist, if not a first time author. Close behind are my two editors, Simon Rae and Sam Alexander – both far better wordsmiths than I will ever be.

I also need to thank veteran soldier and author Harry Bucknall, who made the initial introduction. He is the epitome of 'hail fellow well met', and his many adventures are well worth reading about.

I want to thank two fellow aspiring authors, Katherine Sykes and Adrian Wheeler. They have been unfailingly supportive, and we have shared some of the frustrations of trying to get into print.

Also Jenny Sharkey, who seems to know everything, and Malcolm Tyndall, who seems to know everybody. And two close friends, Peter Haslam and Nicola Venning, who have helped to widen my horizons.

And I do have to thank you, PJ, and you, Ian. I see you, though others may not.

Finally to my wife Claire – without her love and support I would have achieved nothing.

PROLOGUE

KOLYMA, RUSSIA

If the Russian people are ever to be truly free, the Lubyanka, like the Bastille before it, will have to be stormed. And then razed to the ground.

For more than a century, the inhabitants of the imposing building on Dzerzhinsky Square have brutalised the opponents of whichever regime rules from within the crenelated walls of the Kremlin. With time and practice, generations of torturers have perfected their gruesome craft, and become world leaders in the art of inflicting suffering. Physical, sexual, psychological, or pharmacological torture. Whatever is required, whatever works.

The Lubyanka's interrogators drew on all their experience and expertise in their efforts to break one particular prisoner. When torturing their own, professional pride required that extra energy be put into securing a confession.

The prisoner was fastened by leather straps to a heavy iron chair resembling those used to electrocute the inmates on death row in America. One eye was purple, puffed up and closed. His lips were swollen and bloodied, and there were gaps in his teeth. His torso was streaked with blood, and covered in a patchwork of multi-coloured bruises. All of his finger and toenails had been wrenched out, leaving inflamed and infected tips. His scrotum was grotesquely swollen, with angry red marks where the electrodes had been attached.

Yet after weeks of sleep deprivation, near starvation, beatings, electric shocks, and the expert administration of mind-bending and tongue-loosening drugs, no confession had been obtained.

Despite this rare failure on the part of the in-house team, the prisoner was sentenced to 15 years of correctional labour in a secret trial that lasted less than an hour. He became a "58er", sentenced under Article 58 of the criminal code for anti-state activities.

The harshest of punishments are reserved for those who have been inside the system and are then adjudged to have betrayed it. The prisoner, who had fought hard and spied diligently for his country, and who had given up his birth name for the trade name Ivan Ivanov, was to serve out his sentence in the remotest gulag in Russia. He would be consigned to the region of Kolyma, in the furthest corner of the far east, where temperatures regularly sink to minus 40 degrees Celsius.

The prisoner formerly known as Ivanov was crammed into a railway cattle truck with scores of others. There was no heating, and no seating. The captives emptied their bladders and voided their bowels where they stood, cheek by jowl, or buttock by groin. Fortunately, since they were only fed slop once a day, little of substance passed through their systems.

Once a week the train stopped and the doors were flung open by screaming guards, accompanied by frenzied barking dogs. The prisoners were not permitted to disembark. The purpose of these stops was to throw corpses onto the trackside. There they lay unburied, fodder for the packs of steppe wolves that patrolled the railway in the certain knowledge that they would feast.

As the old, the weak and the ill succumbed more room became available in the carriage. Prisoners had space to sit down, and, eventually, take turns to lie down. One corner of the carriage, by silent agreement, became the designated latrine. The comparative comfort of the freed-up space was offset by the plummeting temperatures. There were fewer bodies to warm the carriage, and the train's eastward journey was taking it into ever colder climes.

By the time the train reached its final destination, five weeks after setting out, almost half of the passengers had died. Of the remainder, those considered unfit for labour were either whipped or dragged to a defunct quarry, ordered to kneel on the edge and despatched with a single bullet to the back of the head. Their corpses were tipped into the void. The whole process was designed to weed out those too weak to work.

Their arrival at the gold fields of Kolyma, in the Siberian district of Dal'stroi, completed their transition from human to *zek*. They became nameless, numbered, sub-humans. Machines made of meat and muscle, destined to be worked to death scratching for gold buried beneath the snow-covered hills and frozen valleys.

Between their 14 hour shifts they were housed in unheated huts, with bare bunks to sleep on and a single thin blanket to conserve what warmth their bodies could muster. Night-time was when the fights broke out. When the stabbings occurred. When the gang rapes were orchestrated. Some prisoners regarded this form of physical contact as the last expression of their humanity.

The *zek* once known as Ivanov received particularly harsh treatment. The *storozhi* – guards – expressed their contempt for his supposed treachery towards the *Rodina* – the motherland – frequently and forcefully. The inmates loathed him for his previous life as a secret policeman.

He survived it all. The numbing cold, which induced the frostbite that claimed two of his fingers and three of his toes. The remorseless pressure to dig three thigh-deep holes a day in the rock-hard permafrost. The *balanda* soya and fish-head soup, with minimal nutritional value. The torture at the hands of the *storozhi*, designed to extract a confession he continued to withhold. The attacks by the *vory* – criminal convicts – with crudely fashioned blades, which left his back and chest striped with scars, and a jagged crater in his right shoulder. Under this regime his once robust frame became skeletal, and his hair – head and body – fell out. Yet he survived.

He survived because his upbringing in the Caucasus Mountains had inured him to the cold. He survived because his training had taught him how to fight. Most of all he survived because he believed that one day he would get the chance to avenge himself on the Englishman who had framed him, who had made him out to be a traitor, and who had caused him to be consigned to this hell on earth. In the land of his birth, feuds and vendettas were passed down the generations. He was determined to exact his own revenge in his own lifetime.

As fresh intakes of *zeki* succumbed to the conditions, he continued to survive. He inherited the top bunk in the corner farthest from the door, the warmest and safest berth. He earned the respect of his fellow *zeki*, and in time even that of the *vory* and the *storozhi*. His ability to outlive successive cohorts of fresh inmates earned him a nickname, born of that same grudging respect, and tinged with the fear he instilled in them.

He became Tarakan – the cockroach. The creature that could survive anything.

LIONEL ZETTER

CHAPTER ONE

MILLBANK, WESTMINSTER

Millbank Tower has long loomed over Westminster. It was never called a "monstrous carbuncle" by a former Prince of Wales, though it probably should have been.

The thirty-storey building stands on the site of a prison, where convicts were once held before being transported to Australia. Now it houses an array of quangos, head-hunters, and PR companies, who value its iconic status and strategic location marginally more than they resent the unreliable lifts and eccentric plumbing. The edifice creaks and groans in the wind, as though desperate to belch out the many secrets its steel and glass walls have absorbed over the decades.

The views from the higher floors of the Tower are spectacular. Occupants can look directly down onto Thames House, home of MI5, and across the river to its sister service MI6, in the yellow slab and green-glass concoction at Vauxhall Cross. More importantly, the building provides panoramic views of the neo-Gothic extravaganza that is the Palace of Westminster.

The offices of Beaufort Public Affairs occupied the whole of the 29th floor. It had been decided that, rather than hire a smart restaurant, grand museum or trendy art gallery, that the traditional general election party should be held here once again. For the last few elections the office had been the scene of wild celebrations, as the Conservative Party secured successive victories. Nobody expected a reprise. The Tories were destined for a punishment beating: the only question was... how bad would it be?

Despite the inevitable defeat of the party he had supported since university, consultancy owner Damian Beaufort could not be seen to skimp on the canapés: sushi for the fashionable and health conscious; mini fish and chips and cocktail sausages for those with more traditional tastes. The champagne was Pol Roger – though not vintage. Tequila cocktails, mojitos and even mocktails would be served, as well as limitless bottles of Asahi premium Japanese lager.

The party started at 8.00pm, so that guests could knock back a few drinks before the climax of the evening – the 10.00pm exit poll. As the countdown to the announcement drew near, the room fell silent.

All faces turned to the giant screen that had been hired for the occasion. After the News at Ten bongs, the successor to the Dimbleby dynasty paused, read the slip of paper someone had placed in front of him and passed the death sentence on the Conservative government.

'Our exit poll indicates,' he intoned, 'that the Labour Party has won with a majority of nearly 200. Labour has won with a clear majority, and will therefore form the next government.'

The room erupted in a mixture of groans and cheers. Beaufort caught the eye of Jennifer Bishop, his Labour-supporting fellow director, across the room. She smiled encouragingly, but, despite his brain's instructions, his face refused to adopt a neutral expression. The incompetence of the Conservative administration, and the ineptitude of the party's election campaign, would almost certainly cost him his business.

As a fusillade of champagne corks popped, Beaufort decided he wouldn't try and dampen the celebrations. Over the next few hours, scrolling banner headlines and talking heads chronicled the ousting of scores of Conservative MPs, many of them his friends.

As the drinks flowed, the behaviour deteriorated. Cleaners had to busy themselves with mops and buckets. Queues formed outside the toilets, pressed into service not just for their designated function, but also as venues for shagging and snorting – celebratory or compensatory, according to political leanings.

Inevitably some Labour supporters came up to Beaufort to gloat. Having ruthlessly exploited his connections with the Conservative Party for years, he and his consultancy were dangerously exposed by the change of regime. The air was thick with schadenfreude.

Beaufort put up with the sneering and sarcastic comments, but when the gloating turned to finger prodding, he signalled for security to intervene. As with the refreshments, Beaufort had not skimped in this department. He fancied he could handle most situations himself, but it was never a good look for a host to be laying out his own guests.

For appearances sake, and as a visual deterrent, he had hired two large bouncers to man the door. They were both shaven headed, six feet plus, and well over twenty stone. Experience had taught him to hire two additional security personnel who could blend in and circulate amongst the guests, with a view to pre-empting any disturbances. One, Jean-Pierre, was a former lieutenant with the French Foreign Legion; a tall man, not particularly broad, but calm, polite and hard as nails. He used his height to scan the room for potential flashpoints.

The real star of the security team was Sabina, a slim woman of average height in her early thirties. She was fashionably but practically dressed in a designer tracksuit. Her hairstyle was also contemporary, with one side of her head partially shaved. She was a former captain in the Royal Military Police, and had served four years in the Met's Royal and Specialist Protection Squad.

Frank Hughes, the fleshy trade union general secretary who had reluctantly hired Beaufort's agency during the Tory years, came over with the obvious intention of crowing.

'So, you lot are fucked then,' was his opening gambit.

'We've had a good run,' Beaufort conceded, 'and now it's time to hand over the baton.'

'No, not just fucked. *Royally* fucked. Finished.'

Beaufort shrugged, disinclined to argue. The trade unionist would not let it go. He started yelling in his face, spraying spittle and flecks of half-eaten sausage. Then the finger jabbing became more aggressive. Beaufort looked around for assistance and Sabina read his signal. She came and stood next to Hughes, placing a gentle hand on his shoulder.

'Why don't you and I get some fresh air?' she suggested.

Hughes paused his assault on Beaufort and turned to her, weighing up whether this was a come-on, or some kind of intervention. Deciding it was the latter, he went in hard.

'Why don't you just fuck off, sugar tits?' he replied, mistaking her for one of Beaufort's PR colleagues.

Without any change of expression Sabina tightened her grip on the trade unionist's brachial plexus nerve centre, and used her other hand to lock his elbow joint. Lifting him very slightly, she increased the pressure and whispered in his ear.

'You and I are going to walk quietly out of here. You can look like you've pulled. Or, if you prefer, I will put you on the floor and make you look like a total twat in front of all your mates. Nod if you understand.'

Hughes nodded, and together they walked slowly to the door. Sabina ejected him and instructed the doormen not to readmit him. On her way back to Beaufort she snagged a mocktail from a passing waiter.

'You OK?' she asked.

'Been better. That was impressive. Aikido?'

'Jiu-jitsu. Listen, Beaufort, I imagine that you're pretty good at whatever the hell it is that you do, but I know for absolute sure that I am the best at what I do.'

With a half-smile she turned and resumed her patrol of the increasingly fractious guests.

Spotting Beaufort alone, James Barratt, the owner of a giant software company that had donated millions of pounds to the Tories, came up to him. Barratt leaned forward sheepishly, and half-whispered in Beaufort's ear.

'Damian, we're grateful for all you've done over the

years, but I am afraid we're going to have to terminate your contract. This lot' – indicating the triumphant Labour supporters who were starting to dominate the room – 'are in for at least two terms, and we need an agency with stronger Labour links.'

Beaufort swallowed hard and said:

'Look, James, we're going to pivot. Re-position ourselves. I have friends in the new set-up, and we'll recruit more Labour people. We can still do the business for you.'

The client raised an eyebrow.

'I can give you three months, for old time's sake. But that's all the board will stand for. We have to be pragmatic, and that means switching horses.'

*

As the sun rose and shone hazily through the office's full-length windows the clear-up operation began. The life-size cardboard cut-outs of the party leaders had been defaced, obscenely so in the case of the former Tory prime minister, and were only good for the recycling bin. Empty bottles were piled high in every available receptacle, and a few comatose bodies were still strewn around the reception area.

The two bouncers were tasked with reviving passed-out guests and escorting them to the lifts. A new shift of cleaners arrived to continue clearing up the mess. Beaufort's staffers, those who had not pulled or passed out, began the laborious task of putting the office back together again.

Sabina approached Beaufort. She appeared as fresh as the moment she had arrived in the Tower, over twelve hours previously. She looked him over, took in the dark good looks and athletic build and, deciding that despite being drunk he made the cut, suggested:

'Shall we? I still have a few more moves to show you.'

'I bet you do. Are you still on the clock?'

'Call it a sympathy shag,' she replied, taking him by the arm and escorting him from the room.

*

Beaufort was woken just after midday by the sound of Sabina emerging from the bathroom of his hotel room.

She was naked. Magnificently so. Breasts high and firm, pubic hair neatly trimmed, but not shaved. Her body was un-inked too, apart from the crest of the Royal Military Police high up on her left arm.

Beaufort was usually proud of his body, but on this occasion he decided to remain cocooned in the twisted sheet.

'How about one for the road?' he ventured.

'That rather implies some previous action,' she replied, picking up an unfurled and unfilled condom from the floor, and flicking it at him. 'It wasn't just the Tories that flopped last night.'

She slipped into her thong, tracksuit and trainers, blew him a consolatory kiss, and walked out of the room.

Beaufort swore, switched the TV to Sky News, and began to come to terms with life under a Labour government.

He was fucked every which way, except the pleasurable one.

CHAPTER TWO

EUROPEAN QUARTER, BRUSSELS

Two hundred miles and one time zone away, another party had taken place.

There had been a growing sense of anticipation as the night wore on, and, as the results of the exit poll were revealed, shouts of exultation echoed around the oak panelled rooms of European Commission President Philippe Morand. His suite of offices was on the ninth floor of the Berlaymont, the monolith that dominated the Brussels skyline and housed the thousands of Eurocrats responsible for driving the "European Project".

President Morand was deep in conversation with Edward Gore-Ewing CBE, former permanent representative of the United Kingdom to the European Union – or UKREP for short. As such he should have been the eyes and ears of the British Foreign Office in Brussels. Instead, during his final year in post he had fed the British team a concoction of misleading half-truths and outright lies, whilst passing on top-level intelligence on the UK's negotiating positions to the EU side.

Once Brexit had finally been enacted, Gore-Ewing had immediately resigned from the Foreign Office and applied for French citizenship, which he qualified for via his French wife, a minor aristocrat from the Aquitaine region.

Their children went to the European School of Bruxelles-Argenteuil. They spoke French at home and holidayed in a run-down chateau near Poitiers, where his wife's ancestors had lived for centuries. Gore-Ewing loved his wife, and all things French. He was an ardent Francophile, from the tips of his Savile-Row-tailored shoulders, to the toes of his Jermyn-Street-clad feet.

Shortly after resigning from the British Foreign Office, Gore-Ewing was recruited into the European Commission secretariat. He was put in charge of *Division Bretagne*, within Directorate General NEAR, responsible for European neighbourhood and enlargement negotiations. There he recruited like-minded colleagues from the UKREP office, including his former deputy, Murdo McIntosh. He too had wasted no time after Brexit, resigning from the British diplomatic service and becoming a Belgian citizen.

Once the exit poll sealing the Conservative's fate had been resoundingly cheered, the champagne was opened, and the conversations became even more animated. Murdo McIntosh approached his boss and summed up the situation with typical Glaswegian bluntness.

'Well, that's those Tory tossers screwed then. There'll be a few more Scots in the Labour cabinet – maybe they can teach the Sassenachs some sense.'

Gore-Ewing nodded.

'Perhaps. But it's vital we keep up the pressure, even with the change of cast.'

The host of the event, Commission President Philippe Morand, approached Gore-Ewing, and McIntosh made the wise decision to leave them to it. Morand had been the French ambassador to the Court of St. James during the long and bruising Brexit negotiations, and had never forgiven the British for the numerous slights visited upon him during that fraught period.

'Well Édouard,' – he pronounced the name in the French way but spoke in impeccable English – 'hopefully that's the Conservatives out for a decade. What do you think our chances are of luring the British back into our warm embrace?'

Gore-Ewing considered his answer carefully.

'Labour specifically ruled out re-joining the EU during their campaign. But the British economy is in trouble, and we can make sure things only get worse in the short term. Then, when they really do start to run out of money, we can throw them a lifeline.'

'I agree,' Morand replied, 'but we must be careful not to incite the toxic British press unnecessarily. Speaking of which, I have had to take the photograph off my "glory wall". The one of us all in Oxford. Some nosy British journalist came to interview me about Brexit. He spotted it and recognised us both, and Clem Clark, and of course our lovely actress friend Yvette de Beaufort. He asked me who the fourth man was. I said I could not remember. I don't think he believed me.'

'Good God, Philippe, why did you have it on display? The last thing we need is questions about *him*. Have you destroyed it?'

'Yes, I put it through the shredder and burned the

residue. It is completely destroyed.'

'Good. Enquiries about him could really damage us. And our cause.'

A waiter was patiently waiting to top up their glasses. He was listening intently, but they ignored him completely. Waiters, to members of the elite, are simply not worthy of notice.

*

Once the guests and staff had departed, President Morand locked his office door and opened the wall-safe hidden behind a self-portrait of contemporary Belgian artist Luc Tymans. He took out a framed photograph, and his eyes misted as he studied it.

A small group dressed in evening wear posed for the camera ahead of one of Oxford's infamous May balls. A 17th-century college could be seen in the background. The photograph had obviously been taken by a professional because, although old, the monochrome details were sharp.

Morand and Gore-Ewing were both recognisable as younger versions of the distinguished late-middle-aged men they had become, although the latter had since lost the long lustrous locks – his signature look back in his student days.

Clem Clark, the new British prime minister, had changed surprisingly little in the intervening 40 years. He still looked like a rom-com actor playing the part of a dynamic middle-aged politician. Still had the trademark lopsided grin.

The woman in an off-the-shoulder ballgown was seated on a bench, with the men arranged behind her. She was stunningly beautiful, with jet-black hair and milk-white skin. Her pale eyes flirted with the camera, which loved her even before she was famous.

The fifth figure, the fourth man in the group, had a proprietary hand resting on the woman's bare shoulder. Unlike the others, he wore a hat, a fedora, and his face was turned slightly away, as though seeking out the shelter of the shadow that the hat provided.

*

The James Joyce is an Irish pub located in a quiet street on the fringes of the Brussels European Quarter. It is crowded and noisy most evenings, and its clientele range from off-duty Eurocrats to tourists seeking the legendary Irish *craic*.

Alvariz had signalled his desire for a meeting with a post on X showing a picture of his bookcase and the innocent message: 'quiet night in'. James Joyce's masterpiece *Ulysses*, in the Spanish translation, was on the top shelf, the twentieth book from the left. This system conveyed to his British case officer the proposed venue, the degree of urgency and the precise timing. When one of his followers, a young woman who worked in a local bookshop, "liked" his post, the meeting was confirmed.

The RV was urgent because the more Antton Alvariz replayed the conversation he had overheard between Morand and Gore-Ewing in his head, the more convinced he was that it was important. That was why he had placed the signal book on the top shelf.

Alvariz entered the pub a few minutes after 20.00 hours Central European Standard Time.

Standing beside an upturned sherry barrel that served as a table was the first secretary at the British Embassy, a youngish man, nondescript in appearance, but somehow obviously English. In theory he oversaw consular and visa matters at the embassy. In practice he was the MI6 station chief, operating under diplomatic cover. Two half-litre glasses of creamy black Guinness stood untouched in front of him.

Alvariz knew him as Mr Taylor, but was aware that might not be his real name. Taylor had gone along with the request for an urgent meeting because he knew that the Basque had unparalleled access to conversations and rumours within the Berlaymont building.

Alvariz was primarily motivated by the monthly stipend that the British intelligence agency paid into his numbered Geneva bank account. However, he was also driven by a strong feeling of resentment about the way that the Spanish and French governments, and the European Union, had colluded to deprive his people of the independence that their heritage and history warranted.

'*Topa*,' said the Englishman, toasting Alvariz in his native language and taking a mouthful of his stout. 'I hear you have something important for us?'

'Yes,' replied Alvariz in his heavily accented English. 'I believe so. Last night Morand had a party to celebrate the fall of your British Conservative government. All his people was there, but also Edward Gore-Ewing from *Division Bretagne*. They speak quietly, but I hear them as I wait to serve them more champagne. They speak English, so they think I do not understand. Everybody ignores waiters – we are invisible. Morand talked about a photograph that a British journalist sees on his wall. This journalist asks him about it. It had the two of them, and your politician

Clem Clark, but also the famous English actress with a French name – Yvette de Beaufort. Also, a mystery man. The journalist wants to know about the woman, and the mystery man. Morand tells him about the actress, but lies about the other man – says he had forgotten.'

'And why do you think that was important?'

'Because Gore-Ewing was very worried. Because Morand lied to the journalist. Because Morand has taken down the photograph, and he tells Gore-Ewing that he destroys it.'

The Englishman nodded, and took another gulp of his Guinness. He then reached into the inside pocket of his raincoat and pulled out a folded copy of the *L'Echo* newspaper, within which a number of high-value Euro notes had been folded.

'Good work,' he said, sliding the newspaper across the barrel head. 'A bonus. If you hear anything else about this photograph, there'll be more.'

Taylor took a final swig of his stout, nodded to the Basque, then turned and worked his way out of the crowded pub and onto the rainy street.

He headed back towards his apartment via a circuitous route, using standard counter surveillance techniques. He occasionally stopped to look in curved or angled shop windows, and twice he doubled back on himself, as if lost. As he slowly progressed through the incessant rain, he reflected how much he disliked Brussels – the city itself, but also the institutions it hosted.

CHAPTER THREE

DZERZHINSKY SQUARE, MOSCOW

Fifteen hundred miles and three time zones east of London, a Russian man was watching the UK general election results with considerable satisfaction.

He sat behind an oak leather-topped desk with intricate gold inlay. Its carved legs depicted the two-headed eagles of the Romanov dynasty. The desk had belonged to the last Tsar, Nicholas II, and had been looted from the Winter Palace in St Petersburg.

The man wore the uniform of a colonel general in the Russian Federal Security Service, the FSB. His hairless head shone by the light of the flat-screen television mounted on the wall. The tattoo of a *tarakan*, a cockroach, was partially visible above the collar of his jacket. He had lived up to his soubriquet. He had survived. Not only survived – he had been rehabilitated, promoted, and now ruled over Russia's vast security apparatus.

His extraordinary eyes, which caused unease in most, fear in many, rarely left the screen. Not as he lit another cigarette, and only briefly as he poured another celebratory shot of *Stolichnaya Elit* vodka with his three-fingered right hand.

After the Great Kremlin Palace, the Lubyanka is the best-known building in Moscow. Most of those incarcerated in its cellars beg for mercy in the end. They are prepared to betray everything and anyone – on television or in open court – to put an end to their agony. Some even beg for death, and if they are lucky receive a simple bullet to the back of the head. Others face a ragged firing squad in the Lubyanka inner courtyard, often requiring a coup de grâce to finish them off.

Bodies are stored in a basement mortuary until they make up a lorry load. They are then trucked to a disused salt mine in the Ural mountains and dumped down the main shaft, to join the thousands already rotting there. Generations of rats feast on their corpses and grow fat on the endless supply of rotting human flesh.

The executed are perhaps the fortunate ones. Others are allotted a slow death in the chain of gulags, which have accommodated the opponents of successive regimes over the centuries. They form a vast escape-proof prison, fashioned by nature, where Tarakan himself had been sent to live a non-life, and die a slow death.

Once the fate of the British Conservative government had been confirmed, the uniformed man rose and limped across the fine Persian rug, his missing toes impeding his stride. He gazed through the window that overlooked Dzerzhinsky Square.

An empty plinth marked the spot where a statue of Felix Dzerzhinsky – the legendary founder of the Cheka, which became NKVD, which then became the KGB, which had finally become the FSB – once stood. The statue of "Iron Felix", as he was known to all Russians, had been removed during the glasnost spasm under Gorbachev, but remained in safekeeping in the Lubyanka's courtyard. One day it would be restored to its rightful place.

Tarakan turned and shuffled to the wall, where three large, framed maps were hanging. The first depicted Russia at the height of the Romanov Empire. The second showed an even larger Russia, at its zenith during the glory days of the Soviet Union. The third depicted the Russia of today, still the largest country in the world, but shrunken, and shorn of its vital buffer states.

Finally, he moved to a low table, upon which sat a Fabergé Imperial chess set. He moved the white pawn to E4. The King's Gambit. A new game had begun. It would end, he believed, in the destruction of his opposite number in the British Secret Intelligence Service, Admiral Sir Richard Carr. The only man ever to have outmanoeuvred him.

CHAPTER FOUR

DOWNING STREET, WHITEHALL

The sun was shining as Clem Clark stepped out of the armoured Jaguar just inside the gates of Downing Street. He was alone, apart from his close protection officers. Unlike almost all of his predecessors he had never married and did not have a partner – although he had enjoyed a string of both secret and well-publicised affairs.

A pre-selected crowd of about two hundred awaited him, corralled onto the wide pavements behind metal barriers, enthusiastically cheering and waving miniature Union Jacks. They were all apparatchiks from Labour HQ, newly-elected MPs, or activists who had distinguished themselves during the general election campaign.

The new prime minister worked his way along the serried rows, shaking hands with some, embracing a few, and accepting the occasional kiss on the cheek from those brave enough to lean over the barriers.

After about fifteen minutes of working the crowd, Clem Clark arrived outside the world's most famous front door. There he turned to face the massed ranks of the

British and foreign media, with their batteries of lenses and microphones. Pausing briefly, flashing his famous lopsided grin, and waving his right hand for the cameras, he delivered the now mandatory doorstep speech.

'I want to thank all those who voted for me, and to reassure all those who did not. My mission now is to reunite the country, and mend those institutions that the last government left broken. I will work hard to repair our economy, which has been shattered. I will work closely with our European friends and neighbours to rebuild some of the bridges that Brexit destroyed. My colleagues and I will strive to fashion a nation that looks to the future, instead of being fixated with the past. Thank you.'

Ignoring the barrage of questions that followed his statement, the prime minister turned, and, on cue, the famous black door opened. Then, very much not on cue, the Number 10 cat shot out, heading off to its hunting ground in St James's Park. The new PM paused momentarily to let it pass, and the journalists laughed. So much for clockwork choreography.

The entire Downing Street staff were gathered inside, minus the political appointees who had left with the previous prime minister. They lined the entrance foyer, staircase and landing to clap him in – just as, a few hours earlier, they had clapped out his predecessor.

The official Number 10 photographer was the only one allowed inside the building. He worked hard to capture the moment, for posterity and the next day's newspapers. Cabinet Secretary Sir Adrian Walker was standing in the middle of the entrance hall. He shook hands with the prime minister, and then guided him down the short corridor to the Cabinet Room, with its long coffin-shaped table.

Sir Adrian ushered the new prime minister towards the only chair with arms. It was halfway down the table on the left, in front of the Adam's fireplace, and below the portrait of Sir Robert Walpole, the first prime minister. The cabinet secretary took the seat immediately opposite, where the chancellor of the exchequer would normally sit during cabinet meetings.

'Well, Prime Minister, that was the fun bit. You must be tired, but there are some things that cannot wait. This,' he slid across a thin buff folder with a single red diagonal stripe on its cover, 'is our analysis of your manifesto, and how best to seek to fulfil its pledges. And this,' he slid across a thicker buff folder with two red diagonal stripes, 'is our assessment of the main issues that face your government and the country.'

Clem Clark was indeed exhausted, but up until now he had kept going, buoyed by the surge of adrenaline that his unexpectedly emphatic victory had given him.

'Thank you, Sir Adrian, but I can't look at this now. Apart from anything else, I need to fill these empty chairs and appoint a cabinet.'

'Of course, Prime Minister. I'll put these folders in tonight's red box, along with the Treasury's assessment of the costs of meeting your manifesto commitments. But there are two things that you must do right now, without delay and without interruption. Before we see to them, please let me have your mobile telephone.'

'My mobile? I can't give you my phone. It's my lifeline. Everything comes through my phone.'

'And that is the point, Prime Minister. It will have been

hacked by the Russians and the Chinese. And probably the Americans too. We'll issue you with a secure scrambled device.'

Clem Clark sighed and handed over his mobile.

'Don't you need the PIN code?'

Sir Adrian smiled indulgently.

The prime minister thought it best to ignore this.

'So what are these things I need to do *right now*?'

'First, you must write the Letters of Last Resort to the captains of the four nuclear submarines that carry our strategic nuclear deterrent. You have to instruct them what to do in the event that you – and the entire nation – are obliterated in a nuclear strike.'

Chastened, the PM nodded.

'And the second thing?'

The cabinet secretary withdrew a slim envelope with an old-fashioned red wax seal from his jacket breast pocket.

'You need to read this, Prime Minister. It is from your predecessor.'

*

Clem Clark waited until Sir Adrian had left the room before breaking the seal and opening the heavy cream envelope. It was addressed simply to 'The Prime Minister'.

Inside was a single sheet of Number 10 notepaper, a short letter handwritten with a traditional fountain pen.

As Clem Clark read it, his own hands began to shake.

Dear Prime Minister,

We have had our differences, but it now falls to you to take up the burden of the most important office in the nation we both love so dearly.

It is my sad duty to inform you that Trident, our independent strategic nuclear deterrent, is not worthy of that name. Yes, we build the boats, and yes, we assemble the nuclear warheads. However, the Americans build the missiles, and they can, at will, either divert or destroy them mid-flight. Therefore our nuclear deterrent is not, in truth, independent.

No doubt you will be as shocked as I was when I learned of this situation. We have wasted tens of billions of pounds on a weapons system that we do not truly control. When I learnt of this deplorable state of affairs from my own predecessor I instructed Chief Scientific Officer Sir Paul Trent to assemble a small team at the Atomic Weapons Establishment Aldermaston to develop a method of circumventing the American's override. I suggest that you meet with Sir Paul, and continue with this programme.

Good luck with it all. God knows I have tried my best. Please destroy this letter immediately after reading it.

Yours ever,

The signature at the bottom was an illegible scrawl, but Clem Clark recognised it from dozens of official documents. His hands still shaking, he placed the letter in the grate of the fireplace, and used the lighter that facilitated his secret smoking habit to set it ablaze.

He then pressed the bell to the right of the fireplace, unsure whom, if anybody, it would summon. When his assistant private secretary appeared, the prime minister snapped at him:

'Bring me a pot of coffee, a bottle of single malt and a jug of water. Now. And then I don't want to be disturbed.'

The APS nodded, and swiftly withdrew, wondering whether to add a pearl-handled revolver to the prime minister's list of requirements.

*

Clem Clark drank two cups of coffee and then poured himself three fingers of whisky, adding just a splash of water. The shaking subsided as he began to write, on Downing Street headed notepaper, to the captain of each of the four Vanguard class submarines.

Dear Captain,

If you are reading this our great nation has been destroyed, presumably by a hypersonic nuclear missile strike, against which we have minimal defence.

Our country has been left defenceless by decades of penny pinching short-sightedness on the part of successive governments. But we have, at least, preserved our nuclear deterrent. That which has failed to deter, must now be used to destroy, in the hope of reinforcing deterrence in the future.

Your missiles have been programmed to retaliate against the CRINK states – China, Russia, Iran, North Korea. At this point it is impossible for me to say where the attack that caused you to open this letter originated. However, if the source of our destruction is identified to your satisfaction, use your judgement to strike back with full force. Our great nation cannot be obliterated without there being a price to pay.

Finally, you will have to find a berth after the apocalypse. Do not trust the Americans. They are our allies, but they are not our friends. Please consult your crew and your conscience, but I recommend that you sail to Australia or New Zealand, and try to keep the flame of the ideals that created Great Britain alive. Let this be our enduring gift to the world.

If, as seems likely, the King and the Prince of Wales have perished, I suggest that you swear your allegiance to the King's younger son, whose decision to reside in California will likely have saved his life.

On behalf of the British people, I thank you for your service, and for your acceptance of this heavy responsibility.

God speed.
Clem Clark

The prime minister set down his pen, reached for the whisky, and silently wept.

CHAPTER FIVE

MILLBANK, WESTMINSTER

After Sabina had left Beaufort got up, took a quick shower and brushed his teeth with the hotel's complimentary hygiene kit. He got dressed in the same clothes he had been wearing for the previous 24 hours, and prepared to face a new day. And a new era.

The young woman on reception gave him a knowing smile as he checked out. If only, he thought.

Arriving back at the office he found the furniture back in place, but the office virtually deserted. The receptionist greeted him brightly enough, but the handful of account executives on the open plan office floor studiously avoided his gaze.

'Where's Jennifer?' he asked her.

'In your office. She's been waiting for you.'

Forcing his features into a semblance of a smile Beaufort strode into his office, to find Jennifer seated on the sofa with a mobile phone clamped to her ear.

'Gotta go,' she told the person on the other end of the line.

'Hi Damian, how are you feeling?'

'Never better. I like a challenge. And this is one hell of a challenge. We're going to have to let a few Tory execs go, and cast the net wide for Labour people. A few of the clients will walk. Most will give us some leeway. But I really am going to need you Jen. We need to look at your remuneration package.'

She cleared her throat and shifted uncomfortably before replying.

'Well, here's the thing Damian. I've been offered a post in Number Ten. As a special adviser in the Policy Unit. It's too good an opportunity to pass up. I'm sorry.'

Beaufort felt a surge of resentment. Jennifer had been with him almost from the start, and their relationship had transcended business and become both personal and intimate. The clients rated her. Most of the male ones also secretly lusted after this clever and statuesque young black woman.

'Well, congratulations,' he managed, 'you deserve the opportunity. And let's face it, they're going to need all the help they can get.'

Jennifer rose, gathered up her handbag and laptop, kissed him on the cheek, and left him to sift through the ruins of one of the most successful lobbying consultancies in the country.

*

Sure enough, over the next few weeks, the consultancy began to fall apart.

The loss of Jennifer had been an early blow. She had tried to make up for her departure by arranging meetings at Number Ten for some of Beaufort's clients, but once the "favour bank" had crept into the red these meetings dried up.

One by one Beaufort's senior consultants and account executives left. A fortunate few went to work for the new government; others joined rival agencies untainted by the stench of Toryism that clung to Beaufort. As the staff left, so too did the clients.

Before long Beaufort was left with a skeleton crew of employees and a handful of clients. The staff who remained were either interns taking their first steps into the world of lobbying, or back office staff who focused on research and did not have the people skills to land another job.

The exception was Elizabeth, Beaufort's long-standing PA. She was a woman of great calmness and efficiency, who ran both his business and social diaries. Many, including Beaufort himself, wondered why she stayed.

As for the clients, some stayed out of sympathy, some out of contractual obligation. If the senior, more expensive, staff had not left in large numbers, Beaufort Public Affairs would have been faced with imminent bankruptcy. As it was, the company probably had two months' worth of reserves left.

In an effort to reduce his overheads Beaufort negotiated his way out of his office lease in Westminster and relocated into serviced offices in Holborn. He moved to a small, damp basement flat in Pimlico, and his Porsche was reclaimed by the finance company. Reluctantly he gave up his membership of the RAC Club, where he entertained clients, but also swam and played squash.

Beaufort tried to hold on to his remaining clients by

inviting them to lunch in expensive restaurants, favouring the prestigious Goring in Victoria, or grand Covent Garden eateries such as Rules or Wiltons. The acceptance emails gradually stopped coming in, as clients realised that the cost of these meals were being added to their monthly bills.

In search of political gossip Beaufort went on nightly pub crawls. He would start at the Marquis of Granby, which, despite the party having moved out of Smith Square years ago, remained popular with Tories. He would then move on to the Westminster Arms, frequented by Revival Party MPs and apparatchiks.

At the end of the night he would almost invariably end up in the Red Lion, an old pub with good beer and bad drains situated just behind Parliament's Norman Shaw buildings. Here tourists, journalists, lobbyists, politicians and parliamentary staffers of all parties co-existed in uneasy sweaty proximity.

There was some value in the gossip that Beaufort picked up, and some of it could be traded up for even juicier snippets. The problem was, it was starting to become obvious that Beaufort was going to seed. His Paul Smith suits were crumpled and increasingly threadbare, his Duchamp ties had acquired spots and stains, and his Loake shoes were scuffed and down at heel.

Worse, between the lunches and the evening drinking sessions, and the lack of *dojo* and gym time, his athletic frame now carried a nascent drinker's paunch. His eyes, once clear, bright and discerning, were becoming dull and hooded.

CHAPTER SIX

THAMES HOUSE, LONDON

Dame Sheila Norris, the director general of the Security Service, had been at Oxford with Clem Clark. Not at a fancy college like Balliol or Merton, but Ruskin, the establishment named after the radical socialist John Ruskin. Both had been through the grammar school system, and came from humbler backgrounds than the vast majority of their fellow undergraduates.

Clem had made a pass at her at the time, but she had firmly rebuffed him. She was concentrating on getting the first in Modern History she ultimately achieved. He was determined to bed as many women as he could in his first two years, aiming for a "bonking blue" before focusing on his studies in his final year.

The future prime minister was not offended by her refusal, he simply moved on to his next target. As well as his good looks, he relied on the law of averages to keep his bed-count up. "Don't ask don't get" was his motto, and he asked a great deal.

After university their paths rarely crossed. He became

a successful lawyer, moving in the north London dinner party circuit, before following the well-trodden path into politics. She had received the "tap on the shoulder" while still an undergraduate, and quietly worked her way through the ranks of MI5, becoming director general while Clem Clark was still leader of the opposition.

Whilst climbing the ranks of MI5 Sheila Norris took time off to marry a Treasury civil servant and produce twins, a boy and a girl. Like a certain Conservative prime minister, she managed a "twofer", saving time on the tiresome business of love-making and child-rearing.

Dame Sheila had prevailed on the cabinet secretary to schedule a meeting with the prime minister for the day after his first meeting of the Joint Intelligence Committee. And she had made sure that the meeting would be on her home territory at Thames House, just a few hundred yards from the Palace of Westminster. The Security Service headquarters reflected its occupants: it was squat, dull, low-key, but functional.

As the prime minister was shown into the DG's large but spartan fifth-floor office she rose from behind her desk to greet him. Now that they were alone he had a chance to look over her charcoal trouser suit, spare frame and short iron-grey hair, and wondered why he had ever lusted after her.

They shook hands, and, after a moment's mutual hesitation, kissed awkwardly, continental style.

'Clem, I knew you'd get there in the end, but never anticipated you'd sweep the board in such style. The old Ruskin Marxist Society would be proud of you!'

Clem Clark laughed nervously at the reminder of his

brief youthful flirtation with the hard left.

'Well, I always knew you'd make it to the top of your chosen field, and you beat me to it by a couple of years. To be honest anybody could have defeated the Tories. They were knackered after so long in power, and really scraping the barrel in terms of ministerial appointments. How are you getting on with the home secretary?'

Dame Sheila pursed her thin lips.

'She's fine, as far as she goes, but no match for the foreign secretary. As you know we technically report to her, and MI6 to him, but I'm going to need your help in fighting my corner.'

Clem Clark frowned.

'I did kind of assume we were all on the same side.'

The spy chief snorted derisively.

'Try telling them that. You saw how they behaved at the Joint Intelligence Committee yesterday. They're a bunch of spoiled, snobbish public schoolboys. And they think we're just glorified plods, combining basic counter-intelligence tradecraft with kicking down doors and feeling collars. Just look at our respective HQs. We get a discarded energy ministry, they get a brand new statement building. They should have been left to rot in Century House, along with the ghosts of Philby and Maclean.'

'Surely it can't be that bad, Sheila. Apart from the whole class thing, which I get, what's this really all about?'

The DG paused, and then decided to enlighten the PM.

'Mainly it's about budgets – and of course access to you. But they never forgave us for exposing the Oxford spy ring as Russian agents. In revenge they tried to make out one of my predecessors, Sir Roger Hollis, was a Russian mole –

total nonsense of course.

They then persuaded *your* predecessor as Labour PM to give them intelligence primacy in Northern Ireland, where they licensed British special forces to go around killing people more or less at will. They've always been rogue operators, and under the Admiral they're completely out of control. They need reining in – or even closing down.'

Clem Clark was shocked at the depth of the animosity between the Security Service and the Secret Intelligence Service. He looked for a bright spot.

'What about GCHQ?'

She nodded enthusiastically, before replying.

'They're our saving grace. The bunch of neuro-diverse freaks we have in the "Doughnut" are probably the best cyber-warriors on the planet.'

The PM perked up at this positive response.

'So you have nice things to say about them, Sheila, don't you have any kind words for your sister service?'

Dame Sheila's tried to keep her tone professional, and failed.

'Good words? Do you know what they call *us*?'

The PM said nothing, anticipating he was about to be told.

'They call us Box.'

'Box? I don't understand.'

'When we were set up, in 1909, way before them, we opened a Post Office box called PO Box 500. Loyal citizens could write in to that address and identify traitors and enemy agents. It was simple, but really effective.'

'OK, I can see that's not altogether complimentary. What do you call them?'

The DG smiled thinly.

'They rather grandly call themselves "the Firm", as though they're a branch of the royal family. We call them TSAR.'

'Like the Russian emperors?'

This time her smile was wider.

'No T.S.A.R. – those shits across the river!'

*

From the window of his seventh-floor office in Vauxhall Cross the Admiral stared over to Thames House on the opposite river bank. . He had no idea his MI5 counterpart was at that very moment briefing the new PM against him and his organisation.

He had been appointed following a big clear-out of the upper echelons of MI6 after the agency had failed to anticipate the invasion and partition of Mongolia by Russia and China following the US mid-term elections. This intelligence failure had resulted in the decision to make an external appointment.

Rear Admiral Sir Richard Carr was not a career "securocrat" in the conventional sense. He had previously commanded a Type 42 destroyer, before being posted to Washington as a defence attaché. Success in this posting had led to his appointment as director of Naval Intelligence.

In that capacity he had foreseen the takeover of the Taiwanese Kinmen Islands – just six miles off the shore of mainland China – by a marine division of the People's Liberation Army. Naval Intelligence under the Admiral had been tipped off about the Chinese intention to invade the Kinmens by a young source, born in Hong Kong, and unwillingly conscripted into the PLA. There had been no increase in "chatter" before the invasion, so human intelligence – "HumInt" – had on this occasion triumphed over signals intelligence, or "SigInt".

The Admiral was often regarded as being "old school". He was more than happy for his enemies, at home and abroad, to regard him as a dinosaur, a throwback incapable of grappling with the complicated structure of the modern world's security architecture. By underestimating him, they inadvertently aided him.

On his office wall the Admiral had a framed oil painting of the founder of the Secret Intelligence Service, a Royal Navy commander called Sir Mansfield Cummings. Carr liked to be referred to and addressed as Admiral, but he did not object to being called "C", a tradition dating back to Cummings.

Dame Sheila often employed an alternative "C-word" when discussing her opposite number.

When the Admiral was first appointed he was resented by those MI6 "lifers" who had been unsuccessful in applying for the position. In order to bypass them he had appointed an ambitious young senior field operative to the newly-created post of "Deputy Director, Special Operations".

In appearance – short, stout and bespectacled – Charles Frobisher was the very antithesis of most people's idea of a spy. His background was also unusual for an intelligence operative, his father being an Anglican bishop, and his mother an American from the "Bible Belt" state of Kentucky.

The Admiral and Frobisher both had a strong affinity with the United States. They also believed in the primacy of human intelligence, and regarded MI5 as rivals, rather than partners. In addition, they shared a visceral dislike of the European Union, with its multiple languages, contradictory priorities and conflicting loyalties

Instead, both men favoured the Five Eyes intelligence alliance that had started with the USA and UK after the Second World War, and expanded to include Canada, Australia and New Zealand as the Cold War spread around the globe.

Frobisher had an 11.00am meeting with the Admiral. He arrived in his outer office 10.55am sharp, and stopped to talk to his personal assistant, Ms Danso. She was an efficient young woman of Guyanese heritage who had followed the Admiral from Naval Intelligence.

'What sort of a mood is he in?'

She rolled her eyes.

'He's been like a baboon with haemorrhoids since the Joint Intelligence Committee meeting. You're to go straight in.'

As soon as the door closed behind Frobisher the Admiral launched into a tirade.

'Yesterday we had a four-hour meeting of the JIC. Those bastards at Box have asked for a 20 percent increase in their budget to deal with our home-grown jihadists and knuckle-dragging neo-fascists. They're also pushing for closer co-operation with Europol, the DGSE and the BND.'

'What did the PM say?' asked Frobisher.

'He told them to make formal submissions on both counts at next month's meeting. He didn't push back at all, and neither did the foreign secretary, who's supposed to fight our corner. I don't think he realised that if they do get a budget increase it sure as hell won't come out of GCHQ's slice – it'll come out of ours. And if we start sharing intelligence with the French and the Germans we might as well just blind copy in the FSB.'

Having sat down behind his desk and composed himself, the Admiral asked:

'What's all this about a crash meet in Brussels?'

'Well, sir, we have a good source, a Basque who works in hospitality in the Berlaymont and feeds us grade-A Brexit intelligence. He overheard a conversation between Commissioner Morand and that treacherous snake Edward Gore-Ewing about a photograph. A British journo spotted it and asked about it, and Morand panicked. He and Gore-Ewing then discussed it in front of our man, who they thought didn't understand English, and apparently they were in quite a flap. Morand told Gore-Ewing he'd destroyed it.

We patted the Basque on the back and told him to keep his eyes and ears open. And we're working on options to get hold of a copy of this mysterious photograph.'

The Admiral grunted noncommittally, and then switched topics, as was his habit.

'You know Damian Beaufort, don't you?'

Momentarily thrown by the abrupt change of tack, Frobisher paused before replying.

'Yes of course, sir, we were at school together.'

'What's he like?'

'Clever, brave, and loyal. But also capable of being devious and utterly ruthless. At school he was something of a loner.'

'Seen him recently?'

'No, sir, not for a while. He didn't make the last reunion.

Rumour has it his public affairs business is in trouble.'

The Admiral decided enough time had been wasted in preliminaries and cut to the chase.

'I need you to lure him into our murky little world. He should fit right in. He is a lobbyist, after all – and they're the unfiltered scum of the earth.'

Frobisher paused again before replying.

'Well that should be possible. Just one snag – he's never really liked being told what to do. Can we help his business? I need to be able to offer him something.'

'Oh yes. We need his business shipshape and him grateful, so offer him whatever he needs – within reason.' The Admiral fixed Frobisher with the frosty stare that had terrified many a subordinate and asked: 'Why didn't he fit in at school then?'

'Well sir, he was different, and just a little bit dangerous. He'd been taught martial arts in the school holidays. And he had a temper. When he wanted to, he could really hurt people. He was good looking, even then. The gay boys all fancied him, but he wasn't interested.

He had a famous mother, the actress Yvette de Beaufort, but he didn't appear to have a father. All the other boys had one – or even two or three, what with divorces and so on. So that singled him out. They called him "the bastard" – but never to his face.'

The Admiral considered this, and then issued his orders:

'Well get him on board, and let's put him to the test. We can bankroll him through that Tazmen pervert. Let's get him to organise one of those parliamentary jaunts for the All-Party Parliamentary Group to Tazmenistan. See if we can get the members to the front line, and scare the living crap out of them before we set them up. If we can get something on the chairman, Sir Walter, that would be good. But really we need leverage over Robinson, the foreign secretary's PPS, and Simmonds, who sits on the Intelligence and Security Committee. Let's see what your man is capable of.'

Frobisher nodded, wondering whether Beaufort would be open to the proposal and up to the challenge. As he rose to leave, the Admiral fired one final question at him.

'Is Samantha Ferguson back from New Zealand?'

'Yes, sir, she's been back a week, and has been fully debriefed. She did a great job in Wellington, helping to ensure that the Kiwis stuck with Five Eyes, and steering them towards AUKUS. Now they have a sensible government we don't really need her out there.'

'Good. She can work her magic closer to home. Fix her up with a legend that fits with her movements these past few years, and embed her with Beaufort's consultancy. We need to keep an eye on him, and I have a feeling we're going to need Samantha's skills.'

Frobisher nodded and left, rightly taking the Admiral's words as a dismissal.

CHAPTER SEVEN

CHEQUERS, BUCKINGHAMSHIRE

Despite their historic victory in the general election, and resultant huge majority, things quickly started to go wrong for the newly-elected Labour government. After the briefest of honeymoons, the harsh economic realities soon started to impact on the popularity of the new regime.

During the general election campaign the Labour Party had pledged to stick to Tory spending plans. At the time there had been few protests, as the entire Labour movement had been desperate for power. Now it had been achieved, there was mounting opposition to spending constraints from backbench Labour MPs, party grassroots members, and the trade unions.

The main opposition to the government's policies came not from the decimated Tories, but from within Labour's own ranks. Many of the flood of new MPs swept in on the Labour tsunami had not been expected to win. They had been selected in haste and had not been properly vetted. Many were on the far left of the party, and therefore ideologically opposed to *any* spending constraints, never mind the dreaded "cuts" to public services that were supposed to be the preserve of the hated Tories.

Clem Clark's Chancellor of the Exchequer, who had some experience working in finance, tried to kill two birds with one stone. By clamping down on the privileges of non-doms, and taking away some of the tax breaks enjoyed by private schools, she hoped to both raise revenue, and throw red meat to some of her more left wing colleagues.

To the prime minister's annoyance both policies had backfired, with non-doms fleeing to sunnier climes, and many private schools closing, placing a burden on the state school sector.

Repeated rebellions in the House of Commons, and an austere budget forced on the government by the markets and the Office of Budgetary Responsibility, led to a catastrophic collapse of Labour's standing in public opinion polls. The cabinet did not seem to have any answers, and so the prime minister, deciding to look elsewhere for inspiration, convened an emergency summit.

*

The summit was to be held at Chequers. This mock-Tudor stately home, gifted to the nation by Lord Lee of Fareham, has been the scene of much drama over the years. The last time it was used for an official summit it ended in disaster. The then prime minister's failure to impose a Brexit compromise on her cabinet colleagues had led to the collapse of her government.

In order to avoid a repeat of that catastrophe – and leaks to the press – Clem Clark had decided to keep this gathering small. From within the cabinet he had invited only his chancellor, home secretary, foreign secretary and chief whip.

In view of the failure of his wider cabinet to come up with real solutions to the problems facing the government, Clem Clark had also decided to invite his legendary predecessor, Bill Blythe, who had won three consecutive general election victories before the last extended period of Tory rule. Blythe was encouraged to bring along his fabled spin doctor, Rory Cochrane.

The meeting had been scheduled for 10.00am on a Sunday. It was to be held in the Great Parlour, around the William IV dining table, with Joseph Highmore's portrait of William Pitt looking down on proceedings.

Instructions had been issued to keep the event secret and low key. What that meant, in effect, was no helicopters. As Blythe had bought himself an imposing mansion just down the road from Chequers, that was not an issue.

The PM entered the room five minutes late.

'Apologies everybody. Call from the White House. More long-range missile tests by Pyongyang. Anyway, thanks for coming. I've kept this gathering small, because in government everything seems to bloody well leak. There is no formal agenda as such, but in summary the government's finances are extremely tight, and an expectant electorate – along with our hordes of backbenchers – are looking to us to work miracles. Chancellor, can you outline the financial situation?'

'Thank you, Prime Minister. As you know we didn't anticipate winning on this scale, and in order to convince the voters and reassure the City we felt that we had to promise in the manifesto to stick to Tory spending plans –

and not to raise any of the "big four" main taxes. As a result, we are struggling to fulfil even those modest manifesto commitments we did make. And the markets have made it very plain that if we try to borrow more money, there will be a hefty "moron premium" to pay.'

'Thank you, Chancellor. Home Secretary, can we have your overview?'

'Of course, PM. We inherited a shocking situation from the Tories. Crime clear-up rates are at an all-time low, yet we still have chronic prison overcrowding, and this in turn has led to a succession of riots. What's more, we have been overwhelmed by an armada of small boats packed with illegal migrants. The public are left with the firm impression that we've lost control of our streets, our prisons – and, most catastrophically of all – our borders.'

The prime minister nodded grimly.

'Thank you, Home Secretary. Foreign Secretary, your summary?'

'On the international stage we seem to have lost our USP. We're no longer a bridge between Europe and the United States, and we don't have a "special relationship" with either. We're giving the impression of becoming irrelevant, a small cork bobbing around on turbulent seas.'

'How encouraging. Chief Whip?'

'Thank you, Prime Minister. We won an enormous number of seats in the general election, but the truth is our victory was a mile wide, but only an inch deep. The Tories are no real problem – there aren't enough of them to win any votes, and most of them have gone back to doing what they do best: making money from side-hustles. The problem is within our own party. We can only appoint about a hundred ministers, and that leaves over 300 backbench colleagues with too much time on their hands.

Some of them we can buy off with unpaid PPS roles, others with seats on select committees, or even meaningless trade envoyships, but many of them are becoming unwhippable and ungovernable. I can be pretty certain of winning every vote, but I have no idea of the majority – and that's what the press is fixated on. This isn't 1997, or even 2010 – this time there really isn't any money. This election win is starting to look like the ultimate hospital pass.'

Addressing Bill Blythe and Rory Cochrane, the PM summed up the situation, and the government's predicament.

'So, as you have heard, we have a collapsing criminal justice system, no friends abroad, a rebellious Parliamentary Labour Party, and no money. Our poll ratings have collapsed, and the Tories are just leaving us to it, sub-contracting the job of opposition to our own backbenchers. This is why I've invited you here today. We need a big idea, and we need it fast.'

All eyes turned to Bill Blythe. The former prime minister had a reputation for being able to articulate the wishes and identify the fears of the British voting public.

With his theatrical sense of timing, the former prime minister said nothing. He gazed silently up at the portrait of William Pitt that hung above the decorative fireplace, as though seeking inspiration.

Clem Clark pressed him:

'Bill? Any thoughts? We need something big and bold – and preferably cheap.'

The former prime minister lowered his eyes from the

portrait and ran them around the assembled ministers, before finally turning them on Clem Clark.

'There is one thing I can suggest. It is big, it is bold, and it will cost next to nothing. The question is,' – he gave his successor a quizzical look – 'do you have the balls for it?'

Clem Clark bristled, and shot back:

'I took on the left. I took on the unions. I won the leadership, and I won the general election. Of course I have the balls to make tough decisions. I've proved that, time and time again.'

Blythe nodded, apparently convinced, and continued:

'OK, if you're sure. My Institute has been undertaking extensive polling. Rory will share the results with you.'

A ponytailed tech assistant was summoned to lower the window blinds, bring down a projection screen in front of the fireplace and hook up Cochrane's laptop to a projector.

Cochrane spoke with the authority of someone who had spent decades following – and helping to shape – the ebbs and flows of British public opinion.

'We have been conducting a series of mega-polls, reaching tens of thousands of members of the public. We've also been conducting focus groups in every region of the country. We've asked them a wide variety of questions in order to mask the only one we're really interested in. And the results are unequivocal.'

Clem Clark's patience was wearing thin.

'So what was it, in God's name? What was the question? And what was the answer?'

Cochrane called up a slide with a graph, and replied in the same unhurried tone:

'The question, buried away amongst our decoy ones, was

quite simple. The question was. . .' – he paused for dramatic effect – 'should the UK apply to re-join the European Union?'

The PM, and three holders of the great offices of state, looked stunned. The chief whip choked on his biscuit.

Clem Clark was the first to respond.

'We can't do that! There was a referendum. A clear majority voted to leave.'

Blythe replied calmly.

'We realise that. But that was over a decade ago. And things have not been great since. Rory has some illuminating numbers to share.'

Cochrane pulled up another slide.

'Our polling shows that 68% of all voters would like to re-join the EU. There is a majority for it in every region of the UK. What's more, 71% of all voters now think it was a mistake to leave in the first place.'

The prime minister objected.

'But we can't go through all that again. The referendum was hugely divisive. And the Tory press might just turn those numbers around.'

Blythe looked at Cochrane and nodded for him to deliver the coup de grâce.

Calling up a further slide, he went on:

'With that in mind, we specifically asked those who polled in favour of re-joining if another referendum was necessary.' He paused, building the tension. 'A massive 86% said no, another referendum was not needed.'

The home secretary found her voice.

'But what about the constitutional position? Won't we be accused of ignoring the will of the people?'

Bill Blythe, clearly still irked by the referendum result,

even after all the intervening years, replied forcefully:

'We are a parliamentary democracy. No parliament can bind its successor. It is referendums that are alien to our culture. Even Maggie Thatcher said that.'

Rory Cochrane weighed in:

'Our focus groups back up the opinion polling. Remainers are firm in their desire to re-join. It's the Brexiteers who are flaky, when you push them, when you drill down.'

Bill Blythe stared across at Clem Clark. 'You're looking for bold ideas. You're looking for solutions to your current unpopularity that will cost you nothing. And you're looking for ways to make the Tories actively oppose, thereby reuniting the Parliamentary Labour Party. This ticks every single one of those boxes.'

The PM had one more go at testing his predecessor's argument.

'Brexit has entered the everyday lexicon. It sums up everything the Leavers wanted in one word. We can't combat that with a long-winded Bill title, or even a rational explanation. We need a succinct rebuttal of everything that's encompassed in that single benighted word.'

This time it was Cochrane who replied:

'Obviously, we've thought about that. We've brainstormed it, and focus-grouped it. The counter to Brexit will be "Breturn". When repeated ad infinitum it'll have just as much traction as Brexit, and it sums up the failure of the Leave campaign to deliver on their promises – in one single, memorable, and patriotic word.'

The PM had run out of arguments. He looked across the table at Blythe, considered for a long moment, and then replied:

'OK, let's do it. We will need to draft a short, simple Bill revoking the European Union (Withdrawal Agreement) Act 2020.'

Bill Blythe reached into the folder in front of him, extracted a slim document, and slid it across the table.

'We thought you might say that, so here's one we prepared earlier.'

He grinned his Cheshire cat grin.

CHAPTER EIGHT

HIGHGATE, LONDON

Over the years Beaufort had frequently asked his mother to reveal the identity of his father, and she had always declined to do so. It became obvious to him that the very act of asking the question widened the gulf that had always existed between them.

As a way of getting closer to her world, and perhaps gleaning who his father might be, Beaufort decided to strike up a relationship with his mother's ever-efficient personal assistant. Joan not only managed her demanding employer's schedule, but kept her insulated from the real world, so that the actress could devote her time and energies to the artificial worlds of stage and screen.

Joan had always been polite and superficially friendly towards Beaufort, but – like his mother – she had never really opened up to him. He knew she lived alone in Highgate and decided to invite her for a drink at The Flask, on the pretext that he was visiting a client in the area.

To his surprise Joan readily accepted the invitation and, to his relief, was good company. She thawed as the wine started to take effect, and was clearly attracted to the younger man.

He shared his most scurrilous political gossip, and she in turn regaled him with scandalous tales about actors, producers and directors. Disappointingly, she did not reveal any secrets in relation to her employer.

They were still talking and laughing when closing time was called. Adopting her cougar persona, Joan leaned forward and grabbed Beaufort's knee under the table. She moved her hand up towards his groin and smiled.

'Why don't we take this back to mine? I have an agreeably aged cognac that you can help me with – along with one or two other things that are nicely matured.'

*

Beaufort woke up naked in a double bed to the smell of bacon cooking, and the sound of his mother's PA preparing breakfast in her kitchenette.

His head ached from the wine and cognac, and he felt physically drained from their energetic lovemaking the night before, much of which he could not recall.

Joan had more than food on her mind. Discovering that he was awake, she shed her kimono and pulled back the covers. Massaging him erect, she climbed on top and deftly inserted him.

Then the mobile on the bedside table started vibrating urgently. Pausing in her efforts, Joan picked up the phone, glanced at the caller ID and turned it around to show Beaufort. He saw his mother's name on the screen.

With a wicked smile Joan jammed the still vibrating phone into the point where their bodies joined, simultaneously stimulating his root and her own clitoris.

After a few moments of juddering pleasure she extracted the phone, and returned it to its intended use. Beaufort could hear his mother's voice demanding to know where Joan was and ordering her to report to the film set immediately.

Joan grinned down at Beaufort, and then spoke into the mobile, her voice calm and business-like.

'Yes, of course, Yvette. I am just finishing something off, but I'll come as quickly as I can.'

She hung up, and, laughing at his evident discomfort, began to thrust down hard, before swivelling 180 degrees, presenting him with a rear view, and resuming her efforts.

Beaufort decided it was time to take back control. He grasped Joan's hips, rolled her sideways without disengaging, and hauled them both up into kneeling positions. He now set the rhythm, thrusting energetically and bringing her to a noisy climax, before letting out a low groan of pleasure and finishing himself.

Beaufort dismounted and rolled onto his back. Still panting, Joan reached for a packet of cigarettes on the bedside table. Lighting two, she handed one to Beaufort and lay down next to him. Just then, the smoke alarm started wailing. With a small scream she shot out of the bed and ran naked into the kitchen to switch off the grill.

She returned to bed with a contented smile.

'Perfect timing,' she said, of the smoke alarm.

'Why thank you!' he responded.

They smoked in silence for a few moments, and then Beaufort asked:

'You and my mother get on, do you?'

'Well enough. She is a total diva, of course. And it's very

much a mistress-servant relationship. I'm probably closer to her than anybody, but that's not saying much.'

Beaufort was hurt by the suggestion that he was not the closest person to his mother, despite recognising that it was true.

He asked the question he had been meaning to ask the night before, before the drink and sex had got in the way.

'What about lovers? She's never lacked male admirers.'

'God no. There have been quite a few. Sometimes fellow actors, other times she likes a bit of rough, a scene shifter or a cameraman. The only constant over the years has been Clem Clark. I think that relationship began at university, or shortly afterwards.'

'So he's the love of her life?'

'No, I don't think so. I always get the impression there's somebody else, but not somebody close by. Maybe they're dead, or married, or they moved abroad, but she always seems to be yearning for the one man she can't have.'

'And could that man be my father?'

'I think he might well be.'

*

After a hasty breakfast of burnt bacon and congealed fried eggs, Joan hurried off to attend to her demanding mistress, who had already sent several messages and despatched a car to pick her up.

Beaufort showered and dressed, and then began a leisurely search of Joan's studio flat. He discovered a small selection of sex toys, and a blister pack of Viagra, neither of which had been required during their night-time and morning sessions.

There was a man's razor and a spare toothbrush in the bathroom, and a drawer full of men's clothes, plus some spare rechargeable camera batteries, in the bedroom. Joan obviously had a lover, but apparently not one capable of fully satisfying her.

He then switched his attention to her desk. She had taken her laptop with her, and there were only two drawers to look through.

Bank statements showed that her outgoings exceeded her income, but not by a great deal. Her passport contained visas and stamps for the kind of destinations a PA to an actress would visit – mainly the States, but also Monaco, France, and Morocco. There were a few "artistic" photographs of Joan in suggestive poses, and various stages of undress. He felt himself stirring again at the sight of them.

Pulling the drawers out, Beaufort squatted and examined the undersides. Beneath one was taped a large manila envelope. Careful not to rip it, Beaufort eased open the flap and slid out the contents.

A single photograph. Black and white, slightly blurred, obviously taken through a window with a long lens. It captured his mother in bed, naked, her features screwed up at the moment of climax. On top of her was a thin, bald man, his shoulder muscles knotted with effort.

Beaufort was disturbed, and intrigued. It was impossible to date the photograph, as his mother's face was so contorted. It was also impossible to identify her lover from the rear. He wondered whether Joan was keeping the photograph either to blackmail his mother, or as an insurance policy against being fired.

Having captured the image of the photograph on his

mobile, Beaufort wiped off his fingerprints, carefully slid it back into the envelope, and eased the drawer back into the unit. He let himself out of the flat, feeling slightly guilty, but also pleased with the results of his efforts as a snoop, and as a lover.

He wondered whether a psychiatrist would attribute his lust for the older woman, and his efforts to get closer to his mother, to a deep-seated Oedipus complex.

Sod it, he thought. Joan had got what she wanted, the sex had been fun, and he had at least stripped off one of the many veils that obscured his mother's life.

CHAPTER NINE

KARELIA, RUSSIA

As the Chequers summit started, a very different high level meeting was getting underway fifteen hundred miles east of the English stately home.

The "special military operation" in Ukraine had made the Russian president's favourite holiday retreat, a palatial villa near Sochi, too dangerous to visit. The Ukrainians had constantly buzzed the luxury complex with drones, and even managed to send one crashing into the armoured window of the bedroom where the President normally slept.

When he wanted thinking time, away from the pressures of the Kremlin, the president now retreated to his luxurious dacha in Karelia, near the Finnish border. This was known, implausibly, as the "Fisherman's Hut".

The Ukraine conflict had taken a heavy toll on the president's prestige, and on the resources of his vast, but poor, country. This had, to an extent, been offset by the Sino-Russian invasion and partition of Mongolia, with its enormous tracts of land and almost limitless mineral resources.

The absorption of Mongolia was the most tangible success to date of the CRINK axis, made up of China, Russia, Iran and North Korea. This group of autocratic states had successfully distracted and divided the alliance of Western democracies. As a result, they had failed to respond to the invasion of Mongolia in any meaningful manner, merely imposing easy-to-bypass sanctions.

Although Russia was technically a democracy, governed by a Council of Ministers overseen by the Duma Federal Assembly, in reality the president wielded total power. He trusted only a handful of men, and none of them were members of either the Council or the Assembly.

After more than a quarter of a century in power, the president, known as the *"Malen'kiy Tsar"* – "Little Tsar" – behind his back - was ageing and ill. Like all old men he was in a hurry. He regarded the election of an isolationist president in the United States as his best – and possibly last – chance of establishing his legacy, and elevating himself to the iconic status of the rulers Peter and Catherine, both of whom had been known as "the Great".

The guest list for the unofficial summit at the dacha was select. Lazarev, his long-serving foreign minister. Field Marshal Gazdanov, the head of the armed forces. And Tarakan, the controller of Russia's formidable intelligence agencies.

Unlike meetings at the Kremlin, meetings at the dacha were informal affairs. Instead of a conference table, white leather sofas were arranged around a roaring wood fire. A large marble-topped table was loaded with bottles of premium vodka in ice buckets, silver bowls of caviar and blinis.

The president, instead of his usual two-piece suit, was in jeans and a SKA St Petersburg ice hockey top. The other three men were in chinos and open-necked shirts, the field marshal and foreign minister both looking particularly uncomfortable in this informal garb.

As usual with these gatherings the president began with a tour d'horizon.

'Gentlemen, it is good of you to spare the time. Firstly, congratulations, Field Marshal. The special military operation in Ukraine may have been only a partial success, but the partition of Mongolia was a total triumph. At a stroke we have added 750,000 square kilometres to our land mass, as well as enormous mineral resources. Congratulations also to you, Foreign Minister. Now that the hysteria over Ukraine has died down, and with the withdrawal of the United States from the world stage, we have re-asserted our gravitational pull over many of the former Soviet states. Both NATO and the European Union are in disarray.'

The foreign minister and the field marshal sat back in their sofas, basking in the rare praise from their irascible leader.

Then the president turned his pale and slightly oblique eyes on his spy chief.

'And you, Tarakan, my cockroach, under which particular floorboards have you been scuttling?'

Tarakan had been expecting an inquisition and had a report ready.

'Mr President, we have been active throughout the world, but our focus, as you instructed, has been on Europe and the so-called United Kingdom. I have concentrated on getting our agents positioned at the very highest level of government in both London and Brussels, and we are now in a strong position to action any plan you wish to prioritise.'

The Little Tsar looked unconvinced and, with the vodka starting to take effect, went off on one of his trademark rants.

'The Europeans think we are always the aggressor, but they ignore the fact that we have land borders of more than 22,000 kilometres to defend. And in their arrogance they choose to forget that they stole our buffer states from us!

We are the biggest country in the world, but we only have two assets: mineral resources, and the almost limitless capacity of our people to endure suffering. As long as we keep the price of vodka low, and convince them that we are having successes on the battlefield, they will put up with anything.'

The foreign minister intervened.

'But Mr President, this has always been the case. What has changed?'

The president rose to his feet, smashed his empty vodka glass into the fireplace and shouted.

'China! That is what has changed! They are no longer the younger brother, the junior partner. They are becoming the most powerful nation on earth. In the Pacific, that is America's problem. But to the east, they are our problem.

The time will come when they will not be satisfied with half of Mongolia, and will be emboldened enough to reclaim Siberia. The Ussuri River dispute has been rumbling on since the 1969 war, for fuck's sake. For now, China is our ally, but we must never forget that for three hundred years we suffered under the yoke of the Mongol Asiatic hordes.'

The three men shifted uncomfortably. The set of the president's eyes betrayed his distant Mongol heritage, and it was a subject guaranteed to trigger his volcanic temper.

The field marshal, always nervous in the presence of the Little Tsar, reluctantly decided he had better speak up.

'Mr President, sir, we have stripped our eastern defences by transferring divisions to bolster our forces in the west. We have suffered heavy losses in Ukraine, and Kaliningrad is effectively under siege. How do we balance these commitments? We cannot look west and east at the same time.'

This earned him a withering look from the president. The overweight sweaty man was adept at throwing divisions of poorly trained troops into the meat grinder, but he had no grasp of geopolitical strategy. Many felt he only had a limited grasp of military strategy.

Blanking the field marshal, the president said to the others:

'We balance them by neutralising Europe and removing the threat on our western borders. Make Europe unstable. Either bring the British, our oldest enemy, back within the EU's feeble embrace, or neutralise them. The UK cannot be allowed to remain a bridge between Europe and the America. The Five Eyes alliance must be dismantled. That is your focus. That is your mission.'

Tarakan nodded enthusiastically, and raised his vodka glass.

'My President, this is our time. Democracy is dying. This is the age of the autocrat.'

CHAPTER 10

SOUTHWARK, LONDON

It did not take Frobisher's team long to identify the journalist who had interviewed Morand and noticed the photograph on the Commission president's wall.

Rather than approach the journalist directly, Frobisher went to see his editor, a Fleet Street veteran who was well-disposed towards the security services.

They met in the editor's twentieth-floor corner office at the *Daily Times,* looking out over London Bridge. The editor was a thickset, poorly-shaven, balding Dundonian named Jamie McLeish. He habitually wore red braces to frame his paunch, and would not have looked out of place in the old Fleet Street.

'And what can I do for you this time?' he enquired, with a heavy emphasis on the last two words.

'I need all the photographs your reporter Henry Watkins took when he interviewed Commission President Morand last month.'

'And why do you need them?'

'I can't tell you that. But we would be grateful. We would

owe you one – another credit in the "favour bank".

The editor grunted, turned to his desktop computer and began searching his newspaper's photograph archive. After a few minutes he grunted again, retrieved a memory stick from his drawer and copied a large file.

When the download to the flash drive was complete McLeish held it out to Frobisher and, looking him in the eyes, said:

'Next spook scoop – it's mine, right? If I read something in a rival rag that could have come our way, I will be one very unhappy Jock.'

Frobisher smiled, pocketed the USB and left.

*

Returning to Vauxhall Cross, Frobisher reviewed the contents of the flash drive, and instructed the technical department to enlarge the picture featuring the Commission president's "glory wall".

With the aid of an old-fashioned magnifying glass, he was soon able to identify the most relevant photograph on the wall. He then instructed the techies to enlarge and enhance that particular image, and once they had worked their magic, the features of four men and one woman came into focus.

One look was enough. Frobisher printed out the photograph, picked up the magnifying glass and almost ran along the corridor to the Admiral's office. He rushed past a startled Ms Danso without a word and entered the Admiral's office without knocking. He thrust the photograph and the magnifying glass onto his desk.

The Admiral took one look and, lowering the magnifying

glass, uttered one of his favourite blasphemies.
'God's death. No wonder he took it down.'

CHAPTER 11

VICTORIA TOWER GARDENS, WESTMINSTER

After one particularly heavy late-night session in the Red Lion Beaufort decided to head home on foot to save on the cost of an Uber.

As he was passing the Victoria Tower of the House of Lords, he suddenly felt the urgent need to urinate. Hurrying past the two policemen on duty outside Black Rod's Entrance he took a sharp left into Victoria Tower Gardens, just managing to hold on until he was behind the Burghers of Calais statue.

The relief as he hosed down the plinth of Rodin's masterpiece was almost on a par with that of the surrendering Burghers when they realised they weren't going to be executed by the besieging English after all.

Despite the physical relief Beaufort still felt morose, and he was drawn towards the river. He sat on one of the cast iron benches looking across to Guy's and St Thomas' Hospital, and dozed off.

The sound of grating rusty wheels woke him, and

Beaufort realised he was no longer alone. A homeless man, wrapped in layers of clothes despite the warm weather, had parked a shopping trolley filled with his worldly possessions next to the bench, and sat down to drink a can of Carlsberg Special Brew.

Without a word he offered the can to Beaufort, who accepted the gesture and took a long swig. He handed the can back to the tramp.

'Haven't seen you here before,' was the derelict's opening gambit. 'I come here a lot. It's peaceful, the view is great, and if anything kicks off the coppers are just round the corner.'

'Ur, no, I was just out for a drink with friends and felt like a bit of a sit down on my way home. I do have a home.'

The tramp looked him over and decided to take his word for it.

'Mac,' he announced, holding out a grubby hand. 'I've been living rough for six years. I was a sergeant, Royal Marines, two tours of Afghanistan, and now this.'

'Why? How?' was all Beaufort could think to ask.

'Drink, drugs, PTSD. Like hundreds of others. No sodding use to man nor beast. Unless we come up with another war of course, then it will be like Kipling said: "Thin red line of 'eroes, when the drums begin to roll," and then "come back, Mac, all is forgiven."'

A posh voice from behind startled them both.

'There's a free overnight hostel on Chapter Street, and a late night off-license on Strutton Ground – your choice. Here's twenty quid. Now bugger off.'

As Mac took the money and headed for Strutton Ground, the overweight body that came with the posh voice sat itself on the section of the bench the homeless veteran had just vacated.

'Hello, Beaufort. Long time. How have you been?'

'Hello, Frobisher,' Beaufort replied. 'Must admit, I've been better.'

'Bryant will take you home. Get some sleep, smarten yourself up, and come to the Travellers Club for lunch tomorrow. 12.45 for 1.00. Let's see if we can get your life back on track.'

A well-set man in a chauffeur's uniform coughed gently and gestured towards the black Jaguar I-Pace parked illegally in the bike lane, hazard lights flashing.

'When you're ready sir.'

CHAPTER 12

PIMLICO, LONDON

Once the whisper-quiet Jaguar had dropped him off, Beaufort carefully negotiated the dark metal external stairs that led down to his basement flat.

He managed to retrieve his keys, which had become snagged in the lining of his suit pocket. Then, like drunks the world over, he used the fingertips of his left had to locate the keyhole and guide the key in. Having shoved the door open, and kicked aside the small pile of letters on the doormat, he stumbled inside.

Rummaging around in the small kitchen he found a can of Stella and half a bottle of Pinot Grigio in the fridge, and a quarter-full bottle of cheap *Krupnik* Polish vodka in a cupboard. He placed all three on the coffee table in front of the imitation leather sofa, turned the TV to the BBC News channel and considered what order to drink them in. He started with the lager, followed by the acidic white wine, leaving the vodka to last, in an attempt to knock himself out and get some sleep.

After Frobisher's unexpected appearance, his thoughts

drifted back to his schooldays.

Frobisher and Beaufort had met at boarding school at the age of nine. They were both misfits. Frobisher was overweight and wore thick spectacles and, based on these attributes, had acquired the nickname Frog. He was academic and hardworking, in school terms a swot.

Beaufort was very different to Frobisher, and very different to most of the other pupils at Bloxstead College. At the beginning and end of school terms he was usually dropped off and collected by his mother, the famous stage and screen actress Yvette de Beaufort. The 'de' was an affectation, adopted to add to her allure. She was an extremely attractive woman – judged a "MILF" by the other boys.

From early on, word had got around school that Beaufort had no father. The resultant teasing helped to forge his character at an early age. He was a loner and a bastard, in every sense of the word. When the occasion demanded, he demonstrated that he could indeed be a right bastard.

Despite his fatherless status Beaufort managed to work out the dynamics of the institution he had been offloaded onto. He had sharp instincts, and quickly learned how to judge character. He also had the ability to discern weakness, and to sniff out fear.

Beaufort performed creditably both academically and in the all-important sporting arena. He wasn't a swot, and he wasn't a jock either. Just a good all-rounder. The survival skills he had learned in the fetid and frequently vicious world of boarding school would stand him in good stead for the future.

The incident that helped forge the friendship between

Beaufort and Frobisher occurred after a routine house rugby match. Their house had lost, but Beaufort had performed well on the wing and scored a good try. Frobisher had been pressed into service in the second row of the scrum, and had pushed, puffed and panted his way ineffectually through the game.

After the match, Beaufort showered and changed quickly; he had an essay deadline looming. He was about to leave the changing rooms when he heard loud slapping noises coming from the shower area. He looked in to see Frobisher being whipped with rolled-up towels by Smythe, Barnes and Cooke, the two props and the hooker who made up the house team's front row.

Frobisher was standing there, naked. His soft white belly, back, thighs and buttocks were livid with red weals. His face was crumpled and streaked with tears, and he was whimpering. He had not cried out, or made any effort to defend himself.

The ringleader – the hooker Cooke – wet the tip of his towel to add extra force to the whip action and lashed Frobisher's shrunken scrotum. With a cry of pure agony Frobisher collapsed writhing to the floor.

In a streak of silent fury Beaufort caught hold of Cooke's towel on its next backswing. Wrenching it from the larger boy's grasp, he looped it around his neck, placed his knee in the small of the hooker's back and pulled with all his strength.

Cooke's whole head turned red, then purple, and moments later his legs collapsed. Beaufort let him fall to his knees, and kicked him onto the wet floor. He then turned to stare at Smythe and Barnes in turn. Both backed away, hands half-raised in mute surrender.

Beaufort unwound the towel and threw it at Frobisher so he could cover his nakedness. He then left the shower area and walked slowly back through the crowded but silent changing room; his reputation as a bastard you didn't mess with established, a lifelong friendship formed.

CHAPTER 13

TRAVELLERS CLUB, PALL MALL

The Travellers Club is the oldest of the Pall Mall gentlemen's clubs. It lacks the prestige of the Athenaeum or the Reform, but it makes up for it with an air of relaxed exoticism. Members include explorers, adventurers, spies and retired military types from the lesser regiments that once policed the empire's far-flung frontiers.

It was a natural watering hole for Charles Frobisher. Although he was a senior intelligence officer, his outward appearance was that of a provincial Church of England vicar, or a middle-ranking official in a government department that dealt with statistics. Indeed, if a search of government websites or the Civil Service Yearbook were conducted, that is exactly what his position would be listed as.

When Beaufort received the invitation to lunch, he assumed it was motivated by sympathy for his reduced circumstances. Or perhaps it was an intervention, calculated to shock him out of his spiralling alcohol-fuelled decline. Either way he was grateful for the prospect of a decent free meal.

He turned up on time, wearing an old school tie he found in the back of his wardrobe. If nothing else, this would prevent him from suffering the indignity of being lumbered with one of the ghastly selection of outdated kipper ties, which the porters kept in reserve to embarrass those foolish enough to turn up without the appropriate neckwear.

Frobisher was waiting for him in the long reception corridor. He was worried his guest might need help negotiating his way past the punctilious porters. Beaufort was slightly disappointed; he had planned to stop off at the toilets and help himself to the free cologne, and use the shoe polishing machine.

Frobisher shook Beaufort warmly by the hand, whilst taking in the crumpled suit, slightly frayed shirt collar and unpolished shoes. They went straight through to the dining room, which ran the entire width of the rear of the building, its large windows overlooking the well-tended gardens that ran down to The Mall.

'As it's Wednesday the trolley roast is lamb, and the special is Dover sole. Or you could try the club staple: steak and kidney pudding.' Frobisher offered.

'Steak and kidney sounds good.'

Frobisher decided on the fish for himself. Beaufort was relieved when his host ordered a bottle of white Rioja to go with their smoked salmon starters, along with a bottle of the house claret to accompany Beaufort's main course. Whatever this lunch was about, it didn't appear to be an intervention to address his drinking.

The initial conversation focused on masters who had died and school friends who had achieved a measure of success or, alternatively, disgraced themselves, or experienced some cataclysmic reversal of fortune. The kind of discussions they routinely enjoyed at their regular, if infrequent, meetings.

After a short pause in the conversation Frobisher asked:

'Do you remember that incident in the shower room at school?'

'Of course.'

'I'll always be grateful to you for that. And was it you who carved the graffiti in the bogs, and spread the rumours that Smythe and Barnes were gay?'

'Of course. Revenge – and justice – sometimes take a little time. But that makes it all the sweeter.'

Frobisher nodded, his long-held suspicions confirmed.

After ordering spotted dick for pudding, and two dessert wines, Frobisher straightened in his chair, his body language signalling they had arrived at the point where business was to be discussed.

'Do you remember old Gibbsy taught us Dr Faust at School?'

'Yes, vaguely. Silly old sod even made us read the play! Always struck me as odd that a clever man would sell his soul to the devil for knowledge he could always acquire, or pleasures he could easily afford.'

They paused while the elderly waiter placed the desserts and wines in front of them.

'Thank you, George,' Frobisher murmured. For some reason they all seemed to be called George. 'Here's the thing, Beaufort.' Frobisher looked up and fixed Beaufort with an uncharacteristically direct stare, somehow further focused by his thick, horn-rimmed spectacles. 'We have an offer for you. A deal. A pact. A Faustian pact. A way out of your current predicament. But if you accept, that's it. No change of heart. No going back. No buyer's remorse. Your soul – and your arse – will belong to us.'

'And who is we?' asked Beaufort, although he instinctively knew the answer.

'MI6. Or did you really think I was a government statistician?'

Beaufort shrugged, and decided to try and bluff.

'Things aren't that bad. I can rebuild, it'll just take time. And my lot will be back in power at some stage.'

Frobisher gave him a sceptical look.

'You've moved into a damp basement flat in Pimlico. All your best staff have buggered off, leaving you with a few kids and interns. Your clients are just serving out their notice period.' He glanced at Beaufort's wrist. 'Even your Rolex is a knock-off. Coutts would have debanked you long ago if you didn't owe them so much money. And we both know your party's out for at least two terms'.

Beaufort reached for his dessert wine. He took a sip, and nodded.

'Ok, you're right. I'm on my uppers, and I can't really see a way back. So, what's the deal? What exactly does this pact involve?'

'We have a Tazmenistani oligarch, Usman Abdullaev. Close to the presidential family. Highly successful, very wealthy. We have *kompromat* on him, and he will do what he's told. We'll get him to pay you a monthly retainer, enough to help you rebuild your company and become a player again. But when we ask for something – and we will – you just have do it, without question. Because you have nothing to lose – and nowhere else to go.'

Beaufort looked at Frobisher and began to realise how the bullied swot from his schooldays had risen so far and so fast within MI6. Beneath the Bunteresque appearance he was a ruthless operator.

Beaufort shrugged, and grinned.

'Ok. Yes, I agree. My soul, and my arse, are yours. Though not literally, of course!'

'Good. I would say you won't regret it, but you might. At some stage you'll need to meet my boss. He's a retired Admiral with the image to match: double-breasted suits, ramrod up his arse, drinks pink gin and swears like a matelot. But don't be fooled by that when you do meet him – he has a razor-sharp mind.

He understands how the other side thinks, and he can spot problems coming down the track before anybody else has even begun to imagine them. As a young man he played chess for the Royal Navy. If his career hadn't got in the way he could have played for the national team.

Oh and there's one more thing. We have a new number two for you, to replace Jennifer. She's a Kiwi with impeccable left-wing credentials – or at least she will have when we've finished writing them. She will be extremely useful to you. And she'll keep an eye on you too.'

'Of course. I could do with help building up our Labour contacts, and reviving the agency. That sounds great.'

'Two things. One: in all operational matters you are to do as she says. Two: don't try to shag her.'

Beaufort laughed, and raised his glass. The pact was toasted with Tokay.

CHAPTER 14

VAUXHALL CROSS, LONDON

Frobisher sent a WhatsApp message to Beaufort on the Saturday telling him to present himself at his office at 9.30 Monday morning.

The message instructed him to bring photo ID, and to allow fifteen minutes for security. There was no hint of the agenda, and no allowance for any diary clash which might have precluded his appearance. It was an order, not an invitation.

Beaufort decided to walk from his Pimlico flat. Crossing Vauxhall Bridge he tried hard not to keep looking up at the eccentric but imposing building on the Albert Embankment that housed the MI6 headquarters. Being slightly early he slowed his pace, and timed it so as to arrive at 9.15 precisely.

There were two unarmed civilian security guards patrolling outside the main doors. Inside, it could have been the headquarters of any large corporation, except for the four members of the Met Police's MO19 squad armed with Heckler & Koch MP5 machine pistols deployed around the large reception area.

THE LOBBYIST

As he approached the reception desk Beaufort knew he was being watched. By the guards, by visible and hidden cameras, and through the large mirror on the back wall with what looked like one-way glass.

There were two receptionists on duty. One was already dealing with a visitor, so Beaufort headed for the other.

'My name is Damian Beaufort, I'm here to see Charles Frobisher. I have my driver's licence.'

The woman smiled, checked his driver's licence and handed him a pre-prepared security pass on a lanyard, with his photograph embedded in it. It had a large red 'V' stamped across it to indicate his visitor status. She glanced to her right, and a young British Asian man in a suit came forward and politely invited him to 'Follow me, please, sir.'

The escort used his own security badge to swipe open a frosted glass door at the rear of the reception area. This led to a smaller room, where two more security guards asked Beaufort for his mobile and watch, which they placed in a locker. One of them asked:

'Do you have any chemical, biological, explosive or radioactive material on you, and have you discharged a firearm in the last 48 hours?'

After replying in the negative, Beaufort was asked to step into a tall glass and metal tube, a smaller version of the lifts that service ultra-modern hotels or office blocks. Once the rounded door closed behind him, the air pressure seemed to drop slightly, and there was a faint hum as fans fitted behind a grille in the ceiling began to extract air from the tube for analysis.

After a claustrophobia-inducing thirty seconds there was a barely audible "ping", and the curved doors to the front opened. Had the analysis revealed traces of explosives, chemical or biological agents, radioactivity or firearm residue, the doors would have remained closed. Then enough of the air would have been sucked out to render him semi-conscious. In extreme circumstances incapacitating gas would have been pumped in to knock him out completely.

As Beaufort stepped, unharmed and unhindered, from the metal and glass tube, the guards handed him the numbered key to the locker containing his possessions. His guide gestured for him to follow. They walked along a windowless corridor to a door marked Interview Room 101.

Frobisher was seated at a long conference table. There was a window with thick green glass behind him. Beside him sat a young woman.

'Just our little joke,' Frobisher ventured, referring to the room number.

The young woman rose and held out her hand, which Beaufort shook, noting the strength of her grip. She was tall and slim, a striking redhead, with the pale translucent skin tone and green eyes which often accompany that colouring. Those eyes looked him up and down, spending longer on the appraisal than he would have dared spend looking her over.

'Damian Beaufort, this is Samantha Ferguson. She's one of ours, and now she is also one of yours. Born in Shetland, parents emigrated to New Zealand when she was nine, and she grew up there. She came back to go to university at St Andrews, then returned to New Zealand. She did great work for us in Wellington, helping to keep them vaguely within the fold, and now they have a sensible government she's come home to help to defend the motherland.'

'What do you mean she's now one of mine?'

Frobisher frowned irritably before replying.

'I told you at the club that we would be seconding somebody to your consultancy. Samantha has a politics degree, a background in lobbying in New Zealand, and she worked in Parliament House and the Beehive in Wellington for two years. She has the relevant qualifications and experience, and impeccable "progressive" credentials. She can take over from Jennifer as your second in command, help you get in with the new Labour government and attract clients who are nervous about your Tory background. So, she will be good for your business, and she can be the regular liaison between us. Win-win, I would say.'

Beaufort looked at Samantha and nodded.

'I think that could work well. What is it you want us to do?'

'First, go and see our tame Tazmenistani oligarch. Technically he will be your client, but in reality he's our asset, albeit a reluctant one. You need to show him who's boss, and get him to help to facilitate a trip to Dustana with the Tazmen All-Party Parliamentary Group, which you will be on too. Samantha can fill you in on the details, and mind the shop while you're away.'

With that Frobisher rose, as did Beaufort and Samantha. She led the way out of the room. As they moved towards the door Frobisher gripped Beaufort's shoulder and murmured into his ear:

'Remember what I said, Samantha is important to us. Don't blow her cover – and don't ask her to blow you.'

Beaufort smiled, shrugged off Frobisher's grip and joined Samantha as she made her way along the corridor towards the exit.

It occurred to him that Orwell's original Room 101 had been situated in the Ministry of Love.

*

Frobisher took the lift up to the seventh floor to report to the Admiral.

'Is he free?' he asked Ms Danso.

She smiled.

'Yes, and seems to be in a good mood – for once. Go on through.'

Frobisher knocked and entered, to find the Admiral standing over a low table with a reproduction Isle of Lewis chess board on it, considering a remote opponent's opening move.

'Ah, Frobisher, come in, take a seat. How did it go with Beaufort?'

'Very well sir, I think. He seemed very taken with Samantha – perhaps a bit too taken.'

'Eye for the ladies, that one. Could be his Achilles heel.'

'Yes, sir. But he's good with people generally, not just women. He can use those skills to try and charm the Tazmen oligarch, and if that doesn't work Samantha will just have to wave the big stick at him.'

'Quite so. Anything else?'

Frobisher hesitated, aware that he was about to broach a sensitive topic.

'Yes, sir. We're getting strong indications from Moscow Station that Tarakan is ramping up FSB activity, and shifting his focus to Western Europe. He seems to be moving on from the old Soviet satellite states to target France, Germany – and us. I understand, sir, that you've had direct dealings with him. What's he like?'

The Admiral said nothing for several seconds. His good mood had evaporated. He seemed to be on the verge of bringing the meeting to an end, but instead decided to take his protégé into his confidence.

'Yes, I knew him – or I thought I did. It was in the days when the Cold War was starting to thaw. There was a conference in Odessa to discuss the demilitarisation of the Black Sea. I was a lowly lieutenant in Naval Intelligence, and Tarakan – he called himself Ivan Ivanov at that stage – was something equivalent in what was then the KGB.

After negotiations each day the two sides would occasionally socialise. Ivan – Tarakan – and I would drink, and play chess or snooker. He spoke perfect English, much better than the usual KGB goons. He usually won the chess. I usually won the snooker. Of course we each tried to turn the other, in a very half-hearted fashion. We both knew it wasn't going to work, but it was expected of us by our superiors.'

He paused and Frobisher, eager to hear the rest of the story, urged him on.

'It all sounds very civilised, sir. But I'm sensing that didn't last?'

'No, it didn't. Some idiot in the Admiralty decided that it was an ideal opportunity to check out the propulsion system on a brand-new Russian destroyer, which had berthed in Odessa for the duration of the talks. We sent a diver down, an SBS lieutenant called Sebastian Ames. We were at the Royal Naval College in Dartmouth together. The Russians detected him, captured him, tortured him and killed him. They then used the incident as an excuse to break off the talks.'

'And you believe Tarakan was involved?'

'I know he was. He wanted me to know he was. Ames's naked body was dumped on the bed in my hotel room. It was an indescribable mess. He must have suffered agonies. On top of everything else, they had gouged out his eyes, and hammered snooker balls into the empty eye sockets. One green ball, and one brown ball. Tarakan is heterochromatic – he has a green eye and a brown eye. He wanted me to know that it was him who did for Ames.'

Frobisher absorbed all this, and observed that the Admiral was as close to being emotional as he had ever seen him.

'So what did we do?'

'Nothing we could do, not at that stage. We took the body home and gave Ames a funeral with full military honours. Then began working on a plan for revenge.'

'But how, sir? Presumably Tarakan kept well out of our way after that?'

'We worked on the traditional Russian paranoia. Leveraged the fact that he and I had spent time together, drinking and playing games, that we'd even tried to initiate a defection. And we used the ingrained Russian prejudice against all those with Central Asian blood in their veins – he was quite obviously not pure Rus. We created the impression that Tarakan had been turned, and was about to defect to us. We opened a Swiss bank account in his trade name. We assigned him the phoney codename of the

"Chessman." We sent encrypted messages that we knew might be intercepted and decoded, referring to this great new agent-in-place we'd acquired.

They fell for it. He spent years in the gulag as a result. He survived everything. The horrendous cold. The dreadful food. The grinding work. The brutality of the guards. And the vicious fights – he was stabbed and slashed several times. That's where he got the gulag name of Tarakan – Cockroach. So he went with it, and had the tattoo of a cockroach inked on his neck. But when that bastard double agent Phillips was about to be exposed and fled to Moscow rather than stand trial, he convinced them we had set Tarakan up. After a thorough case review, and further interrogation, he was rehabilitated, and promoted.'

Frobisher puffed out his cheeks.

'And now he's the Russian intelligence chief, the *capo dei capi*. And he has every reason to loathe us.'

'Yes he is. And yes he does.'

CHAPTER 15

HOLLOWAY, LONDON

Beaufort had trained in martial arts since he was a teenager. His mother had decided that he needed to be able to defend himself, and learn how to control his volcanic temper.

He had tried everything from judo to jiu-jitsu, before settling on Shotokan karate. He enjoyed the hard physical training, but also the mental discipline, meditation and feats of memory required to master scores of set-form *kata* sequences.

In recent years Beaufort had started training at a dojo in Finsbury Park, where a world-renowned sensei, a Japanese seventh dan *kyoshi* black belt by the name of Hanata Tshikawa, had established a highly regarded school.

Before the descent caused by the decline of his business, Beaufort had been a model student, training regularly and enthusiastically. He had acquired a firm grasp of the hundreds of moves required to master the intricate patterns of *kata*, and had risen to the rank of third dan black belt, or *sandan*. As a result he was regularly chosen to represent his dojo in competitions and tournaments.

Despite his declining training schedule, Beaufort was picked to fight against the champion of a rival school that practised an alternative form of karate known as *Goju-ryu*. Whereas Shotokan was fast, hard and direct, *Goju-ryu* used more tangential and circular techniques. Both styles claimed to be the foremost school of karate, so it was a needle match.

For the bout of *kumite* full-contact combat, the students of the home dojo were arranged kneeling around two sides of a square on the canvas tatami mat. The visiting students made up the third side of the square, whilst the two sensei from the home and visiting dojos knelt alongside each other on the fourth. Both were senior *kyoshi* sensei, and both were Japanese.

There was no scoring, as there would be in Olympic martial arts contests. The winner would be the last man standing.

The *shinpan* referee, standing in the middle of the tatami, was a fifth dan *Godan* from a neutral dojo. He was there to enforce the rules, which in the case of full-contact *kumite* were minimal. It was simply forbidden to draw blood, break bones or cause permanent injury.

Beaufort and his opponent entered via the fourth side of the square, from behind their respective sensei. Moving to the centre they bowed to their own sensei, bowed to the opposing dojo's sensei, bowed to the *shinpan*, and then bowed to each other. As they performed the last ritual bow the two *karateka* locked eyes. That eye contact was maintained throughout the preliminaries, and for much of the bout.

This was a new opponent for Beaufort, and he only had

a few seconds to size him up. He looked to be Japanese and although they were probably a similar weight, his opponent had a barrel chest and a low centre of gravity. Beaufort was almost six inches taller, and had a correspondingly greater reach, but his opponent had ballast. There was no sign of fear, or even nervousness, in the eyes or the body language of his opponent.

The *shinpan* held his right arm parallel to the ground, and then raised it sharply to the vertical, at the same time crying *hajime*, the signal to begin fighting.

Beaufort's opponent surged forward, sliding his bare feet across the canvass of the tatami at speed, and unleashing a barrage of alternating punches with his short, powerful arms. Beaufort switched stances, pulled back his lead foot, and used a combination of *uchi* inward and *ude* outward blocks to stifle most of his opponents strikes.

Beaufort's gi was already drenched in sweat, and he picked up the scent of his opponent. Often in these bouts he would be able to smell fear, but from this opponent he smelt only raw testosterone. Some of the body punches were getting through his guard, and Beaufort decided he could retreat no further.

He pivoted on his trailing anchor leg and unleashed an *ushiro geri* reverse kick aimed at his opponent's head. He missed, but forced him back a metre. Beaufort followed up with a *mae geri* forward kick, and this time caught his opponent in the solar plexus, partially winding him. He surged forward, intending to finish his Japanese adversary off with an *empi* elbow strike to the side of the head. Then it happened.

A latecomer, a slim young female black belt, flung open

the door to the dojo and rushed in, anxious to witness the fight. For just a fraction of a second Beaufort was distracted.

That was enough. His opponent leaped high and whirled, uttering a spine-chilling *kiai* battle cry, and delivering a devastating *haishu uchi* backhand strike to the side of Beaufort's head.

The tatami rushed up to meet him, and the lights went out.

*

When Beaufort came around, he was lying naked on the treatment table.

His torso had a patchwork of bruises from the punches that had got through his guard, and his head ached from the backhand strike that had knocked him unconscious.

His sensei was sliding his hands down either side of the ridged muscles of his student's abdomen towards his groin, in the process of easing his retractile testicles back into his scrotum.

'What did you learn?', the sensei asked.

Beaufort groaned, and then shrugged painfully, before replying.

'I don't know, sensei. Maybe train harder. Focus more tightly. Don't underestimate your opponent. Drink less alcohol. Lock the door. You tell me, sensei.'

Without hesitation, sensei did just that.

'You are a fat, lazy, stupid *gaijin*, who deserved to be knocked out. Now get up – the first round is on you.'

'What about the concussion protocol?'

'Who is the prime minister?'

'Some lefty called Clem Clark.'

'Who is the King?'
'Little fella, big ears, talks to plants.'
'How many fingers am I holding up.'
'Two – and that's very rude.'
Sensei grinned.
'You are OK – get dressed – let's go.'

CHAPTER 16

HAMPSTEAD, LONDON

Beaufort and Samantha had asked for a meeting with the oligarch Usman Abdullaev in order to discuss the proposed trip to Tazmenistan.

Abdullaev had been reluctant to agree to one, clearly resenting having to pay Beaufort Public Affairs the hefty monthly retainer that he had been obliged to agree to. As an expression of his displeasure, he had insisted on the meeting taking place at his mansion on The Bishop's Avenue, Hampstead, otherwise known as "billionaires' row".

Rather than take the Northern Line, Sam and Beaufort decided to use one of the London black cabs that the Firm maintained in order to facilitate discreet movement around the capital. It might take a little longer, but it would be more comfortable, and with a service driver at the wheel they could discuss the forthcoming meeting without worrying about being overheard.

In the office Beaufort was clearly the boss, and Samantha merely a senior account director recently arrived from

Wellington. In private, and especially when it came to MI6 business, Samantha made it very clear that she was in charge. Mindful of Frobisher's words, and grateful that Beaufort Public Affairs was now solvent and starting to grow once again, Beaufort had reluctantly accepted this role reversal.

As soon as they were in the taxi Samantha began her briefing.

'Abdullaev made his money in the extractive industries – oil and gas, but also rare earth minerals such as neodymium and samarium. These are essential for producing magnets, electric vehicle batteries and solar panels. He also operates as an international arms dealer, buying and selling defence equipment. He deals mainly in old Soviet kit, but he wants to branch out and trade up. He has a young second wife, and two teenage children from his first marriage. He does a reasonable impersonation of a legitimate businessman, and of a family man, but you should know that he's a crook, and a kiddy fiddler.'

Beaufort grimaced and then asked:

'How do we get what we need?'

'Carrot and stick. He spends a lot of his time in the UK, and the kids go to school here. His wife loves the shopping, the theatre, the art galleries. We let him stay, and we don't question his non-dom status. He wants to export his energy and minerals to the West too, to diversify his client base. And he wants to gain access to our sophisticated military materiel. Partly to help his country to keep their neighbours – large and small – at bay, but mostly to sell it on to third parties. '

Beaufort nodded, although he was not totally convinced that would be enough to sway an oligarch who was so used to having his own way.

'And what do we need from him?'

'Three things. We need a good local fixer on the ground in Tazmenistan, support from on high in the capital Dustana in case you run in to trouble, and a compliant hotel manager.'

Unusually the traffic was light, and they were soon pulling into The Bishops Avenue. All of the houses were huge and set back from the road in extensive grounds. Most were owned by foreign nationals, all had elaborate security set-ups.

Abdullaev's house was no exception. Behind the eight-foot metal railings were impenetrable hawthorn hedges. As they drew up at the main gate a guard emerged through a pedestrian wicket-gate and approached with a clipboard.

Having checked their driving licences, which they had been warned to bring, he punched in a code to open the vehicle gates and they drove up to the imposing portico entrance. Even before they got out of the taxi another uniformed guard, with a Doberman straining on a chain leash, appeared from around the corner of the house to check them out.

Samantha instructed the driver to wait, approached the imposing double doors and pulled the heavy doorbell chain. After a few moments a butler in traditional Jeeves garb appeared.

'Mr Abdullaev is expecting you. He is by the indoor pool. Please follow me.'

They followed the butler through the vast hall and a large reception room to a spa complex at the rear of the house. They entered the sultry pool area to find Abdullaev reclining on a lounger in a towel robe, his balding head and hairy chest glistening with sweat.

He waved them over, and gestured towards two chairs. After looking Samantha over, he decided she was too young to be important, and too old to be desirable. He fixed his hard brown eyes on Beaufort instead and asked:

'What do you want? I am a busy man.'

'I can see that,' Beaufort snorted. 'My colleague Samantha will tell you what we need.'

Samantha reached into her bag and pulled out an ultrasonic signal jammer, which she activated and placed on the coffee table between them. It would scramble all mobile signals and recording devices in the immediate vicinity.

'We'll be sending a small delegation from the All-Party Parliamentary Group to Tazmenistan. We need a good fixer on the ground, somebody who speaks English, has zero scruples and can obey orders. We also need a contact in the Presidential Administration who will step in if anything starts to go wrong. We need to take this group to the front line, where there'll be some sort of incident. Either naturally occurring, or prompted by us. And finally, we need a hotel with eight rooms pre-rigged for recording. One for each parliamentarian, plus another four as backup, in case they're smart enough to insist on switching rooms.'

'And what will you do with the tapes from the hotel rooms?'

Samantha raised an eyebrow.

'I think you know the answer to that.'

Abdullaev nodded.

'OK I have a good local fixer, and a good contact in the

PA. I own a five-star hotel near the airport, where we can put them up and set them up. But if I do all this, that's it, we are even and I owe you nothing more.'

'Don't be so naive – you will always owe us,' Samantha replied. 'But if it all goes well, we can lift the arms embargo on your country, and start importing your energy and your minerals. And we can make sure that you continue to live here unmolested. It is so much nicer than Tazmenistan – or even Laos.'

Abdullaev stared at her.

'And if I refuse?' he spat.

Samantha returned his stare.

'Then the *kompromat* we have on you will go to your Presidential Administration – and our Home Office.'

The Tazmen started to respond then shrugged, accepting that he was beaten.

'OK, I will make the arrangements. George will show you out.'

For some reason, they all seemed to be called George.

*

Once they were back in the taxi Beaufort asked:

'What just happened? I thought at one stage he was going to throw us out.'

'He sure as hell doesn't like being told what to do by a woman. He flashed me his hairy balls while we were sitting there – it was a power thing. Truth is, we already have his balls – in a vice.'

'How so?'

'As I said on the way up, he's a kiddy fiddler. He likes them young, really young, and he's into boys as well as girls.

We have video of him abusing young boys in a brothel in Laos, and if we release that he is finished. He'll play his part, and so must you. We need you to go on the Tazmenistan trip. You'll have to lead the parliamentarians into harm's way. Hopefully nobody will get killed, but if they do, tough shit. Whatever happens we need to soften them up. We'll have a nice surprise waiting for them back at their hotel.'

Like Abdullaev, Beaufort decided that this was not the time to argue, and just nodded.

*

They encountered heavier traffic on the way back. After they had both spent some time checking their emails and WhatsApp messages Samantha asked.

'So how did you get in to lobbying?'

'It just sort of happened, I guess. I was at school with Frobisher, and we were both kind of outcasts, for different reasons. I didn't have a father – never had one. That made me a target. He was bookish and un-sporty, which was worse. But I figured out how the system functioned, sussed out what made people tick, and then I worked out how to make them do what I wanted them to do. I also made sure that the other boys were scared of me.'

'And then?'

'I went to Sussex, a very average red brick university, and a very left-wing one. I took over the University Conservative Association, recruited my rugby team mates as members, and made it a force to be reckoned with. I started to help the local Tory MP, and then went to work for him in parliament after I graduated. I did a PhD at the LSE at the same time – another very political, and very left wing, establishment.'

Samantha shrugged.

'You and hundreds of others. What made you a success?'

'It was bit like school, and a bit like university. I figured out how the system worked, and I manipulated it. Most importantly, I saw through Members of Parliament. For all the status and supposed power and influence, they're human like anybody else. Well, not exactly like anybody else: they have even more human foibles and weaknesses than normal people. They're vainer, greedier, thirstier and randier.

And above all, they're chancers. They gamble good careers and stable family lives for the prospect of getting selected, then getting elected, perhaps becoming a minister, maybe joining the cabinet and – who knows – becoming PM. Over the last few years a few of the biggest chancers have succeeded in doing just that.'

'But how did that help you?'

'Having worked out what they want, what they need, I find a way to give it to them. And then I ask for the quid pro quo. My job is getting people to do what I want them to do.

I don't have to threaten them or blackmail them. They just know that I know. Who they are, what they are, what they want, and what they need. . . Lobbying is the art of political persuasion. Knowing what they feel and how they think just makes the process easier. That's how it works. Lobbying in action.'

Samantha nodded.

Politics, lobbying and spying. All just games played by people of high intelligence, but low moral standards.

CHAPTER 17

DUSTANA, TAZMENISTAN

All-Party Parliamentary Group trips are generally scheduled for recess time, and the mission to Tazmenistan was no exception.

This particular trip was to be led by the group chairman, Sir Walter Atkins, who had been a Foreign Office minister in the previous government. A member of the House of Lords, Lord Aled Griffiths of Pontypridd, had also been invited and he had happily accepted. He was a Lib Dem peer, and an energetic champion of the rights of refugees and displaced persons.

As well as the chairman and Lord Griffiths, there were two backbench MPs. Arthur Robinson was a Labour backbencher, but he was also parliamentary private secretary to the foreign secretary. Geoff Simmonds was a relatively new member, having been elected for the Conservatives against the tide of Labour gains. His background working for a defence technology firm had secured him election to the influential Intelligence and Security Committee.

The group met in the airport's VIP lounge well before

the flight. No introductions were necessary, as the group had met several times before to discuss Tazmen affairs. After a round of drinks, Beaufort briefed them on the trip's itinerary, emphasising that it was subject to change. He also updated them on the current security situation on the ground.

'The conflict has heated up recently. We're now entering the fighting season, and the Ujikistanis seem to have got hold of a warehouse full of Russian equipment and large quantities of ammunition. Our guys are holding the line, but without Western help they can't do so for ever. Energy companies – including British ones – are unwilling to make large-scale investments until the geopolitical situation is more stable.'

When the flight was called, the group used their priority boarding and, as is usual for parliamentarians, turned left on entering the plane. After food and drinks had been served, Beaufort, Sir Walter and Lord Griffiths settled down to sleep. Arthur Robinson and Geoff Simmonds continued to make the most of the complimentary drinks. The two had started to form a bond that transcended party lines.

*

There was no formal greeting when they landed in Dustana. The group was met by Faisal, their official guide, interpreter and fixer. He was a dapper young man with gelled black hair, and dressed from head to toe in counterfeit designer clothes. He made sure there was no passport control and no customs – just a two-minute walk to the black Toyota Land Cruisers parked on the apron.

Faisal made sure there were no formalities at their five-star hotel either. They had a swift nightcap, served with a few trays of local delicacies, and were in bed shortly after midnight.

*

The following morning, after a hurried breakfast, the convoy of SUVs headed west. Having experienced the luxury of Dustana, the parliamentarians now needed some gritty photo opportunities. They had to be able to demonstrate to their constituents, and the party whips, that this trip wasn't just a "jolly".

They drove through the suburbs of the sprawling capital city and, after about an hour, arrived at a ramshackle camp for refugees and "internally displaced persons". The camp had grown up around an old Soviet-era barracks. The original buildings were solid enough, but the surrounding land was filled with row upon row of prefabricated huts, patched up against the wind and the rain, and intersected with rudimentary paths and open sewers.

The refugees consisted of ethnic Tazmens who had been living in Ujikistan when the war broke out. They were the lucky ones. Instead of being killed or interned, they had been given the opportunity to flee, leaving their homes and all their possessions behind.

The refugees were heavily outnumbered by the internally displaced persons, or, in UN parlance, IDPs. They included almost all the inhabitants of a small Tazmen border town that had been overrun by the Ujikistanis in the early days of the invasion.

Sir Walter, who as chairman of the group had visited the camp before, warned the group:

'These people don't have much, but they still have their dignity. Let's make sure we don't damage that in any way.'

The convoy of shiny SUVs drew to a halt and was quickly surrounded by small children dressed in ragged cast-off clothes and flimsy footwear. Knowing this would happen, Faisal had issued the parliamentarians with a supply of cheap biros and sweets, to be handed out to the children.

Having dispensed their largesse, Beaufort and Faisal led the group to the old Soviet-era parade ground, where the mayor and his underlings were waiting, clothed in shiny suits and airs of overweening self-importance. The politicians had to stand and listen as the headman regaled them with tales of the demonic cruelty of the enemy, and the limitless bounty of their own president. Faisal conveyed a condensed version of all of this to the group.

'He says the people here are poor, but glad to be alive. One day they will return to claim their ancient homelands. In the meantime, they are grateful to the president for his generosity and support.'

Sir Walter was then invited to reply on behalf of the group. He did so with practised ease, confirming the mayor's account of Ujikistani cruelty, and also praising the president for looking after his people. He was either unaware of the cameras from the local TV news recording his every word and gesture, or happy to go on the record in full support of the Tazmen position.

After that it was time for refreshments, and they were led into the community centre. If the parliamentarians were hoping for some alcohol to lighten the mood, they were to be disappointed. Bottled water, sweet tea and mud-thick coffee were available, but there was no sign of anything stronger. There was, however, plenty of local food laid out on trestle tables – flatbreads, salads, cheeses, fruit, nuts and sweets, but no meat. Being hungry, and not wishing to cause offence, the group tucked into the spread.

Then it was the turn of the ordinary people to denounce the enemy and praise the president. Elderly *babushkas* with flashing gold teeth led the line, followed by a few beautiful young women, some noticeably pregnant. There were no men of fighting age. They had all been conscripted and posted to the front line.

Sir Walter was his usual stiff self, but the two MPs tried to show empathy. Through Faisal, a pregnant young woman told Simmonds that her husband had just been killed at the front; she was a widow before her child had even been born. Robinson nodded sympathetically when an elderly *babushka* explained that she had lost her entire family during the initial Ujikistani invasion. The most genuine empathy was exhibited by Lord Griffiths, who wept copious celtic tears as he listened to the women's stories.

By the end of the morning, despite their irritation at the length of the proceedings, the parliamentarians were convinced. In their eyes these people had been horrendously treated by the Ujikistanis, and were living lives of great hardship, despite the best efforts of a compassionate president.

They didn't realised that this was a reverse "Potemkin village". The originals had been showcase settlements designed and built by Count Potemkin, a favourite of Catherine the Great, in order to convince her that her subjects were not living in abject poverty. This settlement was built with precisely the reverse objective in mind. It had been designed and built in order to convince visiting dignitaries that the refugees and IDPs lived lives of great suffering.

In reality, they all had much better accommodation elsewhere. They were usually smartly dressed and well fed, and had been bussed in for the day to tug at the heartstrings of the visitors.

As the group climbed aboard their now dusty SUVs Beaufort looked across at Faisal and nodded approvingly.

'They put on a great show.'

The cast had played its part to perfection.

CHAPTER 18

BALAGAYUN PROVINCE, TAZMENISTAN

The visit to the camp for refugees and IDPs had been worthy, but deeply dull. The location had provided good content for social media posts and local constituency newspapers but lacked the edge to spice up a parliamentary speech, or enliven an after-dinner talk.

The parliamentarians wanted excitement, and Beaufort was happy to oblige. The front line of the "frozen conflict" was nearly 300 miles from the capital Dustana, and beyond the comfortable range of the Land Cruisers, not to mention the stamina and patience of the parliamentarians.

Through Faisal, Beaufort negotiated with the Presidential Administration to secure the loan of a helicopter. Not the president's brand new state-of-the-art Agusta Westland AW9S Grand Versace. Rather, an old Soviet Mi-I7 with the NATO designation "Hip", retrofitted with comfortable seating, a well-stocked bar, a chemical toilet and upgraded soundproofing.

As the SUV convoy headed towards the nearest airbase,

some 10 kilometres from the camp they had just visited, arrangements were hastily made for the clearance of the flight to a second airbase at a similar distance from the front line.

The politicians climbed the steps to the helicopter and jockeyed for the best seats. Lord Griffiths claimed prime position – front facing and next to the bar – much to the annoyance of Sir Walter. They all declined the proffered headphones in favour of shouting excitedly over the engine noise.

The pilot was a squat balding man in his mid-forties, who looked more Russian than Tazmen. His younger slimmer co-pilot was pure Tazmen. His jet-black hair, Rayban sunglasses and gleaming smile were reminiscent of Tom Cruise in the original Top Gun film. Both wore flight suits but the flight attendant, a young woman called Soraya, according to her name badge, wore the smart blue uniform of a sergeant in the Tazmen air force.

Using sign language, Soraya insisted that the group strap in. Through Faisal she warned them there were in for a bumpy take-off and landing. Then she strapped herself into a jump seat facing rearwards into the cabin. The twin Klimov turbocharged engines spooled up, and the wheels left the ground.

The helicopter climbed gradually to its cruising height of 1,500 feet, and then headed west towards the conflict zone. At this point Soraya opened the cocktail cabinet, which contained premium Scotch whisky – a Macallan 15-year-old single malt – Beluga Gold Line vodka from Russia, Swiss bottled water and ice.

Beaufort and Faisal opted for the water, but Arthur Robinson did not hesitate to order the Scotch.

'Nothing is too good for the workers,' he said, swallowing the first large measure in one.

Lord Griffiths also opted for the whisky, but with ice, whilst Sir Walter and Geoff Simmonds decided to go native and requested the vodka.

As the helicopter drew closer to the line of contact, Soraya cleared away the glasses. This was a necessary precaution: soon the Mi-17 helicopter descended to just 150 feet, adopted an erratic flight line and fired off chaff and flares to decoy any incoming missiles.

The whole battlefront was covered by S-300 surface-to-air missile systems, which both sides had obtained from the Russians. Additionally, there was a plentiful supply of cheap – but effective – SAM-7 shoulder launched missiles, which even poorly trained conscripts could operate.

When, eventually, the MI7 performed a hard landing on the small forward air base, the well-refreshed parliamentarians were more than happy to stumble down the steps onto firm land.

Waiting on the dusty apron was not another fleet of luxury SUVs, but a single battered, olive-green armoured personnel carrier. Like the helicopter, it was a relic of the Soviet era: an ancient BTR-80. Despite its age, the eight giant wheels were more than capable of dealing with the rough terrain, and the heavy armour provided good protection against shrapnel and small arms fire.

As they approached the vehicle Faisal gestured towards two piles of equipment, and politely asked them to don flak jackets and ballistic combat helmets. The politicians, instantly spotting a photo-opportunity, donned the protective equipment, gathered round the APC, with its jutting turret-mounted 30mm cannon, and stared grim-faced into Faisal's camera.

Sir Walter, despite being a widely travelled former Foreign Office minister, had been unsettled by the helicopter's violent manoeuvres prior to landing. He was unconvinced of the need for so many precautions, and perhaps felt foolish in body armour designed for a much smaller man.

'Is all this really necessary?'

Beaufort swallowed his irritation.

'We're heading to the front line as you requested, Sir Walter. This narrow valley opens up into a plain that continues all the way down to Dustana. That's the reason for the trenches. Soldiers – on both sides – are killed here every day. A sniper fires, his opposite number replies. Somebody fires a mortar round, the other side responds in kind. At this point the exchanges usually cease, but it's not uncommon for them to escalate into rocket or artillery fire. Then the UN monitors use their hotlines to phone the senior commanders on both sides and hopefully it all goes quiet again – at least for a while.

In reality all the UN can do is record infringements and negotiate tactical ceasefires. They don't have the mandate – or the resources – to try and enforce peace.'

Sir Walter's shrug was intended to demonstrate that he accepted this explanation, but only with extreme reluctance.

After a short but bone-jarring journey, the BTR-80 drew to a halt in the lee of an earth-covered concrete bunker. This blocked the forward view, but provided some protection against enemy fire. The parliamentarians were ordered to debus, which they were happy to do. The atmosphere inside the APC, which was sealed against nuclear, chemical and biological attack, had grown thick with the fug of diesel fumes and nervous farts.

An officer from the forward trenches had been sent to meet the group and guide them towards the front line. Spotting Faisal, he approached and unleashed a torrent of angry Tazmen.

Faisal turned to Beaufort and translated.

'Captain Baibek is very worried about this situation. He says there have been more exchanges of fire than usual in the last few days and he cannot guarantee the safety of the group. He advises that we do not approach the front line.'

Beaufort frowned and reached into his inside pocket for his iPhone. Checking there was a signal, he sent a WhatsApp message to their contact at the Presidential Administration. A few seconds later the captain's phone vibrated. He glanced at the message, then snarled his acquiescence at Faisal.

'OK let's go,' Faisal urged the group.

They started to follow the captain, whose shoulders were stiff with disapproval.

The approach to the front line was through a series of communications trenches, which zigzagged in a broadly westerly direction. The parliamentarians, all of whom had ignored the warning to wear robust footwear, grumbled as they followed the officer along the muddy trench. Lord Griffiths, the elderly peer, struggled to keep up with the marginally fitter MPs.

When they finally arrived at the front line the group were issued with binoculars to afford them a better view of the enemy trenches. Through them they could clearly see Ujikistani soldiers eyeing them back through their own binoculars and trench telescopes.

Geoff Simmonds, the young Tory backbencher, waved at them. The response was a universally-recognised single digit gesture.

Captain Baibek was obviously still nervous about having a group of foreign VIPs in his sector of the front line. He kept urging the group to keep their heads down. As nothing seemed to be happening, and the Ujikistani trenches appeared to be a very long way away, the group relaxed and began to take selfies, using willing Tazmen soldiers as grinning props.

Beaufort pulled Faisal to one side.

'What sniper rifles do the Ujikistanis have?'

'They use the same as we do. Russian guns, either Dragunovs or SV98s.'

'And what is the effective range?'

'In decent conditions, and in competent hands, either is capable of a clean headshot at 1,000 metres.'

Beaufort smiled, but said nothing.

Sir Walter, all six foot four of him, had been standing on an observation platform for several minutes. His height ensured that his head and shoulders were clearly exposed above the parapet. This proved too much of a temptation for the Ujikistanis.

The first sound was the thump of a 7.62mm high-velocity rifle bullet smacking into a sandbag centimetres to the left of Sir Walter's head. Then came the distant "whump" of a heavy mortar being fired, followed by the whistle of the 120mm shell in flight.

At that point Captain Baibek hurled himself and the chairman off the observation platform and into the trench.

As Faisal and Baibek screamed at the parliamentarians to take cover, the mortar bomb exploded with an ear-shattering roar just ten metres behind the trench, showering everyone with loose earth and stones.

The captain picked himself up and immediately issued orders for retaliation. A Tazmen sniper loosed off a single round, and his comrades fired a shell at the Ujikistani trenches from an identical model heavy mortar tube to the one which had been used to attack them.

Sir Walter stayed down, groaning and squirming in the mud of the trench. A combat medic, with a red crescent armband and medical kit, ran over and crouched by his side. He muttered in Tazmen at Faisal, who informed Sir Walter and Beaufort that:

'The shoulder is dislocated. He will have to put it back.'

Sitting Sir Walter up, the medic gave him a leather strap to bite on. He instructed Faisal to kneel beside him and brace his good shoulder. The medic positioned himself next to the injured shoulder and carefully lined up the dislocated ball with the empty socket. Then, speaking quietly in a soothing voice, and without any warning, he punched the shoulder hard, ramming the ball back into the vacant socket.

Sir Walter spat out the leather strap and roared with pain. The group, who were still recovering from the shock of being on the receiving end of a high explosive mortar round, just about managed to set their faces into an expression that resembled sympathy. The chairman was well respected, but not well loved.

Beaufort did not even bother. He was furious with the Ujikistani sniper for missing Sir Walter, and with the captain for intervening so speedily and so decisively.

A dead or wounded former minister would undoubtedly have forced His Majesty's Government to break off diplomatic relations with Ujikistan. It would almost certainly have unlocked the arms sales he had worked so hard to arrange, and which were currently still held up by the EU-imposed arms embargo.

Close, but no cigar.

CHAPTER 19

EUROPEAN QUARTER, BRUSSELS

This time around it was the Englishman – trade name Taylor – who initiated the meeting with Alvariz. Samantha was in Brussels on one of her infrequent visits, and he wanted her to meet this valuable, but temperamental, asset.

Taylor instructed one of his field operatives to post an envelope containing a beermat from O'Reilly's, another Irish pub, through Alvariz's letterbox. The beermat featured a classic leprechaun figure, and Taylor had defaced it by drawing a vertical biro stroke down the mythical creature's nose, and circling his left eye, indicating a 10pm meeting the following night. It was deliberately messy, as though a small child or a drunken adult had scrawled on it in a fit boredom.

Samantha and Taylor arrived early at O'Reilly's in order to satisfy themselves that there was no hostile surveillance in place. This time Taylor ordered Guinness for himself and Samantha and a Leffe for the Basque, who hadn't seemed to relish the stout at their last meeting. The pub was busy but they managed to secure a small table at the rear, near the toilets.

Alvariz took a moment to spot Taylor at the back of the pub, and hesitated when he saw Samantha. Taylor touched his left ear, giving the safe-to-approach signal, and the Basque walked uncertainly over to the table.

Gesturing for Alvariz to sit, Taylor did the introductions. He used Samantha's trade name.

'Annton, this is Vanessa. She's over from head office in London. She has a very important mission for you.'

The Basque was still wary of the newcomer, but obviously found her attractive.

'What mission? I don't want to lose my job. It is important to me.'

'And you are important to us,' Taylor replied.

'But we do need you to do this. Otherwise we'll have to find somebody else, and then you won't be important anymore.'

Alvariz absorbed the implied threat and took a sip of his beer.

Samantha decided to play on Alvariz's macho nature.

'What's the problem Annton? Are you scared – is that it?'

Alvariz bristled.

'Of course not. OK. What you want me to do?'

Taylor slid a copy of that evening's L'Écho across the table.

'In there you will find an envelope with twenty thousand euros in cash. Also, two small electronic listening devices. They're very sensitive, and don't require any power source. One surface is adhesive, but covered with a plastic film. Just peel off the film, place one under Morand's desk, and the other under the conference table in his office. Be careful not to leave any trace. Wear gloves, and take the plastic film coverings away with you.'

Samantha turned her full charm on the Basque.

'I know you can do this, Annton. It is really important to us, and it will be really lucrative for you.'

Alvariz nodded, picked up the newspaper, and left the pub.

Samantha turned to Taylor.

'Do you think he's up to this?'

Taylor shrugged.

'I don't know. He's nervous, and flaky as hell. But if he gets caught, we just cut him loose. That's the beauty of a deniable asset.'

What Taylor failed to appreciate is that loyalty – or a lack of it – cuts both ways.

*

The following evening, after the Commission president had left for the day, Alvariz slipped into his office.

As instructed, he pulled on gloves – the white cotton pair that he used when serving drinks and canapés at functions. He knelt down, slipped the first bug out of his pocket, removed the plastic film protecting the adhesive and stuck it to the underside of the desk – in a corner, where the Commission president's knees wouldn't dislodge it.

Heart racing, he moved to the long conference table near the window. Just as he withdrew the tiny listening device from his pocket a vacuum cleaner roared into life in the next office. He fumbled and dropped the bug.

Cursing quietly, he picked the device up and tried to attach it, but again it slipped from his shaking hand. Swearing again, he took off his gloves, removed the protective film and this time managed to fix the device under the edge of the table. He clumsily wiped the exposed surface with his handkerchief, and hurried out of the office and down the corridor to the lifts.

*

The range of the listening devices was limited, so Taylor had hired a small office across the square in a building filled mainly with lobbyists intent on acquiring a small fraction of the EU's 200-billion-euro budget for their clients.

A technician had rigged up his equipment to capture and record all conversations. Once the bugs were activated by the peeling off of the adhesive covers, they heard the Basque swearing in his native Euskara, and the faint sound of a vacuum cleaner in the distance.

The techy nodded to Taylor. Both bugs were operational.

*

Russian intelligence maintains a substantial presence in Brussels. Most of the personnel are from the FSB's Foreign Intelligence Service, the SVR, but there is also a strong contingent of GRU officers. These military intelligence personnel are usually *Spetsnaz* veterans, with extensive combat experience.

SVR and GRU personnel alike are based in the large Russian Embassy in Avenue De Fré, in the Uccle district of Brussels. They are all "legals", spies operating as declared diplomats. They are tolerated as long as they don't overstep the mark by breaking the informal code governing the behaviour of spies in peacetime.

Most of their activity is focussed on the NATO headquarters in Boulevard Leopold III, but there are enough of them to also maintain active espionage operations targeting the European Parliament and the European Commission.

The SVR also maintains a strong contingent of local "illegals". These are unacknowledged agents operating under deep cover, and without the protection of diplomatic immunity. Andrezs Ozols was one such operative, a Latvian of Russian heritage who had secured a role as a press officer in Commission President Morand's private office – his *cabinet*.

As a press officer, he had ready access to the Commission president, which was useful, as he was the conduit for transmitting Tarakan's instructions direct to Morand, and relaying intelligence in return.

*

Security is not a strong feature of life in the Berlaymont. However, on Tarakan's instructions, conveyed via the press officer Ozols, Morand had ordered an electronic sweep of his suite of offices. The EU does not have an intelligence service as such, but its Intelligence and Situation Centre (INTCEN) is staffed by former intelligence officers, who work closely with the Belgian and other European spy agencies.

The eavesdropping devices were discovered almost immediately. Morand was furious, and worried about what the bugs might have picked up. Forensic examination revealed a partial fingerprint on the bug placed under the conference table.

All of the officials and ancillary staff who had access to the top floor were fingerprinted. Alvariz the Basque was soon identified as the culprit.

Under interrogation by INTCEN it did not take long for Alvariz to crack and reveal his connections with MI6. In return for his confession, and promise of collaboration, he was not sacked, but instead told that he must become a double agent. He would be played back against his former employees.

The listening devices were left in place, but all sensitive discussions, especially those relating to the UK's relations with the EU, were switched to a secure room in the Berlaymont basement.

CHAPTER 20

DUSTANA, TAZMENISTAN

The journey back from the front line was long, and for Sir Walter, painful. He had been given a shot of morphine by the combat medic, but, even so, the jolting of the APC and the buffeting of the helicopter caused him considerable discomfort.

The helicopter was able to land in the grounds of their hotel, but it was well after midnight before the group finally disembarked.

Beaufort ushered the group into the bar. Local beers were initially ordered to slake their thirst, but then two bottles of premium Russian vodka appeared in ice buckets. The elderly peer Lord Griffiths had one drink and then headed up to his room, but the chairman was downing vodka shots in rapid succession.

'Nothing like a near-death experience to work up a thirst,' he explained.

The hotel doctor, having been woken up by the night manager, came bustling over and insisted on shepherding Sir Walter back to his room to check him over and administer more painkillers. Ten minutes later Beaufort also rose, said goodnight to the two MPs and, after exchanging a glance with Faisal, headed up to his room.

As the night drew on, the high-end escorts started to arrive. Nearly all were tall and blonde, and wore stiletto heels that clicked loudly on the marble floor as they crossed the entrance foyer. The women ignored the reception desk, going straight to the lifts and up to the rooms of the guests who had ordered them.

The Tory and Labour backbenchers, the last members of the group still in the bar, looked at each other.

'What happens on tour stays on tour,' Simmonds said to Robinson.

'Nothing's too good for the workers,' Robinson replied.

Geoff Simmonds cleared his throat and addressed the fixer.

'Faisal, these girls are lovely – really gorgeous. If, hypothetically, one wanted to spend some time with them, how much would that cost?'

Faisal laughed before replying.

'These girls are not local – our women do not behave in this way. They are Russian, Belarusian, Ukrainian and from the Baltic states. They come mainly for the oil workers. It is $100 for an hour, or $300 for the night.'

The MPs exchanged another look, and Arthur Robinson chimed in:

'The thing is Faisal, a day like today makes you realise that life can be cut short at any time. If we wanted to make the most of our precious time on this planet, but didn't have that amount of US currency on us, could they perhaps be put on our hotel bills?'

Faisal laughed again and, instead of answering, made a tablet-swiping gesture to the waiter. He came hurrying over with an iPad loaded with pictures of dozens of glamorous girls.

'You just choose the one you want, and he will send her up to your room.'

Simmonds seized the tablet and began scrolling through the photographs. His forefinger left sweaty streaks across the screen. He came to one girl he particularly liked, and handed the tablet back to the waiter. He keyed in a message, and then looked at the MP.

'Fifteen minutes, sir. This girl will be here.'

Simmonds swallowed his drink and hurried to the lifts.

Arthur Robinson took a little longer. His tastes were more exotic. After ten minutes and many swipes he stopped, letting out a low grunt of triumph. He handed the tablet to the waiter, who keyed in the details.

'Twenty minutes, sir. This girl will knock on your door.'

The MP nodded and, like his colleague before him, hurried over to the lifts.

*

Geoff Simmonds faced a dilemma when he reached his room. Did he have time to shower? Probably not. Instead, he rinsed with mouthwash, slapped on some aftershave and applied deodorant liberally.

No sooner had he finished this rudimentary sprucing-up than there was a gentle tap on the door. The young woman standing there was not a disappointment. She was close to six foot tall, at least in her stilettos, young, slim and blonde. Just as importantly, her lips smiled, and her eyes conveyed the impression that she actually meant it.

'Come in, come in,' said the MP. 'Can I get you a drink?'

She smiled again.

'Vodka please, with just ice.'

Her English was heavily accented, but seemed to come easily to her. The Scottish oil workers were obviously a regular source of income.

'What should I call you?'

'I am Katya. And what should I call you?'

'Call me Dave,' he stuttered, unconsciously echoing a former leader of his party.

She swallowed her vodka in one.

'Shall we begin, Dave?'

'Yes, of course,' replied Simmonds, aware that his one hour had probably started with the first tap on the door.

She reached behind her, unfastened her dress and let it slip to the floor. Underneath she wore nothing – nothing at all. No underwear, but also no piercings or tattoos. Her figure was stunning, and from the way she held herself, she knew it.

Simmonds started to struggle out of his clothes, never taking his eyes off Katya, perhaps fearing that, like a mirage, she might suddenly disappear. By the time he had discarded his briefs he was already half erect, which Katya noted with approval.

She grasped the Member by his member and led him gently to the bed. Pushing him onto the mattress she deftly applied a condom, straddled him and inserted him with professional ease. She gently rode him as he reached up for her breasts, and, very quickly, he arched his back, groaned loudly and spasmed.

Katya smiled and asked:

'Was that good? Shall we try again? You still have 40 minutes.'

Nodding eagerly, Simmonds lay back as Katya pulled off the condom and began to use her mouth to bring him back to life.

*

In the next room a very different scenario was playing out. Arthur Robinson had chosen a dominatrix, who arrived with her bag of tricks.

Olga was shorter and darker than Katya, with studs in her ears, nose and nipples. She wore a black leather gothic corset with a multitude of metal studs. It pinched in her waist but left her breasts free, and her vulva exposed.

As soon as she took off her coat, Robinson moaned with pleasure. She immediately ordered him to strip and get down on his knees. Olga proceeded to push her toes into his mouth, one foot after the other. Then she grabbed him by the hair and dragged him to the bed, ordering him to kneel facing the headboard.

Olga took a silken cat-o'-nine-tails from her bag and began whipping Robinson's backside, gradually increasing the frequency and force of the blows. This was too much for the MP. With a groan he ejaculated copiously onto the bedspread, before collapsing forward into his own mess. Apart from the toe sucking and hair pulling, they had not touched.

The dominatrix looked at him with contempt, packed her whip away, put on her coat and left. This one would not be up to a second round.

Easiest hundred bucks she had earned in quite a while.

*

In an upstairs bedroom converted into a recording studio for the duration of the trip, Faisal turned to the technicians who had been managing the video and audio feeds.

'And that's a wrap,' he announced in a faux American accent.

CHAPTER 21

PRESIDENTIAL PALACE, DUSTANA

The following morning, despite clearly still suffering from the pain of his injury, Sir Walter Atkins was the first down to breakfast, followed closely by Lord Aled Griffiths.

Arthur Robinson and Geoff Simmonds arrived about fifteen minutes later, both looking tired and slightly sheepish. Faisal looked across at Beaufort and grinned conspiratorially.

Beaufort proceeded to brief the group.

'Thanks for being – almost – on time, gentlemen. This is the most important meeting of the trip. President Barakat does not meet every delegation, and it's a sign of how highly he values relations with the United Kingdom that he's agreed to see us. He's well educated: degrees from Oxford and Harvard, and then a diploma from the Moscow Diplomatic Academy.

He speaks perfect English and will have read your biographies. It is very much like meeting the King – you don't speak unless spoken to. The first time you address him as Mr President, and thereafter as Excellency. Any questions?'

There were none. They finished breakfast, then climbed aboard the waiting Toyota Land Cruisers. This time they had a police escort, and made it to the presidential palace – perched on a hill with a panoramic view of the whole capital city and bay – in just 20 minutes.

Much to their irritation the whole party was ordered to go through security scanners at the palace entrance. They were met by an aide-de-camp, a tall, handsome young man in an immaculate uniform. There was also a female translator. She was average height, slight and business-like. She addressed the group in perfect American-accented English.

'Gentlemen, the president is running a little behind schedule, but he has asked me to take you to a waiting room and offer you refreshments. Please follow me.'

They did, and the eyes of Arthur Robinson and Geoff Simmonds followed the undulations of her backside as she led the way up the stairs. Both men turned to smirk at each other.

The translator led them into a grand room with marbled columns, multiple mirrors and dazzling chandeliers. She gestured towards an array of chairs and settees arranged around an ornate coffee table.

'Please, make yourself comfortable. The president will not keep you waiting any longer than necessary.'

Local tea, known as *chai*, appeared, along with thick Turkish-style coffee and a range of cakes dipped in honey and covered with almonds. Conscious of the presence of the guards and the interpreter, the politicians kept the conversation sparse and mundane. After twenty minutes the doors to the president's office were flung open by two guards, and the ADC led them into an even larger and more imposing room.

The president was a tall, striking man with strong features and the style of luxuriant moustache that most of his fellow countrymen favoured. Instead of the military uniform that the group had expected, he wore an immaculately tailored Western suit. Rising from behind his desk, he shook hands with every member of the group, apart from Faisal, whom he ignored.

Gesturing for his guests to sit around a long conference table, the president, clearly pushed for time, and clearly not used to engaging in lengthy dialogue, walked to the head of the table, took a seat and delivered a short monologue. This was diligently captured by a local TV camera crew.

'Honoured guests, you are most welcome. You have been to the front line. You have seen the enemy entrenched in our territory. You, Sir Walter, they even tried to shoot, and their reckless mortar fire could have killed you all. You have witnessed the terrible suffering of the refugees and IDPs, and the conditions they are forced to live in. This is intolerable to our people, and it is intolerable to me.'

The President now raised his voice to emphasise his point. This seemed to be as much for the benefit of the camera crew as for the British politicians seated around the conference table.

'We need modern weapons from your country to help us to defend ourselves, and in order to expel the invaders. And we need your support in the United Nations, where you have a permanent seat on the Security Council. If we do not get these two things from you, we will be forced to look elsewhere. Please convey this to your government.

Thank you for coming.'

With that the president rose, the doors were once again flung open, and the ADC ushered them from the room.

*

On their way out they noticed that there were two men waiting in the antechamber.

One, sitting alone on an elaborately brocaded settee, was tall and skeletally thin, dressed in a simple grey Western suit, with a cream silk shirt and no tie. His head was either naturally bald, or shaven and, despite being indoors, he wore dark wrap-around sunglasses.

The British Parliamentary group were metres away from Tarakan, the feared director of the Russian FSB.

Standing behind Tarakan was a giant of a man, dressed in a black *chokha*, with a shaven head, a luxuriant red beard and ferocious brown eyes.

As the Britons were passing through, the FSB director rose to his feet, and then slowly took off his sunglasses. He singled out and locked eyes with Beaufort, who realised with a shock that he had *heterochromia*: one green eye and one brown.

The ADC nervously ushered them from the room before any words could be exchanged.

*

As they drove back in the same convoy they had set out in, Beaufort asked Faisal:

'Who was that strange man with the sunglasses? He looked more dangerous than the brute of a bodyguard standing behind him.'

Faisal looked uncomfortable, and turned to gaze out of the window before replying:

'I don't really know, sir, and you really do not want to know. He was born here, but he does not live here. Some say he does not live at all.'

*

As the British group left, the giant bodyguard, a Chechen called Dudayev, asked his master:

'Shall I kill the tall pretty one?'

Tarakan turned on him.

'No, fool, you will not touch him, not now, not ever. I will find somebody else for you to kill.'

CHAPTER 22

CHARING CROSS, LONDON

Despite his position on the influential Intelligence and Security Committee, Geoff Simmonds was an opposition backbencher with a safe seat, so he had plenty of time on his hands. It was therefore comparatively easy for Samantha, in her guise as a lobbyist, to persuade him to meet her.

She suggested Gordon's Wine Bar, an ancient establishment in a dark basement in Villiers Street. Its location near the Ministry of Defence and low level lighting made it a favoured venue for civil servants to meet journalists and leak stories.

Simmonds had checked out Samantha's profile on LinkedIn, and her looks had been partially responsible for his accepting her invitation. Despite being married, Simmonds had a roving eye; he had already been warned by the whips to be more careful in his dealings with female colleagues and members of staff.

Catching sight of Simmonds peering around in the gloom Samantha stood up and waved. He came over and they shook hands. She noticed the way he held onto her hand for several moments longer than necessary.

Samantha smiled and said:

'I got us a bottle of house claret. I hope that's OK?'

Simmonds smiled in return.

'Good choice.'

Samantha poured two generous glasses.

'So, to what do I owe the pleasure? I see you have British Defence Industries as a client?'

'Yes, we do. And being a lobbyist is my day job. But I do have a side hustle.'

Simmonds smiled again.

'I'm intrigued. What might that be?'

'I'm an agent for the Secret Intelligence Service.'

Simmonds was stunned by this revelation, not to mention the calmness with which Samantha had announced her connection to the supposedly clandestine organisation.

He adopted a grave tone.

'You know I'm on the ISC. And you also know I've signed the Official Secrets Act. I cannot reveal any details of the committee's work to you – or anybody else.'

Without a word Samantha retrieved her phone from her handbag, navigated to the video of Simmonds in the hotel room in Dustana and handed the device to him.

'Go on, play it. The quality is excellent, both vision and sound – but I suggest you don't unmute it in here.'

As he watched the video of his encounter with the call girl Katya in Dustana, Simmonds visibly blanched. His hand was shaking slightly as he handed the phone back.

'What do you want?'

Samantha told him.

'We're fighting a turf war with Dame Sheila Norris of

MI5, and right now we are losing. My service has kept this country safe from external enemies for over a century, and we're not going to allow ourselves to be side-lined or wound up without putting up a fight.

If you hear anything about the proposed closure of MI6, or a merger with MI5, you will let us know. If this comes before your committee we will find out in due course, and if you haven't alerted us immediately, this video will go to the political gossip websites, to the whips. . . and to your wife. Here is a business card for my day job. If you hear or see anything – anything at all – you call me.'

Simmonds finished his glass of claret in one long gulp, picked up the card, and left.

CHAPTER 23

HOUSE OF COMMONS, WESTMINSTER

The announcement that there would be a statement on Central Asia after Prime Minister's Questions flashed up on the House of Commons annunciator screens mid-morning. Beaufort had persuaded a friendly MP to obtain two tickets for seats in the Strangers' Gallery, one for him and one for the Tazmen oligarch, Usman Abdullaev.

The foreign secretary, James Fraser, a Labour veteran from the Blythe years, rose at the despatch box. His thinking on this issue had been heavily influenced by his parliamentary private secretary, Arthur Robinson. Like Geoff Simmonds, he had been shown the video of his session with the dominatrix Olga, and instructed to use his influence on the foreign secretary. He had readily agreed.

'With permission, Mr Speaker, I would like to make a statement on the United Kingdom's interests in the Central Asian region. It has long been the policy of governments of various hues not to become involved in conflicts in that part of the world, or to take sides. However...' – a murmur of anticipation rose up from all sides of the chamber – 'However, following recent events, I can announce that, with the agreement of my Right Honourable Friend the Prime Minister and of cabinet colleagues, this policy has now changed. Recently an All-Party Parliamentary Group went on a fact-finding trip to Tazmenistan. During the course of that trip, the group came under unprovoked attack by the forces of Ujikistan, and the Right Honourable Member for Atchington sustained a serious injury.'

At this point all eyes turned to Sir Walter Atkins, who was ostentatiously sporting a sling to support his shoulder.

'All members of the group came under mortar fire and were forced to take cover, and an emergency evacuation became necessary. As a result of this incident we have recalled our ambassador to Ujikistan. This morning I summoned the Ujikistani ambassador to the Court of St James to the Foreign Office for a meeting, during which I expressed the utmost displeasure of His Majety's Government.'

A few scattered 'hear hears' rose from the government benches.

'I can also announce that, partly as a result of this incident, the arms embargo put in place whilst we were still members of the European Union will be lifted with immediate effect – but only with regard to Tazmenistan. Furthermore, I can announce that we will shortly be despatching a high-level trade mission to Dustana. This will negotiate the export of British weapons and high-tech equipment to Tazmenistan, and the reciprocal import of Tazmen oil, gas and certain strategic minerals. These measures will provide a welcome boost to British companies, and support our growth agenda.'

The statement was welcomed by the opposition front bench, and by backbenchers on both sides of the House. Arthur Robinson, parliamentary private secretary to the foreign secretary, and Geoff Simmonds, recounted their versions of the incident, and spoke strongly in support of the change of government policy.

However, when the Speaker called Alf Barnstaple, Chairman of the Ujikistan All-Party Parliamentary Group, the House quietened in order to hear what he had to say.

In Commons parlance Barnstaple was a "tanky". This was somebody who was loyal to the Russian-backed Ujikistani regime, and who fondly remembered the glory days of the old Soviet Union. He had stayed loyal despite the Moscow government's decision to despatch tanks to violently put down revolts in Prague and Budapest.

'Thank you, Mr Speaker. I have listened with astonishment to my Right Honourable Friend's statement. The dispute between Ujikistan and Tazmenistan goes back to Soviet times – good times, for some of us.' Hoots of derision greeted these words. 'This incident was clearly staged by the Tazmens, to distract attention from their brutal treatment of the Ujikistani minority in their lands. We should be neutral in this conflict – or even be supporting the Ujiks.'

His words were met with a further chorus of dissent – mostly cheerful.

The Speaker then called Sir Walter, who rose to his full height, holding rough notes in his uninjured left hand.

'Thank you, Mr Speaker. I welcome my Right Honourable Friend's statement. Members of my All-Party Group have made numerous trips to Tazmenistan – but we have never been shot at, or indeed come under mortar fire.

The Tazmens are the wronged party in this dispute, and they have much to offer this country in terms of imports and exports. I look forward to helping to ensure that these opportunities are maximised.'

The Speaker called on the foreign secretary to wind up.

'Thank you, Mr Speaker. I am pleased that this change of policy has received almost universal support in this House.'

Barnstaple yelled out 'Rubbish' from his seat on the front bench below the gangway, where the "awkward squad" tended to congregate.

'I said *almost* universal,' the foreign secretary riposted. 'It is simply not acceptable for members of this House to be shot at, or shelled, and I commend this statement to the House.'

As the 'hear hears' of approval rang out, Beaufort turned to the oligarch sitting next to him, and they silently shook hands.

Lobbying in action.

*

After exiting the Parliamentary Estate, Beaufort and Abdullaev, shadowed by the oligarch's two bodyguards, walked the few hundred yards to the new five-star hotel built within the shell of the Old War Office Building. They headed to the subterranean Spy Bar, where Samantha was waiting with Ewan Farquhar of British Defence Industries.

After being introduced to Farquhar the oligarch ordered champagne.

'A toast,' Abdullaev announced, raising his glass, 'to Beaufort, to His Majesty's Government, and,' looking across at Farquhar, 'to a long and profitable relationship.'

*

In the taxi on way back to the office Samantha turned to Beaufort.

'Well done, you've proved yourself, and shown that old-fashioned lobbying really can work. Frobisher is very pleased.'

Beaufort bowed his head in acknowledgement, and waited for the caveat.

'But that was just an appetiser. It's almost time for the main course. And we'll be playing for higher stakes this time – much higher stakes.'

CHAPTER 24

WESTMINSTER, LONDON

With the help of the large monthly retainer from Abdullaev, and the success in opening up the Tazmen market for British Defence Industries, Beaufort Public Affairs was starting to recover its pre-election status as one of the UK's leading lobbying consultancies.

Samantha's arrival, and her appointment as Beaufort's second in command, had helped to detoxify the brand, and brought on board several new clients from the charitable and not-for-profit sectors.

As a result of this revival of fortunes Beaufort felt confident enough to reinstate his regular lunches for clients and prospective clients. In previous parliaments these lunches had taken place on the last Friday of every month, except in August and December.

Officially the lunches were billed as the "Lobbyists' Lunch". Unofficially, participants referred to them as the "Merchants of Death" lunches. All of those invited were past or present clients of Beaufort's, or those he hoped to add to his client list in the future.

The venue was always the same. A private dining room at the back of Parlamento, Westminster's longest-established Italian restaurant, tucked away in a side street off Smith Square. Nor did the format change. Brief introductory remarks by Beaufort as the host, and then a *tour de table*, with guests giving an overview of developments in their own sectors.

The guest list varied but those invited had one thing in common, over and above their association with Beaufort. The industry the guests represented had to be responsible for the death of a great many of their fellow human beings. The job of the attendees was to make sure that the government of the day continued to allow them to carry on business as usual, since these companies required a licence to operate.

There were eight guests that day. The party was small enough to be intimate, but large enough to provide lively conversation. Beaufort rose to his feet, gently tapping his wine glass with his knife to attract attention.

'Good afternoon everybody, and welcome to this month's Lobbyists' Lunch. You all know the rules – not the Chatham House Rule, not "off the record," but an *omertà*. If you break it, you will be about as welcome in this august circle as a turd in a swimming pool, or a fart in a lift.' He paused to allow the ripple of laughter to subside. 'On a serious note, we all know that gossip is our everyday currency of choice, but discretion regarding these lunches has to be total. What is said here stays within these four walls – and I can assure you they've been swept for bugs!' Another murmur of appreciation. 'OK, most of you know each other, but let's go round the table, introduce ourselves, and set out our credentials.'

Beaufort gestured to the man with a military bearing to his left, inviting him to start the proceedings. He looked like he wanted to rise to his feet, but instead sat ramrod straight in his seat.

'Afternoon everybody. Ewan Farquhar, Major General retired, late of the Scots Guards, now Director of Sales and Marketing at British Defence Industries plc. Currently helping to arm the good guys in Ukraine and the middle east, and starting to supply Taiwan. Also looking forward,' he glanced at Beaufort, 'to opening up new markets in the near future. No sign whatsoever of peace breaking out anywhere any time soon, which is good for our share price, and great for my bonus.'

Appreciative noises from the other guests, and then a throat clearing from the rake thin woman immediately to the general's left.

'Joanna Chamberlain, Director of Comms at Big Burgers, suppliers of fast food to the greedy and indolent. Lots of talk from this new government about clamping down on our products,' she paused, 'but they know their voters are addicted to our fat-infused fodder. Obviously, I never touch the muck myself, but as long as the fat fuckers can fit through our big double doors, and then waddle off to do the odd day's work, I will still be gainfully employed.'

'And if the fat fuckers can no longer waddle into work,' chipped in the young woman to her left, 'we will flog the government our anti-obesity jabs, so win-win I would say!' Fiona Dalmayne, who represented SlimaPharm, turned to high five the fast-food representative seated to her right.

The man to her left chipped in.

'Well our punters – and I use the word advisedly – have more choice.'

Fred Bryant represented Jackpot Bonanza, a gambling company which ran a chain of betting shops and a string of casinos, and had recently acquired an online gambling website hosted in Gibraltar.

'Most of them just like the occasional flutter. OK, some of them are hooked – but we fund a charity that helps them kick the habit if they really want to. Fortunately, very few of them really do!'

Joe Thomson represented British BrewDistil, a major drinks company whose portfolio encompassed everything from a nationwide pub chain to breweries in the north of England, vineyards in France, and whisky distilleries in Scotland.

'We're the good guys,' he pronounced, tongue firmly in his cheek. 'Not least because we're supplying the drinks for this lunch!' A ripple of appreciative laughter went around the table. 'Seriously, we have been around for centuries, and you have to work really hard, over a long period of time, to kill yourself with our products.'

A rangy Australian, a newcomer dressed in chinos and a crumpled linen shirt, introduced himself:

'Hi, I am Jack Shaw out of Sydney, New South Wales. I represent Payday Mayday in the UK. Now that you Brits have left the EU we see plenty of scope to develop this market. We offer payday loans at not entirely unreasonable rates – assuming you can find the money to repay on time. And if your compatriots want to carry on eating crap food, drinking, gambling and smoking, well, some of you are gonna need our help. Pleased to be invited, and delighted to be of service.'

That was Beaufort's cue.

'And talking of smoking, last, but by no means least, our friend from big tobacco.'

Brian Swayne, the representative of the Global Tobacco Corporation, had patiently been waiting his turn.

'Come on you guys – this is amateur league. We manage to kill off half of our customers! No other industry in history has killed as many people as us. But it's all legal. And it's your job,' pointing at Beaufort, 'to make sure it stays that way.'

Just then the door opened and a compact man with a crew cut and dressed in a Brooks Brothers suit appeared. Beaufort gestured for him to take the empty seat next to Ewan Farquhar. The latecomer shook hands with Farquhar, and then addressed the group.

'Hi everybody, I am Brad Kowalski from the good old US of A. I used to fly fighter-bombers, and now I sell them for Granthorne Aviation. Me and my good friend Ewan here are going to be working with Dr Beaufort to persuade your new government to provide end-user certificates so that we can sell our joint-venture products to a wider market in this dangerous world we all live in. Honoured to be invited to join this select group, and apologies for being late – most un-American.'

Words of welcome echoed around the table and Kowalski was soon in animated conversation with Farquhar. Beaufort, who thought the American might have chosen to duck the lunch, looked on with relief.

As the main course was served, and the wine continued to flow freely, the conversations became louder and more fractured, with guests talking to their neighbours left and right, and leaning across the table to make their points to those sitting opposite.

Conversations roamed across the political scene, with hot gossip on who was sleeping with whom, who was on the take, who was on the way up, and who was heading for a fall. One topic dominated – how long would the new Labour government continue to tolerate industries which preyed on their own electorate?

After dessert had been served and the port decanter circulated Beaufort tapped his glass again and began winding up the event.

'Thank you all for coming, old friends and,' looking at the American, 'new. The one thing that unites us around this table is a belief in freedom of choice. We believe that adults should be free to eat what they like, drink what they like, and – within reason – smoke what they like.'

This veiled reference to the possible future legalisation of cannabis raised a laugh.

'We have a government that fundamentally believes that the man – or woman – from Whitehall knows best. If they could, they would ban, or at least severely limit, most of the products you sell. But for now, they can't. They need the excise revenue you contribute, and they need the jobs which you create and sustain. And as long as that is the case, and as long as they remain scared of the "nanny state" label – and, of course, as long as you keep the donations flowing into their party coffers – they will continue to meet you, and at least pretend to listen to you. But make no mistake: they hate you, and everything you stand for, and if they get the chance, they will rein you in and ultimately wipe you out. That is why you need lobbyists. That is why you need me.'

There were murmurs of agreement around the table and then, seemingly by pre-arrangement, Joanna Chamberlain, who had stuck with Beaufort through the lean times, tapped her own wine glass and gave the vote of thanks.

'We all owe Damian Beaufort a great deal, not just for these lunches, but also for helping to steer us through a change of regime. So, the toast is to Damian – our very own Dr Death.'

The guests rose to their feet, and noisily echoed the toast:

'To Dr Death.'

Farquhar added a gravelly adjunct:

'May he keep our industries alive.'

*

Ewan Farquhar and Brad Kowalski had been in deep conversation throughout most of the lunch. They were the only pair who worked in the same sector, and were bored by the conversation of the consumer-facing lobbyists around the table.

As the lunch wound up Farquhar suggested they continue the conversation at the Special Forces Club, of which he had been a member since a stint in the SAS as a young officer. The club was founded in 1945 by SOE survivors, and its membership consisted of an esoteric collection of spooks and special forces veterans, plus a handful of war correspondents with frontline experience.

Having ordered pints to wash down the wine they had consumed over lunch, they sat at a remote table and

Farquhar broached the subject he had not been able to discuss over lunch:

'How important is the Trident missile contract to your company?'

'Extremely important. The contract to supply missiles to your Trident boats is big, although the contract to supply them to the US Navy Ohio class boomers is massive. Why do you ask?'

'Here's the thing. Our new government came in thinking that since we built the boats and the warheads we must have total control over our nuclear deterrent. Clem Clark was briefed by the outgoing Tory PM that because your company assembles the missiles – both the hardware and software – you and the president have an effective veto over its deployment. He is more than a little disturbed by this, and has ordered the ramping up of a programme to develop a work-around to your software, so we could have total control. They plan to use our new Tyche satellites rather than your NAVSTAR system for guidance, and to have a test launch in a few weeks' time.'

Kowalski was visibly shaken by this news, and took a long pull at his beer before replying.

'OK two questions. First, how do you know this? And second, why are you telling me?'

'I can't name my source, but let's just say he belongs to something that likes to call itself the Senior Service – an insult in my view to both the army and the air force. As to why, from a commercial point of view British Defence Industries has far more collaboration projects with you than with the Europeans. And, from a personal point of view, I can't stand Clem Clark and the bunch of second-rate

Trots he's surrounded himself with.'

Kowalski looked Farquhar square in the eyes, nodded, and raised his glass.

'OK thanks. I'll pass your intel on to the Pentagon. I'm sure they'll be grateful, and that they'll express their gratitude in tangible form.'

CHAPTER 25

BELGRAVIA, LONDON

Half a mile away, on the Belgravia Victoria borders, another lobbyists' lunch was being held.

Instead of the plush Italian restaurant, this was in an unpretentious Indian eatery. Instead of fine wines, the drink was lager, mineral water or fruit juice. And instead of rich Italian meat dishes, the Ashoka restaurant served up curries, many of them vegetarian or vegan.

Samantha had started convening these lunches to coincide with Beaufort's "Merchants of Death" gatherings. The guest list could not have been more different. It was made up of charity representatives from the worthy third sector, those who aimed to save lives, instead of ending them. As such, instead of Merchants of Death, they had christened themselves the "Angels of Mercy".

As the attendees could attest, angels could be male or female, or even something in between.

The ambience and the fare may have been very different, but the format was identical. Samantha tapped her beer glass with a knife, and stood up to get the proceedings underway.

'Good afternoon, everybody, and welcome to this month's alternative Lobbyists' Lunch. Obviously, we have nothing to hide, but perhaps it would aid discussion if we all agree that everything said at these events is kept between ourselves. We're all professionals, and despite our undeniably worthy intentions, we are realists: we understand there is a need for discretion if we're going to express ourselves freely. So anyway, enough from me. Most of you know each other, but why don't we go round the table and introduce ourselves?'

The young, slim woman with purple died hair and dressed in denim dungarees seated to Samantha's left, took her cue.

'Afternoon everybody. Most of you know me. I'm Jo Bennett, Head of Public Affairs at the Child Poverty Fund. As a charity we're obviously not allowed to lobby. But we do try and shape the policy agenda to ensure as many children as possible are lifted out of poverty. Our stated aim is to eliminate child poverty, but of course by constantly changing the definition of what child poverty is, we can make sure that will never actually happen!'

Jo turned to her left, and the sickly-looking young man sitting there seemed surprised to find himself in the spotlight.

'Oh, yes, sorry, hi everyone. I'm Alan Honeyball, and I am Head of Research at British Animal Action Alliance. We make sure that the rights of animals are defended in Westminster and Whitehall. Again, as Jo has said, as a charity we cannot lobby, but we make sure that parliamentarians and civil servants are fully aware of the cruelties inflicted on the animal kingdom in our - for now at least – United

Kingdom. I would like to thank you all for choosing the vegetarian options. Eating dead animals is not only cruel, it's also bad for human health.'

Next to speak was an earnest middle-aged woman wearing dark-rimmed thick-lens spectacles, and with her hair captured in a severe bun.

'Good afternoon, everybody. I'm Dr Yvonne Kantar, Director of Advocacy at Cancer Cure UK, one of the UK's leading cancer charities. I think we're all aware that up to half of us around this table will contract one form of cancer or another. We're also aware that lifestyle has a significant impact on the odds of our doing so. That being the case I am proud to be not just a vegetarian, but a vegan. And very happy to stick to fruit juice. I just wish that our lords and masters in Westminster would do the same.'

An overweight man with a florid complexion was next in line.

'Afternoon one and all. I am Andrew Bancroft, and I'm Director of Strategy for the UK Heart Campaign. Over 25,000 people a year die from some form of heart disease, and we aim to bring those numbers down dramatically. But we need the government to play its part, by clamping down on the type of harmful behaviour that causes coronary issues. We've tried to educate and explain, and it is simply not working. The government needs to start outlawing harmful behaviours, and our aim is to make sure that they do so.'

His speech was somewhat undermined by the faintest hint of whisky on his breath, and the yellow nicotine stains on the fingers of his right hand, but in that company, nobody was about to challenge him. Do as I say, not what

I do, was the unspoken but widely accepted maxim of the voluntary sector.

The last guest to introduce himself was a well-dressed late-middle-aged black man who spoke with a strong West African accent.

'Thank you for the invitation. I have not been to one of these lunches before. I am Dr Amadi Abdoulahi, Executive Director of the Global South Reparations Campaign. I have worked for many years on the ground and in the field, and I have seen first-hand the poverty and hardship that war and climate change have inflicted on my continent. Most of our troubles can be traced back to the ravages of colonial rule, and my job, and my mission in life, is to make sure that reparations flow from the former colonial powers to the descendants of their victims.'

There was a strong groundswell of agreement around the table in response to this passionate address.

Then, as a plethora of dishes for the main course arrived, the conversation fragmented. The main themes, however, were consistent. The Tories were bastards, who ground the faces of the poor, sick and disadvantaged into the dirt. Labour, on the other hand, had the interests of the deprived at heart, but had been left no money with which to help them, thanks to the greed and incompetence of the previous Conservative government.

After the healthy mango and coconut-based desserts had been consumed, Samantha began bringing the proceedings to an end – much earlier than at Beaufort's equivalent event. For the second time that day she tapped her glass to attract attention before saying:

'Thanks for coming everybody. I hope you have found

the discussions interesting and useful, and our thanks to Iqbal and his team for looking after us so well. After more than a decade of Tory governments – under various leaders – we now have a chance to claw back some of the ground, and some of the funding, that we lost. I left New Zealand because the Right came back to power there, but my aim, now we have a Labour government in the mother country, is that the voluntary sector enjoys its time in the sun. We know the Tories always find a way back into power, so we must use these years to good effect.'

The vote of thanks came from Jo Bennett, who had begun proceedings.

'Thank you, Samantha, for those words, and for arranging today. We're all fighting for slices of the same pie, so we must make sure that the pie itself is as large as possible. And if that means having to soak the rich, or having to borrow more money, then so be it. Our time has come, and as you so rightly said, we must make the most of it.'

*

Beaufort and Samantha had arranged to meet after their lunches at Davy's, a wine bar just off of Piccadilly.

It was underground, and had a suitably conspiratorial air. More importantly it was unlikely that any Westminster people would bother to walk across St James's Park in search of drink or company.

Beaufort took a taxi, and arrived first. Samantha, who had walked from Belgravia, spotted him at the corner table he had secured and flopped into the empty chair opposite him.

'Jesus, I need a proper drink. Those do-gooders make

me want to puke.'

Samantha's Kiwi accent was thickened by her disgust.

'All they do is scrounge off society and encourage victimhood amongst their clients. Meantime they work in fancy offices, earn good salaries and expect a big fat bonus for distorting public policy and changing the law.'

Beaufort signalled for the waiter and ordered a bottle of house claret.

'Yes, at least my lot are nakedly cynical. But we need your rabble to give us cover and to open doors that would otherwise remain closed to us. So, here's a toast – to the Merchants of Death, and to the Angels of Mercy – who fly top cover and provide them with first rate air support!'

CHAPTER 26

VAUXHALL CROSS, LONDON

The Admiral was becoming increasingly angry about the attitude and activities of the recently-elected Labour government.

By time-honoured practice the head of MI6 had always been granted unrestricted access to the prime minister, and other senior cabinet ministers. Under the new regime it was Dame Sheila Norris of MI5 who had the PM's ear. The Admiral was frustrated by his lack of access, and by the marginalisation of the agency he led.

He had tasked Frobisher with addressing the problem, and arranged a meeting with his protégé to discuss potential solutions.

This time, when he arrived for the meeting, Frobisher was nodded straight through by Ms Danso. He found the Admiral standing at the window of his office, arms clasped behind his back, glowering in the direction of the Palace of Westminster. Without turning round he snapped:

'So what have you got for me?'

'It's difficult, sir. Their people are excited to be back in government, and have a reformist zeal to save the nation – as they see it. Their focus, as with most new governments, is on domestic policy. They can lift their gaze as far as Europe, but anything beyond that seems beyond them.'

The Admiral turned and glowered at Frobisher.

'You're telling me what I already know. What is your proposed solution?'

'Of course, sir, in time we'll either be able to suborn one of their people, or infiltrate their ranks with one of our own. But we don't have the resources here in the UK that Box have. So we need to be patient – or try something radical.'

'We don't have time to be patient!' the Admiral barked. 'That lot,' he nodded towards Thames House, 'are running rings around us. What's your radical solution then?'

Frobisher told him.

CHAPTER 27

PALL MALL, LONDON

When he received the invitation from Frobisher to a second lunch at the Travellers Club Beaufort assumed it would be for a routine review, or a thank you for the Tazmenistan trip. He was therefore not altogether surprised to find that Samantha had also been invited.

When Beaufort arrived at the club Frobisher and Samantha were already seated at the former's regular table, by a window in the far corner. Frobisher stood up to shake hands, but Samantha remained seated. Beaufort thought she was looking uncharacteristically uncomfortable.

After George had taken their food and wine orders, and a bottle of house champagne had been poured, Frobisher deployed all his bonhomie to toast the pair of them.

'Here's to the two of you – you have done a fantastic job. The Ujikistanis have been put back in their box, the arms embargo on the Tazmenistanis has been lifted and British Defence Industries has landed a few chunky contracts. The UK has also started to buy Usman Abdullaev's minerals. So,' he raised his glass to Beaufort, 'you have fully justified our faith – in particular my faith – in you, and in the power of lobbying.'

'Thank you Charles. It's good to be back at the highest level of the lobbying game – and to have such an able colleague alongside me.'

He raised his champagne flute to Samantha. She raised her glass in return, but did not meet his gaze.

The conversation then turned to the unseasonal weather and its effect on the sporting calendar. The main course having been finished and cleared away, Frobisher finally raised the real reason behind the meeting.

'When I said you've done a great job I meant it, Damian. But we – Samantha and I – have a very demanding boss in the Admiral. He's worried about the current government's direction of travel, and feels we are being kept in the dark on various vital issues. The upshot is, we need somebody on the inside.'

'That won't be easy,' Beaufort replied, 'these people are fanatics – they're on a mission. A handful of them are sensible though. Have you tried tapping up my old number two, Jennifer?'

Looking embarrassed Samantha replied:

'I probably should have told you, Damian, but I've been out for drinks with Jennifer a couple of times. We got on very well, but my assessment is that she's fully committed to the government's agenda.'

Beaufort stared at Samantha, silently seething at the fact she had bypassed him to approach his former colleague.

Frobisher noticed the frisson of tension, but decided to plough on.

'The thing is, we are getting pretty desperate.' He paused,

looked at Beaufort, and continued. 'Like you were desperate. After the general election. When we bailed you out.'

'I know that, and I am grateful. But I've delivered on the Tazmens, and my agency provides cover for Samantha. I don't see what else I can do to help.'

Frobisher decided the time had come to stop prevaricating and cut to the chase.

'It's really simple, but at the same time really difficult. We need you to defect to the Labour Party.'

'You have got to be fucking joking!' Beaufort slammed his champagne flute down, spilling half the contents. He grated out a response: 'I've been a Tory all my life. I hate Labour, and they hate me. And nobody likes defectors, they're beneath contempt. The party they leave hates them – the party they join never trusts them. I cannot do it. I will not do it.'

Heads turned as Beaufort rose, flung his napkin at Frobisher, and stormed out of the room.

'Well, that went well,' Samantha said. 'I did try to warn you.'

'I thought that he would probably react like that. It's natural, and I do understand. But we're going to have to talk him round. More specifically, you are going to have to talk him round.'

'How in God's name am I supposed to do that? You saw how he reacted.'

'Any way you can, Samantha.'

'Any way?'

'Any way.'

CHAPTER 28

PIMLICO AND VICTORIA, LONDON

Having stormed out of the club, Beaufort decided not to go back to the office.

Instead, he returned to his flat, turned his phone off and his TV on, and proceeded to drink his way through his remaining stocks of vodka and wine. His mood slipped back into the despondency of the immediate post-election period, when his business was collapsing and his life unravelling.

Beaufort's depression gradually morphed into anger. His fury was initially directed at Frobisher, who to his mind had betrayed the friendship they had kept up since their schooldays.

Then, to his surprise, he realised that he was more hurt by Samantha's role in trying to persuade him to do the unthinkable and desert the Tories for Labour. Although he had only known her a few months, she had used her intelligence, beauty and charm to infiltrate not only his business, but also his affections.

Using an app, Beaufort ordered more wine and vodka. As

an afterthought he added a couple of pizzas. He considered sending for a call girl, or putting in a booty call to his PA Elizabeth, but then rejected both ideas.

Sitting alone, Beaufort ate, and drank, and thought. He considered his options. Having done so, he realised he had very few. On reflection, he had none.

*

Samantha had been trying Beaufort's mobile repeatedly since the lunch, but his phone was switched off.

When he did not turn up for work the following morning she called Elizabeth into her office.

'Have you heard from Damian?'

'No, nothing at all.'

'We had a bit of a falling out yesterday. You know him as well as anybody. What is it that makes him tick?'

Elizabeth thought before replying.

'He's quite a private person. He's had plenty of relationships, but none of them really last. He's attractive to women – and some men – and he knows it. He uses his looks and charm to get his way – in life, in work and in politics. He flirts a lot, and sometimes he follows through. But when a relationship looks like getting serious, he ends it.'

'And why do you think that is?'

'Classic commitment issues. He never had a father, and his mother didn't have much time for him. She was – and still is – a great beauty, and a fine actress, if rather typecast. Over the years she's had a string of high society boyfriends, but she's never told Beaufort who his father is which he resents. That's what's made him the way he is.'

'And what exactly is that? The way he is?'

Elizabeth considered again.

'He is undeniably manipulative, scheming, and ruthless. He can also be vengeful. When a senior member of staff left the consultancy and then poached one of his clients, he waited almost a year before taking his revenge. He knew that this guy was a heavy cocaine user. He waited until he found out he was organising a big reception on the Commons Terrace for the client he'd stolen from us. Knowing that this former colleague couldn't handle the stress of organising a large event without the aid of some Bolivian marching powder, Damian tipped off the Palace police.

Normally visitors are just scanned for weapons, but this guy was properly searched on entry, and the drugs were found. The quantity wasn't enough to send him to prison, but he was utterly ruined. And Damian got the client back.'

Samantha cut in, interrupting Elizabeth's flow.

'You're making him sound like a total bastard.'

'He's not really, no. I have to be fair and say that he has many laudable attributes, to counter-balance the negative ones. He's intensely patriotic, and consistently loyal to his friends and his colleagues. As you know he's charming too, which is a major plus in our business. But never forget that beneath that sometimes smarmy exterior he is genuinely clever – he got a doctorate while holding down a full-time job working for an MP, and that takes some doing.'

'You're really quite fond of him, aren't you?'

Elizabeth blushed.

'Yes, yes I really am. There's so much more to him, I know, more than he chooses to show the world I mean. I've seen that side of him.'

Samantha sat there, absorbing this insight into a man she thought she had come to know well. Then she asked the question, the answer to which might decide whether he could continue to be an MI6 asset.

'And, in your experience, does he ever change his mind?'

'Not as far as I know, no. Never.'

CHAPTER 29

PARK LANE, LONDON

After her discussion with Elizabeth, Samantha messaged Beaufort.

'I know you are pissed off. Let's have a drink and discuss. Vesper Bar @ Dorchester - 6.30.'

There was no response for over an hour, and then a terse 'OK.'

Samantha left work early and went home to change.

She dressed carefully, in a green silk dress that hugged her figure and highlighted her green eyes and red hair. She applied a dab of Chanel Coco Mademoiselle behind each ear, and chose a red Gucci clutch bag, to complete her preparations.

Beaufort deliberately arrived ten minutes late, unshaven, dressed in jeans, a crumpled polo shirt and a black leather bomber jacket. He sat down without a word and waited for Samantha to speak.

'I really am sorry about all this, Damian. I told Frobisher you wouldn't like it, but he'd already told his boss this was the only solution to our lack of access to the Labour government. Just think about it, and let's talk about other things. Martini – shaken, not stirred?'

Beaufort relented, half smiled, and nodded. When the drinks arrived, Samantha proposed the toast.

'To us, and the Firm.'

'Which bloody firm? Sometimes I don't know which one I'm working for.'

'Welcome to my world. Look, if you could bring yourself to do what Frobisher asked, it would keep our boss happy, and it would be good for business. And I would be really grateful.'

'How grateful?'

'Why don't you let me show you?'

*

They took the lift to the fifth floor, standing apart, neither speaking nor touching, barely glancing at each other. Beaufort picked up the subtle scent of her perfume, which she didn't usually wear to work.

Samantha had pre-booked a room overlooking Park Lane. Like all the bedrooms in this five-star hotel it had a luxurious marble tiled bathroom. She ordered a bottle of champagne from room service, went into the bathroom, and returned wearing one of the hotel's complimentary dressing gowns.

When the champagne arrived, they sat at a small table in the window alcove. She leaned forward when pouring their drinks, just enough to show him that she had discarded her bra. Leaning back she crossed her legs, affording him a momentary glimpse of what lay between.

Beaufort appraised her carefully and then asked:

'I'm not complaining, but is this work or pleasure?'
'Why can't it be both?'

*

Once room service had delivered a second bottle of champagne, Samantha suggested they make use of the large free-standing bathtub.

Beaufort undressed self-consciously and stepped into one end of the bath, which was still filling up from the centre taps. This particular tub was designed for sharing.

Samantha did not display the same shyness. She slipped off the bathrobe, and stepped unhurriedly into the other end of the bath, allowing Beaufort a lingering look at her alabaster white body, lightly dusted with freckles.

'Cheers,' she said, lifting her champagne flute and touching it to his.

'They say cleanliness is next to godliness.'

'They do. And this could be regarded as most men's idea of heaven.'

Samantha turned off the taps and stared into Beaufort's eyes. Without breaking eye contact she positioned her feet either side of his growing erection. Moving them slowly and rhythmically she brought him to a convulsive climax, which sent bathwater cascading on to the marble floor.

'Jesus, did they teach you that at spy school?'

'No. I grew up in New Zealand. We had to make our own entertainment.'

*

When they eventually climbed out of the bath and tumbled onto the king-sized bed, their love-making was urgent.

Despite the convulsions in the bathtub, Beaufort did not suffer a recurrence of the problem that had both amused and disappointed Sabina in the aftermath of the election night party.

What with the alcohol and their exertions, sleep came quickly. They awoke just after seven, and Samantha messaged Elizabeth to say she would be late into the office. Beaufort, after his absence the day before, did not bother.

They ordered room service and ate at the small table in the bay window, clad only in their hotel bathrobes.

'I think I might keep this,' Samantha said, fingering the softness of the collar, and running her fingers over the stitched hotel monogram.

'I wouldn't if I were you. They'll add at least a hundred quid to your bill. Besides, we don't have any suitcases.'

She laughed, and then asked the question that had never been far from either of their minds.

'So are you going to do it? Are you going to rat on your party? Are you going to join Labour?'

'I was going to do it anyway. I just wanted to see how far you'd go to persuade me.'

'Oh my God, you really are a bastard.'

*

An hour later Samantha's phone vibrated with an incoming message from Frobisher.

'How did it go? Did you manage to persuade him.'
'Yes, I think so'
'What did you have to do to change his mind?'
'Don't ask, don't tell.'

CHAPTER 30

PETTY FRANCE, LONDON

When Samantha messaged Jennifer suggesting a drink after work she readily accepted. They had met twice before, and got on well. Both were in their early thirties, single, and supposedly politically aligned.

The Blue Boar Inn was agreed as a venue, being equidistant between Victoria Street and Downing Street. It was part of the Conrad Hotel, and although the front area had large picture windows looking out onto Tothill Street, the rear section had low lighting and discreet booths.

Jennifer was running late, and Samantha was already seated with a bottle of New Zealand Sauvignon Blanc in an ice bucket on the table when she arrived. The graceful young black woman turned heads as she strode through the bar.

'Sorry, sorry – work is mental at the moment. How are things with you? And how's Damian?'

Samantha poured out two large glasses of wine.

'Work is fine. We've clawed back some of the clients we lost after the election, and we've added a few interesting new ones.'

'So I hear,' Jennifer replied with a chuckle.

'Actually, it's Damian I wanted to talk to you about.'

A look of concern crossed Jennifer's gold-flecked hazel eyes.

'Is he OK?'

'Yes, he's fine. Still misses you of course! But the thing is. . . he's thinking of leaving the Tories.'

Jennifer fumbled her wine glass back onto the table.

'Damian – leave the Tories! I thought he was a lifer – Thatcher underpants, Brexit coffee mugs, blue blood in his veins and all that.'

'He is – or he was. But he thinks the Tories are out for at least two terms, and he wants to get closer to the action. In fact, he wants to join Labour.'

Jennifer's eyes widened in shock.

'You must be joking! What did you do – shag him into submission?'

Samantha shifted uncomfortably in her seat.

'You did, didn't you! You shagged him! What was it like?'

'Well you should know – you got there first.'

Both women collapsed in laughter, and Jennifer raised her glass.

'Got to be said, he is a seriously good fuck. To Damian Beaufort, and all who've had the pleasure!'

A second bottle of wine was ordered and then Samantha returned to the topic in hand.

'Seriously, Jen, he does want to move over to our side, but he wants reassurance that the move will be worthwhile, that he'll be welcome. Can you fix up a meeting with the prime minister?'

Jennifer considered carefully before replying.

'Sure, why not. It could be win-win, and Brownie points all round. Worth pursuing.'

And so it began.

CHAPTER 31

DOWNING STREET, WHITEHALL

Most visitors to Number Ten Downing Street arrive through the famous shiny black front door. On entry they are relieved of their mobile phones, but having already passed through strict security at the front gate, and with all visitors being pre-announced and pre-vetted, security is otherwise low key.

Beaufort had been told to avoid this more public entrance and instead report to the rear entry point in Horse Guards Road. This is used for vehicular access by the PM, the chancellor of the exchequer, and distinguished overseas dignitaries. And by visitors who want to avoid the permanent press presence in Downing Street.

Jennifer was waiting to escort him and, after Beaufort had shown photo ID to the armed police officer on the turnstile pedestrian gate, she ushered him through the back entrance of Number Ten.

As they ascended the staircase lined with pictures of previous prime ministers Jennifer briefed him in a low voice.

'Clem is not as tribal as most of his colleagues, and now the initial honeymoon period, such as it was, is over, we're in the market for good news. The chief whip will be there, and he's probably the one you're going to have the most trouble convincing.'

Beaufort nodded, and felt a momentary pang of guilt for playing his former colleague, even though she thought that she was playing him.

All prime ministers have their favourite rooms to work in, and Clem Clark had decided on the White Drawing Room, sandwiched between the Pillared Room and the Terracotta Room. It overlooks the garden at the rear, and is quieter – and more secure – than any office located at the front of the building. Margaret Thatcher used it as her office in a bygone era. Her portrait still hung above the fireplace, staring balefully down at the Labour interlopers.

As Beaufort and Jennifer reached the top of the stairs the PM's private secretary was waiting for them. He led them along the corridor past the State Dining Room, knocked on the PM's office door, opened it without waiting for a response and announced them.

There were two leather Chesterfield sofas arranged either side of a low oak coffee table. Beaufort's took in the charismatic figure of Clem Clark, who rose and extended his hand, his face assuming its characteristic lopsided grin. As they shook hands the PM said:

'Welcome, pleased to meet you. Jennifer's told me a great deal about you. This is Bert Withers, my chief whip.'

An overweight balding man in an ill-fitting suit rose slowly to his feet, and extended his hand with every show of reluctance.

'And *I've* heard a great deal about you as well,' he growled in a Geordie accent, not bothering to disguise his disdain.

The PM laughed, and offered whisky all round. No choice of drinks, and no choice of how to take it. But the Scotch was a single malt from Jura, the island the PM's ancestors hailed from, and the measures were generous. It was starting to occur to Beaufort that the British state was almost entirely fuelled by Scotch whisky.

'So we know a lot about you,' the PM said, sitting down again, 'but what we don't know is why you want to join us?'

'And why we should take you,' the chief whip added.

Beaufort had already rehearsed his answer in his mind, but he paused as though considering the question for the first time. He knew he would only get one shot at convincing two of the most powerful men in the country.

'As you know, I'm a lifelong Tory. And, as you also know, I'm a lobbyist – ranked somewhere in the public's affections between estate agents, traffic wardens, and. . . politicians.'

The PM and Jennifer laughed. The chief whip glowered.

'But lobbying is just business,' Beaufort continued, 'we take every brief that comes along – like lawyers, or taxis, or prostitutes.'

Again, a smile from the PM and Jennifer, but no reaction at all from Withers.

'Politics is just a game. We all know that. A serious game, a game with high stakes, a game for grown-ups, but a game all the same. Government is where the real action is. You seem destined to remain in power for the foreseeable future, and I want to be part of it.'

The chief whip looked unconvinced, but the PM turned to Jennifer.

'What do you think?'

'I've known Damian for years, and I worked for him for quite some time. Without wishing to blow smoke up his arse, he's clever, and he understands how government works. As you know, I head up the industrial team in the Policy Unit. We're trying to set up an Industrial Advisory Council, and it's proving tricky. Business is still wary of us – it still needs convincing. Damian could be a real help, and his defection would be a PR coup for us too.'

The Prime Minister nodded, and got to his feet, signalling the end of the meeting.

'Thanks for coming in. We'll be in touch, through Jennifer.'

As Beaufort and Jennifer left, the PM turned to the chief whip.

'So what do you think then Bert?'

'I think he's a smarmy bastard and I wouldn't trust him as far as I could throw him,' was the blunt response.

The PM laughed.

'You're right. He is a smarmy bastard. But the question is, could he be our smarmy bastard?'

CHAPTER 32

GREAT GEORGE STREET, WESTMINSTER

Despite the chief whip's misgivings, the decision was made by the prime minister and the party chairman to admit Beaufort to the Labour Party. Jennifer was put in charge of the plans to smooth his way into the party, and then of generating as much positive publicity as possible from his defection.

The timing of the announcement was carefully choreographed to achieve maximum impact. It had been scheduled for 10.30 on a Wednesday, ahead of Prime Minister's Questions at midday. This would allow the Westminster press pack ample time to cover the announcement, and still get back for the midday kick-off of the week's premier scheduled political event. It would also enable Clem Clark to taunt Chloe Baverstock, the leader of the opposition, with this high-profile defection.

The venue chosen for the press conference was the Smeaton Room in the Institution of Civil Engineers, just off of Parliament Square.

This was the same venue that a former shadow chancellor had chosen to deliver his disastrous pre-election shadow budget, which many believed had cost the Labour Party victory in 1992. Very few of the current press pack had been on the Westminster scene in those days, and none seemed to have made the connection.

The event was chaired by the secretary of state for business and industrial strategy, Mary Myers. She sat at a table on a low dais at the Great George Street end of the room, with Jennifer seated to her left. A chair to her right was empty. The press had been briefed to expect a "major announcement" relating to industrial strategy.

Jennifer stood up and approached the podium, situated to the right of the table. She spoke into the twin microphones.

'Ladies and gentlemen of the business press, members of the lobby and the press gallery, thank you for attending this event at such short notice. Allow me to introduce the business secretary, Mary Myers.'

There was a smattering of applause from the civil servants and Labour staffers scattered around the room, and the minister took to the podium.

'Thank you, Jennifer. As you all know we came to power inheriting one of the worst economic situations since the second world war. The economic climate globally is far from benign, with political and military tensions in eastern Europe, the Middle East and the Far East disrupting trade, and dampening business confidence. This has had a negative impact on both the UK stock exchange, and the value of the pound. It has also brought with it inflationary pressures. We are working hard with business to mitigate the effects of these global headwinds, and my job is to ensure that relations between this Labour government and the UK business community are strong. We want a partnership with business.'

This last statement was greeted with scepticism and muffled guffaws by the assembled press pack.

'With that in mind we are today announcing the setting up of an Industrial Strategy Council. What is more, I can also announce that the first person to join that Council, and indeed the latest member to join the Labour Party... is Dr Damian Beaufort!'

On cue Beaufort entered via a side door and climbed onto the low dais.

He and Mary Myers embraced awkwardly, then shook hands and turned to meet the barrage of flash photography being unleashed. Beaufort was well known to many of the journalists present – but they knew him as a die-hard Tory, and his appearance on a platform with a Labour cabinet minister was astonishing.

Returning briefly to the podium Jennifer announced:

'Damian Beaufort will take a few questions.'

Beaufort walked across and placed himself behind the podium, using it as a psychological and physical shield. He posed for the cameras, leaning slightly forward with a hand either side of the podium, trying to project a façade of calmness. Many of the hacks were on their feet, desperate to get a quote for their newspapers, or a clip for their news channels.

'Yes, Craig Thorpe, BBC,' Beaufort said, following the established precedence for these occasions.

'Frankly, I don't where to begin,' was the BBC political

editor's opening gambit. 'What on earth persuaded you, a lifelong Tory, to join a party you have campaigned against all your adult life?'

'I'm not surprised that you're surprised,' came the response. 'The reality is that we live in a time of tumult, and I think that I have something to offer on the economic front. I am putting country ahead of party.'

ITN was next in line, its political editor John Sopwith asking:

'But what exactly are you going to be contributing? You have minimal political experience, and no friends or allies in the Labour Party.'

'I understand your scepticism. But as a public affairs consultant I have advised many of the UK's leading companies, and many of the largest overseas inward investors. My previous party never developed an industrial strategy. My new party is in the process of doing so, and I want to be part of it.'

By convention Sky News was next in line, and their Whitehall correspondent Martin Beckworth tried a slightly different tack.

'You're a lobbyist by trade, and you've represented a few pretty dodgy nation states, as well as some multinationals whose products do a great deal of harm to their consumers. How do you reconcile that track record with your sudden Damascene conversion to public service?'

Beaufort had been waiting for a question along these lines, and he, Samantha and Jennifer had rehearsed the answer.

'You're right Martin, I have been a public affairs consultant – a lobbyist if you prefer – all of my working life. My view, and the view of my colleagues in the industry, and the view of our professional body, is that if a country is recognised by the United Nations, it is entitled to be advised and represented. And if a company sells a product which is judged – by our own Parliament – to be legal, then that company is entitled to be advised and represented. There is no shame in being a lobbyist – in fact I am proud to have been one.'

Another three questions along similar lines followed, which he dealt with comfortably. Then, just as proceedings were winding down, and it began to look like Beaufort was going to emerge unscathed, he realised that he had not called for a single question from a female journalist. Aware of how this might look, he called for one last question from a persistent young woman who had made her way to the front in order to catch his eye.

'Belinda Smith, UK News. I've listened to all this and frankly it sounds like business as usual – politicians, lobbyists and mainstream media all looking after each other. But let me tell you what my viewers will be thinking. They'll be thinking that in reality you are motivated solely by ambition. And the question they will be asking themselves is this: aren't you just a greedy, treacherous bastard?'

The room erupted in a cacophony of laughter, catcalls and ironic cheers.

Beaufort was furious, partly with himself for taking that one last question, and partly with the attention-seeking rudeness of the UK News correspondent. He was about to angrily respond, but found that his microphone had been switched off. The press pack surged forward, scenting blood. Labour staffers formed a human shield around the dais.

Jennifer rushed onto the podium, grabbed hold of Beaufort and half-pulled him off the platform towards the side door. The secretary of state followed, pausing briefly to try to thank the journalists for coming, before she herself was hustled through the exit by her special adviser.

*

The secretary of state's official car was outside the main entrance in Great George Street, and she was quickly ushered into it and driven the short distance back to the Department on Victoria Street.

Samantha had been watching from the back of the Smeaton Room. When she saw that the press conference was descending into chaos she had ducked out, cut through the main foyer to intercept Jennifer and Beaufort as they emerged. Grabbing Beaufort by the arm she led him across the foyer and down the stairs, past the toilets and the cloakroom, and out through the service door that opened onto Storey's Gate.

The three of them, having successfully lost the press pack, headed round the corner to the same bar that Samantha and Jennifer had met for a drink in the week before. After securing a booth at the back they bracketed Beaufort, Samantha by his side and Jennifer opposite. Samantha urgently signalled to a waiter and ordered three large Scotch whiskies.

'What the hell have you two made me do?' Beaufort snarled.

The two women took it as a rhetorical question.

'It was fine,' Samantha responded unconvincingly. 'Until that bitch from UK News weighed in. Anyway, it's done now. There's no going back.'

Beaufort took a huge gulp of his whisky and vented:.

'Everybody hates traitors. Turncoats. Defectors. Rats. Scum. I've really screwed up.'

Jennifer reached across the table and gripped his hand.

'You have not. It'll blow over. The party will look after you. The prime minister likes you.'

Beaufort snorted.

'And the chief whip hates me – he made that bloody obvious.'

Jennifer gripped his hand tighter and smiled.

'He's the chief whip in the Commons. And you're not going to the Commons. You're going to another place.'

CHAPTER 33

VICTORIA, LONDON

Beaufort's fears were at least partially realised.

His former Tory colleagues treated him with disdain, or even outright contempt. The right-wing press was incensed by his defection, and the social media pile-on reached epic proportions. AI-generated memes appeared of Beaufort as Neville Chamberlain, Vidkun Quisling and even Judas Iscariot. He was forced to close his X account, and stop posting on LinkedIn.

This negativity was balanced by the ecstatic reaction of the Labour-supporting press. They hailed the wisdom of the Labour government in opening itself up to outside talent, and for recognising the need to attract business people. The Financial Times did a particularly fawning interview, hailing Beaufort as a champion of business, with the connections and clout to persuade foreign companies to invest in the UK.

Beaufort's clients were delighted by his switch to Labour. None of them withdrew their business, and several former clients re-joined. This included Frank Hughes, the trade union leader who had insulted Beaufort at the general election party and was escorted out of the event by Sabina.

With this inflow of new clients, the consultancy was able to move into luxurious offices on the top floor of a prestigious office block on Victoria Street, which had been built on the site previously occupied by New Scotland Yard. The company was also restructured, with Beaufort moving to the role of chairman, allowing him more time for his duties on the Industrial Strategy Council. Samantha took over the day-to-day running of the agency in the role of chief executive officer.

Along with other senior members of the team they embarked on a campaign of lavish corporate entertainment, using the terrace of their new offices when the weather was fine, and securing seats and boxes for a range of hot-ticket cultural and sporting events. Even the most senior politician loves a freebie.

They also ensured that their clients attended and sponsored a wide range of Labour Party fundraising events. The party was keen to move away from its dependency on trade unions for its funding, and donations from big corporations reinforced the message that the party, like the country, was open for business.

The rapid expansion of Beaufort's consultancy also ensured that it won a number of awards, and Beaufort was elected president of the industry's trade body. This achievement resulted in his being featured in all the advertising, marketing and public relations trade journals.

Lobbying is all about access, and Beaufort and his consultancy now had unprecedented access to the upper echelons of government. The new business opportunities kept on coming, nearly all of them stimulated by the privileged access that his defection had secured.

*

Logisticalis were private-sector providers of services to government. They had suffered a series of scandals and failures, but due to a lack of alternatives they remained on the government roster of preferred suppliers.

When Labour came to power ministers quickly realised that overcrowding in prisons would inevitably lead to riots. Having released many prisoners early, they were still faced with a massive capacity problem, and turned to the private sector to provide a solution.

Having decided to award a contract for five new prisons, they had narrowed the field down to two potential providers: Logisticalis, which was British, and the American Correctional Solutions Corporation. The indications were that the US company would get the nod, in view of Logisticalis's multiple failures on other contracts.

Beaufort and Samantha were invited to present to the board of the British company. The CEO, Tom Agaris, summed up the brief.

'Our reputation is crap over here because it's home territory, and our bloody press pick up on everything. We need you to dig up some dirt on the yanks, and make sure that it finds its way into the British press. Then we need to make sure it's picked up by the kind of political publications and websites the key decision makers read and pay attention to. This could be a huge field for us, and we need this contract. Can you do it?'

Beaufort looked at Samantha and waited for her nod, before replying:

'Of course. It's lobbying in action. It's what we do.'

*

William Hanson was the owner of a hedge fund that had previously backed the Tories.

He contacted Beaufort and they had a lunch at Nobu. After the main course, having discussed a wide-ranging brief covering all aspects of financial services, Hanson cut to the chase.

'This Industrial Strategy Council. It can't be all spanner men and metal bashers. It needs somebody with financial expertise. Somebody like me. Can you arrange that?'

Beaufort, who had figured out the way the conversation was heading, paused briefly before replying.

'Of course. It's lobbying in action. It's what we do.'

*

Michael Raynsford, the owner of Raynsford Retail, invited Beaufort into his offices in Portland Square.

He was a self-made man, and well known for his blunt speaking.

'We already have a public affairs consultancy. They do store openings, store closures, planning disputes and all that type of bollocks. Frankly, they're bloody useless, but then I think most of you lot are. I'll fire them and appoint you – but there is one thing I need you to do.'

'Which is what?' Beaufort asked.

'My son has just been turned down by Oxford. He wants to read PPE. He has all the grades, but they told him to go away for a year and broaden his experience. I don't want him swanning around Asia doing drugs and banging prostitutes – and I don't want him digging latrines in Africa either. I want you to get him an internship at Number Ten. Can you fix that for him?'

Beaufort barely hesitated before replying.

'Of course. It's lobbying in action. It's what we do.'

*

Alan Margrave, the chairman of Walthamstow Waste Management, visited the new offices of Beaufort Public Affairs and sat in the boardroom with Beaufort and Samantha. After a brief discussion about the company's priorities and their need for better access to the upper echelons of the Labour government, Margrave got down to the real point of the meeting.

'I got a CBE under the last lot, having supported them publicly and donated half a million pounds. I was promised a knighthood, but it never materialised. If I do the same for this new crowd, will they let me have one? Not for me, of course. The wife would very much like to be Lady Helen. Can you make that happen for me, for us – for her?'

Beaufort smiled, looked at Samantha and said:

'It's lobbying in action.'

Samantha smiled back, and completed the mantra:

'It's what we do.'

CHAPTER 34

DOWNING STREET, WHITEHALL

After the Chequers summit, the prime minister called a meeting in his office in the White Drawing Room in Number Ten.

The purpose of the meeting was to discuss the introduction of the European Union (Application for Readmission) Bill, already dubbed the "Breturn Bill" on the advice of spin-doctor Rory Cochrane. The only other attendees were the chief whips of the House of Commons and the House of Lords.

As the Bill, being of constitutional importance, would have to be initially introduced in the House of Commons, Clem Clark turned first to the Commons chief whip, Bert Withers.

'Well, Chief, how do you see it panning out?'

'Procedurally, it shouldn't be a problem. We keep the Bill short, with clauses authorising us to negotiate with the EU for re-accession, and a schedule to revoke the EU (Withdrawal) Act 2020 – at a time of our choosing and using Henry VIII powers. We have a massive majority, and we'll introduce a "guillotine" timetable motion, so I'm confident the Bill will pass on schedule and without amendment.'

The PM nodded, and then turned to Lord Anstruther, Withers's opposite number in the Upper House. He came from a traditionally Tory-supporting landed family, but had been turned against the Establishment by his years at Eton. He had joined the Labour Party while he was reading human anthropology at Corpus Christi, Cambridge.

'I wish I could say the same for their lordships, PM. There will be substantial opposition from the Tories, who seem unabashed by their electoral drubbing. We'll also have problems with the constitutionalists, who will object to a measure that was approved by referendum being overturned without a second one, and will also object to the reliance on Henry VIII clauses. Finally, as this measure was neither in the King's Speech, nor our manifesto, it will not be protected by the Salisbury Convention. As you will be aware, Prime Minister, under this doctrine a precedent was established in the 19th century, and re-affirmed after the Second World War, that no Bill introduced by a government, having previously been presaged in their manifesto, should be voted down by the unelected House at second or third reading.'

Clem Clark was exasperated by Anstruther's lecture, and by his negativity and procedural pedantry.

'To hell with all that. Brexit has been a disaster, and we must reverse it with Breturn for the sake of the nation. If necessary, I'll accelerate the expulsion of the hereditary peers, pack the Lords with life peers and ram it through, like Asquith threatened to do in 1911. I have a plan. I'm going to appoint Damian Beaufort as a peer and a minister, and charge him with piloting the Bill through the Upper House. As a lobbyist he knows all about parliamentary procedure, and as a former Tory, and what's more a former Brexiteer, he knows the weak spots in the opposition's armoury.'

Both chief whips looked at each other doubtfully. It was Bert Withers who articulated what they were both thinking.

'But can we trust the treacherous bastard?'

Clem Clark chuckled, and Lord Anstruther backed his colleague.

'Hardly a laughing matter, Prime Minister, this is serious. The Upper House regards itself as an honourable institution, and we've all seen Beaufort, and his ilk, in action.'

This time Clem Clark laughed out loud.

'Apologies for the levity, gentlemen, but we ran him through the developed vetting process. I can tell you that he really is a bastard – no trace of a father! The point is, he may be a bastard, but now he's our bastard."

*

Jennifer was instructed to invite Beaufort to a meeting with the two chief whips at No 12 Downing Street. She met him at the gates, and eased him through security. It was only a short walk, so she briefed him rapidly.

'That may be the last time you need to go through all that security palaver. They're going to offer you a peerage and a ministerial job. For some reason Clem seems to like you – though the two chiefs aren't so keen.'

'What the hell? I've only just joined the party. This is crazy.'

'We need to burnish our business credentials, and they have a specific project in mind for you. Promise me you won't just turn this down? Promise me you will at least think about it? Clem wants you on board, and I have staked a lot of credibility on you.'

Beaufort nodded in what looked like reluctant agreement. He had already been ordered by Frobisher to accept the ennoblement that Jennifer and her Labour colleagues were working hard to persuade him to receive.

They turned and walked through the less famous black door.

*

Beaufort and Jennifer were shown through to Bert Wither's office, where Lord Anstruther was already installed. Both men rose and offered their hands, and then waved them to two vacant chairs set around the small conference table.

Withers was the first to speak.

'Right, Beaufort. Let me be quite clear. If you relay a word of this conversation to the media, or anybody else for that matter, you will be finished in Westminster. You've joined Labour, and I have to believe that your conversion to the people's party is sincere. On that basis, we would like to offer you not just a life peerage, but a role as minister of state in the Business Department.'

Beaufort pretended to be surprised, and asked the obvious question:

'But why me?'

Lord Anstruther stepped in.

'We need to reinforce our business credentials, and we want to form a "government of all the talents". Frankly, we would rather have you inside the tent pissing out, than outside the tent pissing in.'

'OK I get that – but why me specifically? There are dozens of businessmen who would chew off their own gonads for a peerage.'

This time it was Withers who responded:

'The PM has taken a shine to you. Your defection is one of the few good news stories we've had since the election. And we have a specific job for you. One that requires expertise in parliamentary procedure, but also the ability to suborn, manipulate and if necessary blackmail. Skills which you, as a lobbyist, possess in spades. It will get out soon enough, but here's a sneak preview for you. We intend to re-join the EU. In short order. And without another referendum. And we want you to pilot the Bill through the House of Lords.'

This time Beaufort was genuinely shocked.

*

Beaufort allowed Jennifer to shepherd him out of Downing Street. Then he headed for the office on foot, using the short walk to get his head around the bombshell that had been dropped on him in Downing Street.

Samantha saw the look on his face and followed him into the office. She shut the door behind her.

'What the hell happened to you? You look like you've been goosed by Thatcher's ghost.'

Beaufort recounted the meeting with the two chief whips.

Samantha arranged a hasty meeting with Frobisher.

*

They met in St James's Park, and as they walked around the ornamental lake Beaufort gave Frobisher a blow-by-blow account of the meeting with the two chief whips.

Frobisher was unfazed.

'We were kind of expecting this. There was a summit at Chequers with the old Blythe lot, and that's where the rejoin plan was hatched.'

As you know Jennifer and Samantha are drinking buddies, and Jennifer has been talking you up ever since you joined the ranks of the great unwashed. And Clem does seem to like you – God knows why.'

Beaufort was still unconvinced.

'I'm not sure I should accept. What about the company? And what about my reputation? I've always been known as a Eurosceptic, a Brexiteer.'

'Beaufort Public Affairs will be fine with Samantha at the helm. She'll probably run it better than you. And your reputation was shot the minute you defected. You have to accept their offer. We need somebody on the inside who can tell us what the hell is going on with this government. And that somebody is you.'

Beaufort nodded his reluctant agreement.

After all, he had signed up to the Faustian pact.

CHAPTER 35

HOUSE OF LORDS, WESTMINSTER

Within a week the King had approved the peerage. As a ministerial nominee Beaufort jumped the queue and was scheduled for an accelerated introduction into the Upper House.

He was to be introduced between the government chief whip, Lord Anstruther, and another former lobbyist, Lord Ken Knowles, who had raised a great deal of money for the Labour Party and been ennobled as a reward. Lord Anstruther had quickly discovered that there were not many Labour peers who were willing to take part in the ritual to introduce this despised turncoat.

The ceremony had not changed for centuries. Beaufort and his two "supporters", Lords Anstruther and Knowles, entered the chamber wearing the full regalia of scarlet wool robes with white miniver fur collars. The mothball smell from the robes fought a losing battle with the aroma of damp tweed and wet dog that pervaded the ornate chamber.

A large contingent of parliamentary sketch writers had decamped from their usual perch in the Commons Press

Gallery to come and witness this unusual event. It was not often that a lifelong Tory defected to Labour, and was then ennobled and given ministerial office as a reward.

More than that, it was unique for a confirmed Brexiteer to change codes, and then be entrusted with the task of steering a vital piece of legislation such as the Breturn Bill through the Upper House. The proceedings promised to provide rich copy for the press pack.

Once Beaufort had been escorted in, he handed his writ of summons to the bewigged clerk, who read it out word for word, appointing him Baron Beaufort of Pimlico 'In pursuance of the Life Peerages Act.'

Beaufort swore his allegiance to the King and 'all his heirs and successors' on the Bible, and then signed the massive leather-bound register resting on the despatch box. Finally, as custom dictated, Beaufort walked across and shook hands with the Lord Speaker, who remained seated on the woolsack. Normally at this point a hearty rumble of 'hear hears' would ripple around the chamber. In this case it was a low and reluctant muttering.

Leaving the chamber to change out of his robes Beaufort was torn between exultation at his elevation, and doubts about his future role. He had lobbied the House of Lords for years, but never imagined that one day he would join its ranks.

He scanned the government, opposition and cross benches looking for a friendly face.

There were none.

CHAPTER 36

DOWNING STREET, WHITEHALL

Acting on the advice of his predecessor, Clem Clark invited the chief scientific officer, Sir Paul Trent, to Downing Street for a meeting.

Despite the protests of his principal private secretary he insisted on holding the meeting with no civil servants present. Sofa government had returned.

The CSO, having been invited to sit, perched on the very edge of the chair, and stared expressionlessly at the PM. Clem concluded that the rumours were true. Sir Paul was brilliant . . and autistic. Perhaps he was brilliant because he was autistic.

Deducing that the usual niceties were not required, the prime minister came straight to the point.

'My predecessor left me a note with some disturbing news. He informed me that Trident, far from being the UK's independent nuclear deterrent, is in reality only able to be deployed with the agreement of our American allies. Is that correct?'

'That is indeed correct, Prime Minister.'

'He also told me that he had instructed you to remedy that unfortunate situation?'

'That is also correct, Prime Minister.'

'And how is that going?'

'The project is progressing very well. The first problem we needed to overcome was that we were entirely dependent on American satellites to guide the missiles to their target. We now have our own independent Tyche satellite system, developed and manufactured in the UK, and fully controlled by us.'

'So that means we can now launch and target the missiles independently?'

'Unfortunately not, Prime Minister. The Americans inserted lines of code into the launch software, which means that they can override our targeting instructions, or abort any launch seconds after it occurs. We believe we have developed software code that can work around their override – but it will need to be tested in real world conditions.'

'Then I suggest you do that, Sir Paul. With an isolationist president installed in the White House we need control of our own nuclear deterrent – and the sooner the better.'

'Of course, Prime Minister.'

Without another word, the CSO rose and left. He did not offer to shake hands. Like the US president, he was a germophobe.

CHAPTER 37

ST JAMES'S, LONDON

The Admiral liked to hold some of his meetings away from the eyes and ears of Vauxhall Cross.

When he did so his favoured venue was the Naval and Military Club, known to its members as the "In and Out". For most of its history the club has been based on Piccadilly. Its one-way U-shaped carriage drive explains its strange alternative title.

Frobisher had been invited for a pre-dinner "chat". He was not fooled by the informality of the invitation. The Admiral did not believe in wasting time – least of all his own. Frobisher made sure he was appropriately dressed, but even so the ex-military doormen regarded his short, plump, bespectacled personage with disdain.

They did not like the cut of his jib.

Nevertheless, the Admiral was a revered figure in the club, and Frobisher was escorted promptly to him in the near-empty library. His host did not rise, or offer his hand, but simply gestured to the leather wing-backed chair opposite his own.

Two pink gins magically appeared. This was the Admiral's preferred tipple, but as Angostura bitters were not widely available, he often had to settle for alternatives.

The Admiral raised his glass and gave the traditional Royal Navy toast.

'To a willing foe – and sea room.'

Frobisher raised his own glass, and echoed the sentiment.

Then the Admiral got down to business, having reinforced his cover as just another old sea-dog pensioned off to a life ashore. His dress, his manner, his choice of club, everything about his outward appearance screamed naval officer, rather than spy chief.

'I wanted to talk to you about Damian Beaufort. He seems to be settling in well, though you and Samantha still need to keep an eye on him. It's common knowledge his mother is Yvette de Beaufort. But you said that at school nobody knew who his father was, and publicly at least that still seems to be the case. Now there are rumours flying around, fuelled by Beaufort's meteoric rise, that his father is none other than our new prime minister, Clem Clark. I can tell you that those rumours are completely wrong.'

Frobisher looked around nervously at the other occupants of the room.

'Don't worry about them, they're all as deaf as posts.'

Reassured, Frobisher ventured an opinion.

'I guessed as much. Clem is too cautious a politician to take a risk like that, if Beaufort were indeed his by-blow. But if it isn't Clem, who is it? Who actually is – or was – Beaufort's father?'

The Admiral leant forward and whispered a name.

Frobisher was stunned.

CHAPTER 38

CHELSEA, LONDON

Yvette de Beaufort was well-known for her *salons*, her soirées, and her dinner parties. These were held at her townhouse in Cheyne Walk, in fashionable Chelsea, and were attended by the leading lights of London's political and cultural circles.

In opposition Clem Clark had always been warmly welcomed into these gatherings. Now that Labour were in government, with budgets to balance, his welcome was sometimes less warm than previously, although being able to boast about having supper with a sitting prime minister undoubtedly had a cachet all of its own.

Yvette liked to keep her gatherings intimate and discreet, so numbers were usually low. For this particular dinner she had invited older guests, knowing they would want to leave at a reasonable hour. She sat at the head of the table, with Clem, the only other singleton, opposite.

Two couples made up the guest list. The first was an elderly thespian on the threshold of national treasure-dom and his tiny, almost mute, wife. Sitting opposite them were a bombastic right-wing journalist and his eccentric fashion designer wife.

The conversation rarely strayed far from the world of theatre and the arts. As the evening wore on, Yvette used her expressive eyes to convey two things to Clem. Yes, we will be making love. And yes, I have news.

As the two elderly couples air-kissed their way out of the door, Yvette took hold of Clem's hand and led him up the stairs to her first-floor bedroom. They made leisurely love, with the familiarity and fondness of those whose relationship stretched back over many years. Knowing his habits, Yvette had placed an ashtray, a lighter, and a packet of Dunhill cigarettes by his favoured side of the bed.

Clem lay back on the pillows, smoking and admiring the naked woman stretched out beside him. Her figure was virtually unchanged since their student days, still smooth, lithe, unblemished and desirable.

'Have you heard from our mutual friend?' he asked.

'Yes. He's so proud of you for becoming prime minister. He asked me to congratulate you. And instructed me to tell you that you must pursue your project to re-join the European Union with – and you'll recognise the phraseology – determination, speed and vigour.'

'But why? I would have thought a stronger EU would be against his interests?'

She took the cigarette from his mouth and took a deep drag before returning it.

'I don't know. He doesn't share his reasoning with me. I'm just the messenger. He also asked about Trident.'

'What about Trident?'

'He wants to know if it works, and whether it can be

launched without the Americans' permission.'

'Tell him that it doesn't, and it can't. But I have good people working on both aspects of the problem as a matter of urgency.'

Clem asked the question that always concerned him after they had sex.

'Do you still think of him, when we make love?'

'Of course not,' she lied.

Clem nodded, anxious to believe her. Then, deciding that there wasn't time – and, in his case, energy – for a second bout, he stubbed out his cigarette and got dressed. Yvette put on a silk kimono, and they both went downstairs. Yvette opened the front door, and they kissed chastely, like luvvies, not lovers.

As the prime minister got into the back seat of the car, his personal protection officer and his driver exchanged knowing glances. Good old Clem, the look seemed to say. Still got it.

*

Across the road, leaning on his high-powered Honda motorbike, lurked a pot-bellied middle-aged man with long greasy hair captured in a ponytail. He was dressed from head to toe in black leather, with Hells Angels colours on the back of the jacket.

Snyder was a paparazzo, and had been hoping for a candid shot of the famous actress, perhaps without make-up, or in her dressing gown or tracksuit. Instead, he now had pictures not just of her dishevelled and scantily clad, but also bidding farewell to the prime minister.

Amongst the paparazzi Snyder was a legend. He had

been the lead guitarist in a heavy metal band in his youth, but when the band split up he turned from hunted to hunter. He swapped his guitar for a camera and long lens and began hanging around outside the kind of venues he had previously frequented, snapping celebs in various stages of intoxication and undress.

Normally he sold his pictures to the tabloids, but these shots might fetch more from his Russian friend. He called himself Oleg, which wasn't his real name, but was easy for foreigners to remember, and easy to pronounce. He wore ill-fitting suits and scuffed suede shoes, but always seemed to have ready cash to spend on good snaps and juicy gossip – especially relating to politicians.

Snyder thanked his lucky stars, and his lover Joan, who had tipped him off about the assignation.

CHAPTER 39

WESTMINSTER, LONDON

Beaufort had never consulted a psychiatrist. Had he done so he would no doubt have been told that he had both mother and father issues.

As a lobbyist Beaufort had operated in the shadows throughout his career.

Because of his mother's fame he had occasionally featured in gossip columns, but since they rarely met, and lived very different lives, this had never been much of a problem. Or at least it wasn't until his high-profile defection to the Labour Party. Followed shortly afterwards by his elevation to the House of Lords. Followed almost immediately after that by his appointment as a minister.

The right-wing press, which had never been inclined to give the new government the benefit of the doubt, took every opportunity to criticise the elevation and appointment of a lobbyist with a long list of unsavoury clients. They also used their considerable resources to try and solve the great mystery that surrounded Beaufort's parentage.

Gossip is the currency of both politics and lobbying,

and it is also traded energetically in the subterranean world of espionage. The rumour that the explanation for Beaufort's meteoric rise was that Clem Clark was his father gained traction amongst the cognoscenti, and soon became conventional wisdom. Snyder's photographs of the prime minister leaving the actress's Cheyne Walk town house in the small hours of the morning only served to give credence to these rumours, once Oleg had given the paparazzo permission to sell them to the tabloids.

Tory MPs used parliamentary privilege to ask pointed questions at Prime Minister's Questions. Where the mainstream media feared to tread, social media filled the vacuum. Various anonymous tweets on X showed the two men in profile, and drew attention to a supposed likeness.

Finally, a political gossip website named after Watt Tyler, the leader of the Peasants' Revolt in the 14th century, took the plunge. Alongside similar profile photographs that had been circulating on X, it asked the question the mainstream media dared not ask.

'Is a blood relationship the key to this man's unprecedented rise?'

Beaufort sought advice from government lawyers as to whether he should take legal action against this scurrilous website. The advice was unequivocal. Since nobody knew who hid behind the nom de plume "Wat Tayler", and since the website was hosted on a server in Delaware where it was protected by the First Amendment, there was no point in trying to sue.

This was yet another negative consequence of leaving the shadowy – but shaded – world of lobbying. He would just have to suck it up, and, privately, continue to wonder if the rumours were true.

*

Although Beaufort had never really pressed his mother to name his father, in the light of his raised public profile, and the resultant media and social media speculation, he decided now was the time to do so.

He and his mother rarely met, and almost never spoke on the telephone. They had never actually fallen out, nor become estranged in the strict sense of the term. They had just started out with some distance between them, and gradually drifted even further apart.

Beaufort therefore decided to write a note, pressing his mother to put an end to the mystery once and for all and reveal who his father was. He instructed his government driver to hand-deliver the note to her town house in Cheyne Walk.

And then he waited for a response. A return note. A text message. A phone call. An invitation to meet.

None of these were forthcoming.

CHAPTER 40

INDIAN OCEAN

Due to the delay in bringing the new class of Dreadnought nuclear strike submarines into service, the operational life of the Vanguard class has been extended. Both the Dreadnought and Vanguard are officially designated as SSBN – Ship, Submersible, Ballistic, Nuclear.

One submarine from what the Royal Navy calls the "boomer" flotilla is always on patrol. This is termed "continuous at sea deterrence". A second boat undertakes overlapping patrols, whilst a third is always on standby at HMS Naval Base Clyde at Faslane, undertaking training duties. The fourth boat is usually in dry dock, undergoing routine maintenance.

Vanguard submarines can dive to a depth of 500 metres, but have to rise to 100 metres in order to fire their missiles. The submarines can carry up to 16 missiles, with five warheads on each. Each missile has a range of 12,000 kilometres, and each warhead a maximum yield of 100 kilotons – eight times more powerful than the nuclear bomb that devastated Hiroshima.

The task of testing the Trident D5 missiles, with the new bespoke UK guidance system, had fallen to HMS Vanguard. The British government had notified all of the signatories to the Treaty on the Prohibition of Nuclear Weapons of their intention to conduct a launch trial. They had not warned the Americans that the missile had been adapted to be targeted solely by Royal Navy personnel, and guided by British Tyche satellites.

Normally the Royal Navy would test its nuclear missiles from the US Trident Test Range, situated offshore from Cape Canaveral in Florida. Clem Clark was adamant that this American test range should not be used on this occasion. The submarine had therefore headed for the Indian Ocean, parts of which reach depths of over 7,000 metres.

The plan was to fire one test missile from a point 250 nautical miles east of the British base on Diego Garcia. A Type 45 destroyer and a Type 26 frigate, both carrying Lynx helicopters, would be deployed to monitor and film the launch.

The missile would then be routed to overfly the vast 47,000 square mile Royal Australian Air Force Woomera Range Complex, where vital telemetry data would be collected. It was then scheduled to splash down 100 nautical miles west of the British-owned Pitcairn Islands, in the Pacific Ocean. Another destroyer and another frigate would then use their helicopters to film the splashdown, and deploy their Royal Marine contingent on rigid hull inflatable boats to retrieve any floating debris for analysis and disposal.

The test launch was scheduled for 16.00 GMT, so that footage could be featured on the BBC early evening news.

Clem Clark had gathered his closest cabinet colleagues in the COBRA centre under the Cabinet Office. The military top brass were all assembled in the Operations Control Room at the Strategic Command Headquarters in Northwood.

The captain of HMS Vanguard was a Scot, Commander Iain Ferguson, who had grown up on the banks of the Clyde within sight of the Faslane facility. He could only fire his missiles – test or real – with the receipt of a code from Northwood, and with the concurrence and cooperation of his boat's executive officer, a first lieutenant by the name of Fred Ince.

For the purposes of this exercise the warhead from the missile to be test-fired had been removed, and the co-ordinates for splashdown pre-programmed. As the ship started to rise towards its operational firing depth the captain and the XO went to the safe in the wardroom.

Under the gaze of the armed COB – chief of the boat – they retrieved the two keys needed to initiate the firing sequence. As this was a test launch, with no live warhead, the captain did not need to open and read the "Letter of Last Resort" from the prime minister. Both officers were aware that although there was no warhead, the stakes were still high.

Ferguson and Ince, escorted by the COB, made their way to the bridge, holding the printed launch codes in plain sight of the crew. They inserted and turned their two keys on the launch console, and began the firing sequence.

The submarine was steady at 75 metres depth, the weather up top was clear, and the weapons launch console showed an unbroken array of green lights. Sonar indicated that no other vessels, friendly or hostile, were in the immediate vicinity.

Thirty seconds later the codes had been punched in and the launch sequence was completed. A thump of compressed air from the number one tube reverberated throughout the boat, indicating that the missile had launched. The two senior officers exchanged satisfied looks, and the boat rose to optronic mast depth to observe the missile's progress.

The XO, who was manning the modern equivalent of a periscope, turned to the captain with a look of horror. Seconds later sonar reported contact, as the missile struck the ocean surface close to the submarine and disintegrated.

*

Twenty thousand feet above, a Poseidon maritime patrol aircraft relayed live pictures to a horrified Operations Control Room in Northwood. A bevy of gold-braided admirals exchanged looks of incomprehension.

*

The United States Navy had also maintained a careful watch of the launch from its Naval Support Facility in Manama, Bahrain. There the top brass exchanged looks of satisfaction. That would teach the Limeys to try and go it alone.

*

The air of expectation that had permeated COBRA turned to one of despair as the near live images showed the missile striking the sea surface barely half a mile from its launch position.

Clem Clark was white with fury, and Sir Paul Trent grey with shock.

'I thought you told me this would bloody well work,' the prime minister snarled at the chief scientific officer.

'I am most terribly sorry, Prime Minister. The satellite is in the correct orbit, and we tested the software time and again. The Americans appear to have somehow overridden our override.'

The prime minister turned to his director of communications.

'Use the Musk gambit. Tell the media we had to test the missile to destruction to iron out the bugs. This was a test missile, and the failure was event specific, I repeat, event specific. The live missiles are still fully-functional and fully-operational.'

Without another word Clem Clark stormed out of COBRA and re-entered Number Ten through the secure door linking the two buildings.

CHAPTER 41

PORTON DOWN, WILTSHIRE

The sprawling and heavily guarded facility just outside of Salisbury is officially entitled the Ministry of Defence Science and Technology Laboratory. In practice it is always referred to simply as Porton Down.

Since its establishment at the height of World War One in 1916 it has gained a reputation as the world's leading establishment for identifying and countering chemical, nuclear and biological weapons. It is guarded and patrolled by highly trained and heavily armed members of the Civil Nuclear Constabulary.

When Russian military intelligence, the GRU, was ordered to assassinate an FSB defector and his daughter, chance placed them in Salisbury, in close proximity to Porton Down. This enabled the variant of Novichok used in the attempted killing to be speedily identified, and effective treatment to be rapidly administered. The defector and his daughter survived, as did the first policeman on the scene, who was also contaminated.

Months after this assassination attempt the chance

find of a discarded perfume atomiser led to the near fatal poisoning of a British civilian and the tragic death of his partner. The perfume dispenser had contained enough Novichok to wipe out a small village. It was taken to Porton Down, analysed and then locked away in a secure lab.

Every quarter an audit of all the hazardous material stored in the many warehouses and laboratories located around the top-secret site is conducted.

Everything from WW1 mustard gas and chlorine shells to sarin, used by Syria's former dictator against his own people, has to be accounted for. The material is required to be either securely stored, returned to its source of origin, or destroyed in special ultra-hot furnaces.

Porton Down has, over the years, received multiple samples of Novichok, garnered from the scenes of FSB, SVR or GRU assassination attempts in the UK and around the world. But the Salisbury sample is the jewel in the crown of the collection.

Fully 78ml of the 100ml capacity of the atomiser remained unused from the original attack, after the fatal accidental application and the testing process. Except that when this particular sample was checked by the chief compliance officer, a Welshman called Gwyn Roberts, only 70ml appeared to be present.

Roberts immediately asked for a meeting with the director of Porton Down, Dr Chris Saunders. That same afternoon he walked into the director's office and delivered the worrying news.

'Dr Saunders the annual audit is nearly complete. It's all in order, except for one thing. The Salisbury sample appears to be 8ml short.'

The colour drained from Saunders' face.

'But that's impossible. It's held in our most secure lab. Has there been a mistake? Could some of it have been drawn down for further testing? Could the measurements be off?'

'I don't believe so, Director. I have checked and double-checked the measurements, and I've checked the logs for any requests for sample testing. There doesn't appear to be a mistake.'

Dr Saunders recovered his composure.

'OK leave it with me, Gwyn. Tomorrow we'll have another look and triple check it together.'

That night the director worked late, which was not unusual.

When all was quiet, he used his security pass to access the laboratory where the Salisbury Novichok was stored. Drawing on his extensive scientific expertise, and with a steady hand, he introduced precisely 8ml of distilled water into the atomiser containing the Salisbury sample.

CHAPTER 42

LONDON, BRUSSELS, MOSCOW

It had been several weeks since Beaufort had sent his mother a note asking her – begging her – to end the uncertainty, and tell him who his father was.

He waited as patiently as he could for a response. He hoped that she would invite him round to her town house, or that they could meet for lunch in a neutral venue.

As the weeks passed, he gradually realised that not only was she unwilling to divulge the information he had by now become desperate to obtain, but that his request had driven an even larger emotional wedge between them.

Then everything changed. Beaufort's mother was cast to play an ageing femme fatale in a romantic comedy being filmed at Elstree Studios in Borehamwood. After repeated retakes of a love scene, and tense exchanges with her co-star, a handsome young male lead with halitosis, she collapsed.

On-site medical staff succeeded in stabilising her, and an air ambulance was called to take her to the Royal Berkeley Square Clinic, a discreet private hospital in central London. Because of the effect it might have had on the film's financial backers, news of her sudden illness was kept under wraps.

The prognosis was not good. Yvette de Beaufort, a lifelong smoker, had suffered a massive heart attack, and some of the damage was irreversible. If it had not been for the speed and skill of the studio medics, she would have died on the film set.

Although the doctors made encouraging noises, the number of machines she was hooked up to, and the worried looks on the nurses' faces, convinced Yvette de Beaufort that she might not have long to live.

The actress sent for Joan, her long-serving and long-suffering assistant. Joan had disliked her demanding employer for years, and often thought about trying to secure another position. But the pay was good, and her lover, Snyder, was desperate for her to stay on.

As private secretary to one of Britain's biggest stars Joan had access to a steady stream of show business gossip. Her employer's known association with the new prime minister and her son's rapid political rise were all the more reason for her to remain in the job, as far as the paparazzo was concerned.

Secretly, Joan was also hoping for a repeat of the extended and satisfying sex session she had enjoyed with the actress's son the previous month. She still fantasised about Beaufort, whether she was in Synder's arms, or alone with her Rabbit.

When Joan answered the summons and arrived in her employer's private hospital room she was expecting to be sent out on an errand to buy a packet of forbidden cigarettes.

She was surprised when the actress instead ordered her to take dictation, and hand-write a short note for her to sign. She was even more surprised when she found out that the recipient was to be Beaufort, and more shocked still by the content.

My Darling Son,

I am sorry that I did not get back to you. I have been busy – too busy – and as you know the subject of your father has always been painful and difficult for me.

Yesterday I had a heart attack on set, and the prognosis is not good. Come and visit me at the Royal Berkeley Square Clinic and I will answer all of your questions and tell you all that you need to know.

Please contact Joan and confirm that you will be coming, and when. I urge you, do not delay.

Your loving, and ailing,
Mother.

This last line and the signature were scrawled by the actress in her own hand, in order to add force and authenticity to the note. Then the letter was sealed in an envelope in front of the actress, and Joan left to order a courier to hand deliver it.

On the way she slipped into the ladies' toilet, slit open the envelope, and photographed the contents. She then resealed the letter in a fresh envelope, and left it at the reception desk for collection by the courier service.

Snyder would be delighted with her efforts, and might even take her out to dinner, and then back to his Soho flat for a night of the steamy S&M sex they both enjoyed.

*

When Snyder received the WhatsApp with the copy of the letter attached from Joan, he immediately recognised its importance. He sent Oleg, his Russian contact, an urgent message on Telegram. The Russian acknowledged receipt, and congratulated Snyder on his scoop.

He promised him a hefty reward, and warned him not to share the contents of the letter with any of his other contacts.

*

Beaufort was in Brussels engaged in interminable Breturn negotiations with the former UKREP, turned head of the European Commission *Division Bretagne,* Edward Gore-Ewing.

The British were still obsessed with trying to secure the return of the "Thatcher rebate", which they had previously enjoyed. The EU side had in turn suddenly introduced a stipulation that the UK would have to join the European Defence Community if they were admitted.

The EDC was formed following the American refusal to guarantee the security of European states that did not meet their uplifted NATO commitment to spend 5% of GDP on defence. The implication was that if the UK joined the EDC, their Trident nuclear submarine fleet would come under its command.

When the envelope arrived at his departmental office in Whitehall, Beaufort's private secretary was torn. The envelope was marked "Personal", but it was also marked "Urgent". Spurred on by her sense of duty, and her natural curiosity, she opened the letter and immediately understood why it was marked as it was.

Without delay she scanned the letter and sent it to Beaufort's secure government mobile, with apologies for having opened it.

Beaufort replied immediately, and instructed her to book him on an overnight Eurostar back to London. He then messaged Joan, and told her he would come by to see his mother the following day. She too replied immediately, urging him to hurry.

Beaufort thanked Joan for her dedication to his mother, and promised her another drink when the crisis was over. Joan replied with a heart emoji.

*

Oleg showed the duty officer at the *residentura* the message he had received from Snyder. Without hesitation he telephoned the *rezident*, who hurried into the embassy to view the message. He ordered it to be encrypted and sent to the Lubyanka, where it was rushed to Tarakan's office.

For once the FSB chief's composure slipped. He swore viciously, and immediately sent for Dudayev. Within the hour the Chechen was on his way by private plane to Helsinki, where he caught a connecting scheduled flight to London Heathrow.

*

Security at the Royal Berkeley Square Clinic was good, but nowhere near good enough.

Private security guards from a well-respected company manned the reception desk during the evenings, and also patrolled the corridors. The security company provided ex special forces bodyguards for close-protection work with celebrities, politicians and senior businesspeople. Those allocated to routine duties at institutions such as the Royal Berkeley were of a lower calibre.

As Dudayev was heading to Heathrow via Helsinki a GRU "active measures" team kidnapped one of the clinic guards who was asleep at home after his night shift, and was due to be back on duty that evening.

The man was tortured for information relating to the security regime at the hospital. His uniform was taken off him, and the jacket let out to accommodate the shoulders of a much broader man. His security pass was doctored, an east European name inserted, and the photograph replaced with one of Dudayev.

The security guard's body would be found several weeks later in a disused quarry in Bedfordshire, its teeth smashed to fragments and its fingertips cauterised, in order to hinder identification.

*

Dudayev was met at Heathrow by an embassy driver in an unmarked BMW and driven to a safe house in Highgate.

He was then issued with the fake ID badge, kitted out in the kidnapped security guard's altered uniform, and dropped around the corner from the hospital in a nondescript white van.

The Chechen deliberately arrived a few minutes late for the shift he was covering. He wanted to stimulate anxiety in the day shift, who would then be even more keen to get away. His English was adequate, but his accent heavy and identifiable as Russian, or at the least eastern European. He did not want to engage in a long conversation during the handover.

Looking up from the reception desk the uniformed man simply asked.

'Where's Joe?'

'Called in sick.'

'Have you been briefed on the routine?'

'Sure.'

'Just to be certain, it's two hours on the front desk, then Pete will replace you, and you go and patrol the ward corridors on all three floors. Then reverse and repeat. There's a VVIP in Room 39 on the top floor. She is not to be disturbed – and no photographs.'

'Got it.'

The daytime security guard headed for the door. He had a hot date that night.

Dudayev settled down behind the reception desk, patiently waiting to be relieved of his static duty and freed up to roam the ward corridors.

*

The security guard who arrived to replace Dudayev after his two hour stint on the reception desk was a retired police sergeant who looked like his active-duty days had long since passed.

'Where's Joe?' came the inevitable question.

'Called in sick.'

'Right. All quiet down here?' the ex-policeman asked.

'All quiet. Upstairs?'

'No dramas. Check the fire escape doors are properly shut. Some of the patients – and some of the nurses – nip out for a crafty fag, and they don't always shut the door properly.'

'Sure. See you later.'

*

Dudayev ignored the first two floors and headed straight up to the third.

He nodded to the sleepy duty sister on the nurses' station, and headed towards the fire door at the end of the corridor. Having checked it was firmly closed, he walked back down the corridor, and then slipped into Room 39.

As soon as he entered Yvette de Beaufort woke up.

Her eyes, which had lost none of their lustre, locked on his, and she instantly understood. Something about the way he stood looking expressionlessly down at her, about his broad shoulders and massive chest, his untamed red straggly beard, told her this was no ordinary security guard. That and the fact he was pulling on blue surgical gloves.

Still looking him full in the eyes she asked:

'Did he send you?'

Dudayev nodded.

'There is no point, you know, I'm dying anyway.'

Dudayev shrugged, and moved towards the bed. He moved the alarm button out of her reach, took the pulse oximeter off her finger, and fixed it to his own. Slowly, almost gently, he slipped one of the two pillows out from under her head.

She looked up at him, unprotesting, resigned to what was to come.

'Tell him I forgive him. Tell him I love him. Tell him I have always loved him.'

The Chechen nodded again and spoke for the first time, in Russian.

'It is an honour to take such a life.'

He held the pillow over her face. She lay unmoving, and only towards the end did her hands reflexively rise to feebly try and push the pillow from her face.

Dudayev checked for a pulse to make sure she was dead. Then he replaced the pillow under her lifeless head, crossed her arms across her chest and folded her hands into fists. In one he placed a green snooker ball, in the other a brown ball. He had orders to make it painless, and to leave the face and body of the actress as beautiful in death as they had been in life.

He also had orders to leave a message that one man alone would understand.

*

Half an hour later a nurse coming in to check on the patient immediately spotted the disconnected pulse oximeter and the lifeless patient. She pressed the alarm and scrambled the crash team, but nothing could be done.

The hospital's senior management team convened an emergency Zoom meeting. The private security company alerted the Met Police, who quickly informed Special Branch, who in turn notified Thames House and Vauxhall Cross.

This particular corpse was a celebrity, with connections to the prime minister, and the rising political star Lord Beaufort of Pimlico.

Alarm bells were ringing, and not just in the hospital.

CHAPTER 43

VAUXHALL CROSS, LONDON

The Admiral arranged for Beaufort to be met off his Eurostar from Brussels and driven straight to Vauxhall Cross. When the lobbyist-turned-spy-turned-politician was brought into his office he offered him a seat and a drink.

'I'm fine standing, thanks, and it's a bit early for me, sir. What's going on? I only just got back from Brussels. My mother's very ill – I was on my way to see her in hospital.'

'I know. I'm sorry, my boy. I wanted to tell you face to face, man to man. Your mother is dead.'

'Dead? How? I don't understand. . .'

Beaufort slumped into the chair he had previously declined and shook his head in incomprehension and denial.

'She was very ill, sir, but they'd stabilised her. . . She asked me to come and see her. . . She was going to tell me about my father, at last, after all these years.'

'I'm really sorry, Damian, but that's why she was killed. Precisely so she couldn't tell you about your father.'

Beaufort leaped back to his feet.

'Killed? By whom? And why? Why does it matter to anybody else who the hell my father is – or was?'

The Admiral made soothing motions with his hands.

'I have to be honest with you Damian, we've known for quite some time who your father is. And he is very much alive.'

Beaufort shook his head again, and asked in a quieter voice:

'So why didn't you tell me, sir. If I'd known, maybe I wouldn't have pushed my mother to reveal it. Maybe she'd still be alive.'

'We thought it might be best if you didn't know. You were unhappy not knowing, but we calculated you might be unhappier still if you did know.'

'It's bloody Clem Clark, isn't it? Those rumours on the blogs and in the muck-raking press are true, aren't they? That's why he made me a peer, and a minister.'

'No, it isn't Clem – you might wish it were. But you were indeed the result of an Oxford liaison.'

'Not that creep Morand? Don't tell me I am the son of a Belgian Eurocrat?'

'I'm sorry Damian, but it's far worse even that that. Your father is Russian. Well, half-Russian, half-Tazmen, to be precise.'

'Russian? Tazmen? So, who is he? Enough games, sir, please – just tell me.'

'You father is Tarakan, the head of the Russian intelligence service, the FSB. He was at Oxford with your mother. He ordered her killing so that she couldn't tell you that he was your father.'

Beaufort's head was spinning.

'I will have that drink, sir, maybe a whisky.'

The Admiral rose and poured two large Scotches into crystal tumblers. He handed one to Beaufort, and waited for the inevitable question.

'But why kill a defenceless old woman? She was just an actress, and she was already on her deathbed. I just don't understand.'

'Your mother was much more than just an actress, Damian. She was a very clever, and highly motivated, woman. She studied Russian literature at Oxford. She won awards for her portrayal of Anna Karenina and Lyubov Ranevskaya in films. She loved Tarakan, she loved Russian culture, in fact she loved all things Russian, no matter what flag the motherland was wrapped in, and no matter who was at the helm. She even named you after the great Russian poet Demyan Bedny.'

'I still don't understand. What exactly are you saying?'

'You mother was seduced by Tarakan, both sexually and politically. She was an active Russian agent, and a communications conduit between him and three of the most important agents the Russians have ever had in the West.'

Beaufort took a gulp of his whisky.

'What agents? Who?'

'The Admiral rose, went to his wall safe, opened it and extracted a buff folder with three red diagonal stripes. It was marked 'Top Secret – UK Eyes Only.'

He sat down, opened the folder, extracted a photograph, and slid it across the coffee table to Beaufort.

'Who do you recognise?'

Beaufort studied the slightly blurred print of the old

photograph.

'My mother, of course. And yes, Clem Clark. I knew they were at Oxford together – and so do the bloody press. And is that Philippe Morand?'

'Yes, that is the man who is now the European Commission president.'

'And who is this guy with the long hair, standing next to Morand?'

'That is Edward Gore-Ewing, late of the Foreign Office and UKREP, now of the European Commission. He has changed a great deal in appearance, and he has changed sides, but he's the same man you were negotiating the details of the Breturn arrangements with just yesterday.'

'So the fourth guy, the one standing directly behind my mother, with the hat, and his hand on her shoulder? That's my father?'

'Yes, that is Tarakan. He was at Oxford. He'd stolen the persona of a Czech called Karel Kucera, a true patriot killed by the *Statna Bezpecnost*, the Czech secret police. Tarakan assumed his identity and came to study at Oxford as an *émigré*. This is the only photograph we have of him.'

Beaufort studied the face. The high, prominent cheekbones were striking. The lips, twisted into a sardonic smile, brought the lower half of the face to life. But the eyes were invisible, shaded by the fedora hat.

'So this,' he jabbed the face in the photograph, 'this is my father?'

'Yes, Damian, that is your father. A man of great ability. A man of great patience. A man without conscience or scruples. And a man who controls our prime minister, the Commission president and the EU's chief Breturn negotiator. And the man who ordered your mother's assassination.'

Beaufort looked at the photograph for a long time, and nodded calmly. After all these years, all the rumours, all his own guessing and imaginings and fantasies, he had finally found out the truth.

His father was alive, and his father was a murderous psychopath.

CHAPTER 44

LUBYANKA, MOSCOW

The flash signal came through from the London *residentura* that Dudayev had successfully completed his mission and was on his way back to Moscow, via Dublin and Istanbul.

Tarakan was not surprised. The Chechen never failed.

*

The following afternoon, after his circuitous return journey, Dudayev presented himself to his boss in his top-floor corner office.

Tarakan looked up from his ornate desk.

'Was it quick and clean, as I ordered?'

'Yes, General. She was ready. There was no struggle, and no pain. I left no marks on her.'

'Did she say anything?'

Dudayev told his boss the actress's last words.

Tarakan nodded, and dismissed the Chechen with a wave.

He sat silently, perfectly still, his mind returning to his university years, when he had seduced, and been beguiled in turn. Of all the things he had done to safeguard the *Rodina*, this was the hardest.

After several minutes he rose from the desk, and limped across to the chess board. He sighed deeply. If he still knew how, he might have wept.

He reached out his three-fingered hand, and toppled his own queen.

CHAPTER 45

COVENT GARDEN, LONDON

Because of the manner of her death, there had to be a post-mortem before the actress's body could be released for burial.

This confirmed she had been murdered, with asphyxiation given as the cause of death. The tabloids made the most of the sensational story and ran it for several days, even though all mention of the snooker balls were hushed up on national security grounds.

The funeral took place at St Paul's Covent Garden. Known as the Actors' Church, and designed by Inigo Jones, it has famous thespians such as Corinne Redgrave and Vivienne Leigh buried in its churchyard, and plaques for the likes of Charlie Chaplin and Noel Coward on its walls. As such it was a suitable last resting place for the much-loved actress.

The service was billed as private, which meant "no fans". Beaufort had no living relatives on his mother's side, and after the Admiral's shocking revelation he had no idea how many he had on his father's. Not that he would have invited them, of course.

Frobisher went to the service ostensibly to provide comfort and support to an old school friend, but in reality to keep an eye on the other mourners. Joan attended as the deceased's confidante and longest serving employee. Clem Clark, Philippe Morand and Edward Gore-Ewing were in attendance as old university friends.

The rest of the congregation consisted mainly of actors, directors, writers, technicians and crew from the worlds of stage and screen. Many of them had worked with the actress multiple times over the years, and most seemed to have been genuinely fond of her.

The vicar conducting the service wore suitably bright vestments. The ceremony was being live-streamed for those unable to fit into the small church, and the priest made the most of his time in the limelight, behaving as though he was auditioning for a part in 'Four Weddings and a Funeral'.

Beaufort kept the eulogy short, aware of the fact that many of those present knew his mother better than he did. His final words hinted at the bitterness he felt at the state of the relationship between them.

'My mother lived for her work, and her work was acting. She was a great actress, on screen, on stage, but also in real life. Many of you knew her for decades, and it was a tribute to her versatility – and to her vitality – that she remained so much in demand even in her later years.'

In the churchyard a small group of fans stood, some weeping silently, some holding photographs of the actress in her prime. The paparazzi were out in force, including Joan's lover Snyder. They managed to snap all the politicians and celebrities, but Frobisher slipped out unobtrusively through the vestry.

At the church entrance there was a mountain of cheap cellophane-wrapped bouquets of flowers from fans, and a small number of more formal floral tributes. One of these was a stunning wreath of white lilies, with a simple note in English. It read: 'Thank you, for everything, and I am truly sorry.'

It was signed with a single letter 'T'.

*

The wake was held in the River Room at the Savoy on the Strand, five minutes' walk from the Actors' Church. It had been Yvette de Beaufort's favourite hotel, and the doormen, concierges and bell boys all wore black armbands in tribute.

Beaufort was still in a state of mild shock, and Samantha turned up to offer him emotional support. Where others shook his hand and offered formal condolences, she walked up and embraced him.

'Are you OK?'

'Not really, no. I can't help blaming myself. If I hadn't pushed her to name my father, she might still be alive.'

Samantha hugged him again, and led him by the arm to the bar, which was serving White Ladies, his mother's favourite cocktail.

She ordered two, raised her glass, and proposed a toast.

'Here's to Yvette – a hell of a woman, who led a hell of a life.'

They clinked cocktail glasses, and Beaufort smiled gratefully.

Clem Clark, Philippe Morand and Edward Gore-Ewing were standing drinking champagne in a quiet corner. The Commission president asked the British PM:

'How's the Breturn Bill progressing?'

'Very well. It sailed through the House of Commons, and my chief whip is confident that he can get it through the Lords, now that we've expelled the hereditaries and packed the House with Labour life peers. Trust me, it'll happen.'

Morand and Gore-Ewing both grinned the former gripping the PM's shoulder to ram home the congratulations.

'We must push this through – before your people turn on you, and before my people change their minds. Together we can make history. And it seems to be what *he* wants.'

The prime minister nodded. The Bill had passed through the Commons unscathed. He had gerrymandered the composition of the House of Lords, and put a former Tory Brexiteer in charge of steering the Bill through.

What could possibly go wrong?

*

Samantha stayed behind until the last guest had departed, all repeating their condolences, sincere or otherwise, on the way out. She ordered another drink for them both, cognac this time.

'I'm sure your mother was a lovely lady,' she said, 'but her taste in drinks sucked! Anyway, here's to her, once again.'

Beaufort was starting to look at Samantha differently. Not as a PR colleague, not as his MI6 handler, but as somebody who cared for him, and whom he cared for.

'Come on,' she said, 'let's see if this fancy pile of bricks has a spare room. I know just what you need to cheer you up.'

There was a room, and she proceeded to cheer him up in it. Not the kinky bathroom sex of last time, nor its frenetic aftermath in the giant bed at the Dorchester. But slow, deep, meaningful love-making, that relieved his sadness, and left them both sated and sleepy.

After a while Beaufort stirred and asked:

'Was that a sympathy shag?'

'Only if you want it to be.'

CHAPTER 46

CHARING CROSS, LONDON

The following day Samantha received a message from Geoff Simmonds requesting an urgent meeting.

They met in Gordon's Wine Bar, the same venue as their last meeting, when Simmonds had stalked out having been shown the sex tape from Dustana.

This time Simmonds arrived first, and chose a table on the ground floor. He ordered a bottle of Merlot and two glasses.

As Samantha entered Simmonds rose from his seat and embraced her, planting an unwelcome kiss on both of her cheeks.

'Marvellous to see you. And looking so lovely as well.'

Samantha smiled and said.

'You're looking good yourself, Geoff. What have you got for me?'

Simmonds reached into the briefcase at his feet and extracted an A4 House of Commons envelope.

'This is dynamite. Top Secret, restricted, numbered copies to each member of the committee, so be careful who you show it to. Don't look at it here.'

Samantha tucked the envelope into her shoulder bag and asked:

'So what is it Geoff? What's so explosive?'

'This submission is from the PM's national security adviser. It recommends the merger of MI5 and MI6. It talks about the efficiencies and cost savings that a merger could achieve. And it talks about bringing an end to the century-old rivalry between the two agencies. It is exactly what you asked me to look out for.'

He sat back with a triumphant grin, waiting for praise and expressions of gratitude.

'It is indeed Geoff, thank you. My masters will be most appreciative.'

Samantha rose to leave but Simmonds grabbed her wrist.

'Is that it? I've risked my career getting this to you. Don't I get some sort of payment? Won't you at least destroy the video?'

Samantha wrenched her arm free, leaned forward and whispered into Simmonds' ear.

'You don't understand how this works, Geoff. You ceased to have a career the moment you shagged that escort. The way it works is this: you give, we take. Just be thankful it was us recording your antics, and not the FSB.'

She turned and left, leaving Simmonds to finish the bottle of wine, and curse his overactive libido.

CHAPTER 47

EUROPEAN QUARTER, BRUSSELS

Talks between the UK and the EU were being conducted in parallel with the Breturn Bill progressing through the Westminster Parliament.

Most of the detailed negotiations were conducted by officials, with the UK side represented by staff from the British Embassy in Brussels, reinforced by trade and legal experts seconded from Whitehall. On the EU side, Edward Gore-Ewing's DG NEAR team was negotiating on behalf of Commission President Morand.

The bugs planted in Morand's office by Alvariz had been left in place, so as not to reveal that he had been trapped and turned. They continued to provide the British with some intelligence. However, as Morand and his team were aware of them, and as negotiations were reaching a critical phase, most of the internal discussions took place in the "bubble", a Perspex sphere suspended from cables in the basement of the Berlaymont.

The EU's intelligence agency, INTCEN, was determined to use Alvariz to gather evidence proving that "Perfidious

Albion" was up to its old tricks. They wanted to ensnare not just the local MI6 station chief, but any senior intelligence officers they could lure over from Vauxhall Cross.

The Basque was ordered to request an urgent meeting with Taylor. The British spy chief in Brussels suggested that they meet in the Parc Leopold. Strolling around the formal lake they would be well out of range of any fixed microphones, and it conformed with the Hanslope Park dictum: whenever possible hide in plain sight. What Taylor did not realise was that the Basque would be "mic'd up", and every word of their conversation would be overheard and captured.

Brussels was a relatively benign environment for a British spy. Nevertheless, Taylor practised basic tradecraft. He arrived twenty minutes early and wandered apparently aimlessly around the lake until he had satisfied himself that the rendezvous was not staked out.

When he spotted Alvariz hurrying into the park, nearly ten minutes late, he signalled to him it was safe to approach by transferring his umbrella from his right to his left hand.

'You're late,' was Taylor's opening gambit.

'I have job. Is not easy. Is easy for you. Not for me.'

'OK. Well, what have you got for me?'

'Not for you. Is big. Is for beautiful lady.'

'For God's sake Alvariz, this isn't a dating show. I'm your case officer, and if you have something you give it to me.'

'No. You threatened me. You do not respect me. I like her. Get her to come here. Tell her it is big. Tell her to bring gold.'

Too furious to trust himself to speak Taylor nodded curtly and strode towards the exit.

*

What neither MI6 nor INTCEN realised was that Alvariz had been working for the FSB for years.

In his youth he had associated himself with the Basque separatist group ETA, and their main paymasters were the Russians. When he got his chance to work for the EU in Brussels, the FSB had got back in touch with him, and given him small tasks to perform in order to establish his loyalty and assess his potential usefulness.

Now he found himself serving three spymasters, which was a bit like playing three dimensional chess. Sometimes he couldn't work out whether he was a double agent or a triple agent, and the complexity of his situation gave him headaches, and caused him to sleep too little and drink too much.

Alvariz did have one hobby that helped him to relax. Like a lot of Basques, he liked to shoot. Not the anodyne clay pigeons of the bien-pensant middle class, but real, live, fast-flying birds. If he was lucky, he occasionally got to hunt wild boar.

The FSB kept the Basque on a loose leash. When a meeting was required, they usually arranged for it to take place at the Forest of the Prince hunting ground in the Ardennes region.

Alvariz's FSB controller was an amiable, burly man whose trade name was Viktor. In contrast to his relationship with Taylor, Alvariz got on well with Viktor. They shot together, drank together, and occasionally whored together in Brussels's red-light district in Rue de Brabant. The Russian also spoke Spanish, following a five-year posting to Madrid.

Stalking through the woods as a gun pair, the Russian asked Alvariz in Spanish:

'So, do you have anything for me, my friend?'

'The Breturn negotiations are progressing. The British are desperate for any information on the talks. They made me plant electronic bugs in Morand's office, but INTCEN found out, and decided to leave them in place. They make me work for them, and now they have ordered me to trap Taylor. He is a typical arrogant English bastard, so I am happy to do this. But now they have told me to lure his lady boss over from London, on the promise of a piece of prime intelligence, which I do not have yet.'

'OK this is good – you are a master spy! We know all about Taylor, his tradecraft is sloppy. But we would like to "meet" this woman. When you have the details, let me know.'

A stag sprang from cover and made off at speed. They had no license to hunt deer.

Viktor shot it anyway.

CHAPTER 48

KENNINGTON, LONDON

When Taylor contacted Samantha and told her about his meeting with Alvariz, and the Basque's insistence that he would only divulge his latest information to her, she was torn.

On the one hand she did not want to undermine Taylor, and she could sense the station chief's irritation with his volatile agent. On the other hand, she had the lobbying agency's Brussels office as a watertight alibi, and MI6 needed to produce intelligence on the EU negotiations to shore up its increasingly precarious position.

Samantha therefore told Taylor to confirm the meeting, and prepared to travel to BXL on the "red eye" Eurostar the following morning.

Since their night together in the Savoy, she and Beaufort had been carrying on a clandestine relationship. The night before she left for Brussels, he came over to her small flat in Kennington to discuss developments, and to make love.

It had been agreed between them that he would not stay the night, because of her early start. He called an Uber just before midnight, and as they kissed on the doorstep he whispered:

'Be careful over there. Some of those *moules* can be lethal.'

She laughed, and pushed him towards his taxi.

CHAPTER 49

WATERLOO, BELGIUM

Alvariz was now in a difficult position. INTCEN wanted him to entrap Samantha, and record her asking for intelligence on the EU's strategy for the Breturn negotiations. At the same time the FSB were insisting he create an opportunity for them to kidnap and interrogate her.

On instructions from Viktor, Alvariz suggested another outdoor meeting, this time at the site of the Battle of Waterloo, approximately 20 kilometres outside Brussels. And close to the Russian ambassador's country residence north of Nivelles.

Taylor insisted on accompanying Samantha and checking out the rendezvous. She agreed, but asked him to stay out of sight, in view of the deteriorating relationship between him and his "Joe".

When they arrived, Samantha headed straight for the Lion's Mound, the centrepiece of the battlefield memorial site. Taylor, having checked out the surroundings for the presence of hostile agents, retreated to the nearby Rotunda café in order to remain out of sight.

The FSB, meanwhile, had inserted a seven-strong GRU team into the area: five men and two women, operating under Viktor's command. Taylor had failed to spot them.

One man-and-woman team made their way to the top of the Mound, whilst a second man followed shortly behind them, masquerading as a solo tourist. Two men went to the Rotunda to maintain eyes on Taylor, and another man-and-woman team stayed in the car park in a ubiquitous white Renault Trafic van. Viktor also remained with the vehicle, in radio contact with the other teams.

Samantha wandered around the top of the mound, trying to act like any other tourist. She had spotted the Slavic-looking couple, but they seemed to be absorbed in the view, and in each other. The solo male tourist seemed solely intent on using the elevation of the mound to get the best shots with his expensive-looking camera. She observed Alvariz making his way breathlessly up the steps of the mound, and used her left hand to remove her sunglasses, to signal that it was safe to approach.

When the Basque finally reached the viewing platform, she turned to him, smiled and held her arms out for an embrace. He moved forwarded obediently to wrap his arms around her, feeling guilty as he did so.

'Are you alone?' he whispered.

'Yes, of course,' she lied.

'OK good. I have something for you. Do you have gold?'

'Yes. Are sovereigns OK?'

'Better than OK. What I have is good – also pure gold!'

Just then the GRU couple approached, and the woman asked Samantha in heavily-accented English:

'Will you take our photograph – with the Lion behind?'

Although irritated at the interruption Samantha agreed, rather than cause a scene. She took several shots, and didn't object when the woman huddled up to her in an effort to view the phone screen in the shadow cast by their bodies.

At that point the man approached, leaning over as if he too wanted to view the photographs. As he did do, he jabbed Samantha in the thigh with an EpiPen filled with a fast-acting date-rape drug, designed to incapacitate her.

As Samantha collapsed Alvariz and the GRU man went through the motions of giving her CPR, and the second GRU man with the expensive camera rushed over as though offering assistance. The woman pretended to be hysterically phoning for an ambulance.

Then the two male GRU operatives picked up Samantha, wrapped her arms around their shoulders, and started to carry her awkwardly down the steps of the monument. The woman was still keeping up the pretence of talking to ambulance control, and Alvariz trailed behind, feeling bewildered and unsettled by the speed of events.

Taylor, seeing Samantha being carried down the steps by the two GRU man, turned from the café window and rushed towards the exit. The two-man GRU team that had been tasked with shadowing him blocked his path, bundled him into the men's toilet and administered a lethal dose of cyanide into his neck, via another EpiPen.

They shoved him into one of the toilet stalls, perched his body on the seat, and secured it upright by swivelling his tie 180 degrees and knotting it to the downpipe. One of the GRU men then locked the cubicle from the inside, before sliding out through the gap at the bottom of the door.

In the fake electrician's van in the car park, the two

INTCEN operatives heard the initial chaos over Alvariz's microphones, and then the feed went silent as the GRU woman ripped the listening device from Alvariz's chest and dumped it into a litter bin. They radioed for orders, but were instructed to stay in the van until backup arrived.

Samantha was placed in the back of the Renault Trafic. At the last moment two of the GRU men grabbed Alvariz and flung him in after her. He had served his purpose, and outlived his usefulness.

A lethal cyanide dose was jabbed into his neck too. As he lay dying, he looked reproachfully up at Viktor, who shrugged apologetically.

The Basque was once, twice, three times a traitor. Nobody would mourn him.

*

Plenty of witnesses saw the abduction of Samantha, but none could agree on the description of the kidnappers, or even how many of them there had been. Several described the van accurately, and one even remembered part of the license plate number, but as the plates were false this piece of information did not significantly help the investigation.

*

Just fifteen minutes after the abduction, the Renault swung through the gates of the Russian ambassador's country retreat. The ambassador resented having his premises used by spies, but knew he would be overruled by Moscow if he objected. As a compromise he instructed the GRU team to avoid the main building, and confine their activities to the stable block.

The vehicle itself was driven straight into the stables, out of sight of any loitering drones or orbiting satellites. Samantha was carried through to the old tack room, still unconscious.

The body of the Basque Alvariz was chain sawed into pieces and then shoved through a wood-chipper. The resulting slurry was fed to the ambassador's herd of pedigree pigs.

Karma for all the wild boar he had shot over the years.

*

When Samantha regained consciousness, she was naked, and strapped by her wrists, waist and ankles to a stainless steel autopsy table. The tack room was cold and damp, and there was a bright a bright overhead light shining directly down into her eyes.

Recognising the gravity of her situation, Samantha attempted to retreat deep inside her own mind. She pictured happy moments from her childhood, and tried to mentally put herself back amongst the soaring mountains and deep valleys of the New Zealand of her childhood.

Over the next three days the GRU team ran through their entire repertoire of interrogation techniques. First, they tried depriving her of dignity, warmth and sleep. She was given no food, and only enough water to prevent her organs from failing.

When this treatment failed to produce results, her tormentors tried a variety of chemicals, designed to disorientate, and to loosen inhibitions and tongues. When these drugs also failed to break her resistance, they resorted to the old NKVD techniques of electrocution, punctuated by savage beatings and torture with an array of implements neatly arranged on a surgical trolley within her view.

In her more lucid moments, drawing on the resistance-to-interrogation training she had received at Hanslope Park, Samantha gave her interrogators snippets, near useless pieces of intelligence that would at least convey the pretence of cooperation. This tactic was designed to bring about some temporary relief from the incessant pain, and buy some time for her rescuers to find her. Somewhere deep inside Samantha still believed that colleagues from the Firm would locate and liberate her.

Once Samantha had started to offer up the "chicken feed" of minimally useful information the interrogators, rather than scaling back the torture, redoubled their efforts. They asked her about the Trident test, and whether the failure had been staged. They asked her if the UK would really hand over control of its nuclear deterrent as the price for re-joining the EU. They asked her about the Admiral, and they asked her about Beaufort.

When they questioned her about her lover, Samantha shut down completely, retreating to the very deepest recesses of her mind. At that point the interrogators gave up on getting any useful information out of her.

That is when Dudayev was sent for. To inflict the final indignities.

*

Samantha's body was left, naked, battered and bloodied, stretched out on the slopes of the Lion's Mound, scene of Britain's greatest military victory on land.

Taylor's was discovered in the Rotunda toilets, but

in view of his status as MI6 station chief, this news was suppressed. The Belgian government convened a crisis meeting of the Cabinet Security Council. INTCEN and the Belgian State Security Service, the VSSE, were in a state of turmoil.

The whole area around the Waterloo battlefield site was closed and cordoned off for two days in order to allow the forensic teams to do their work.

Samantha's body was taken to the main Brussels morgue in the Rue Montserrat for storage, and placed in a refrigeration chamber next to that of Taylor. The British insisted that both Taylor and Samantha had diplomatic immunity, in death as in life, and therefore no autopsy should be conducted.

Frobisher was sent over on an RAF Hercules to repatriate the bodies, and liaise with the VSSE. The Belgian intelligence agents were embarrassed by what had occurred on their patch, but they were also anxious to find out what operation MI6 had been running on their soil, at the site of the nation's most famous landmark.

CHAPTER 50

VAUXHALL CROSS, LONDON

When Frobisher arrived at Vauxhall Cross, having accompanied both bodies back to the UK via RAF Brize Norton, he immediately reported to the Admiral. He walked straight past an unusually subdued Ms Danso, and entered the Admiral's office without knocking.

'How the hell did this happen?' the Admiral roared. 'Taylor and Samantha were both highly experienced operatives, but they seem to have walked into this with their eyes closed.'

'It was the Basque, Alvariz, sir. He set them both up. And now he's disappeared.'

The Admiral moderated his tone.

'Samantha would have talked, I imagine?'

'Anybody would have. They had her for nearly a week. But she was very strong, and very stubborn. It's possible she died without giving anything vital away.'

'Any signs of snooker balls?'

'Not in her eyes, and not in her hands. We'll have to wait for the autopsy to be sure.'

Beaufort had not heard from Samantha for several days. This was not unusual, given the complex, multi-layered lives they both led.

When he got the call to meet the Admiral, he felt uneasy, and hurried over to Vauxhall Cross. One look at Ms Danso's red-rimmed eyes and strained face confirmed his fears.

The Admiral got up from behind his desk, came round and put his hand on Beaufort's shoulder.

'I'm terribly sorry, my boy. Samantha is dead. Tortured and killed by the Russians. We have brought her body home.'

Beaufort said nothing for several seconds. Then he reached up and flung the Admiral's hand from his shoulder.

'First my mother, and now Samantha. The only two women I have ever really loved. What a filthy, disgusting world you live in.'

'Your world too now, I'm afraid. We cannot be sure what Samantha told them under interrogation. We have to assume they know about you.'

'Who did this?'

'The FSB, with their GRU thugs.'

'But who specifically?'

'A Chechen called Dudayev. GCHQ hacked the CCTV at Brussels airport, and spotted him coming in and out. But he was acting on orders. Orders from your father, orders from Tarakan.'

'He has to pay for this. They both do. I don't want to be a lobbyist anymore. And I don't want to be a politician. I want to be an agent. I want to be an assassin. I want to kill him – I want to kill them both – Dudayev and Tarakan.'

'Tarakan rarely leaves Russia, as you know. If we ever hear that he has plans to set foot outside Russia again, we will get him, I promise you. If you want to do it yourself, if you want to become one of us rather than just being an "external", you'll have to go to Hanslope Park to be trained up. But before that, we have one final job for you to do – as a politician. Despite everything, I think you might rather enjoy it.'

CHAPTER 51

AROSA LENZERHEIDE, SWITZERLAND

For the Brussels duo a weekend trip to the exclusive Swiss ski resort of Arosa Lenzerheide did not present any logistical challenges. Commission President Philippe Morand left it to Edward Gore-Ewing to hire a remote chalet just outside the main resort, on the slopes of Monte Valbella.

Having arrived on the Friday evening the two men spent Saturday exploring the more advanced black runs. Both were expert skiers, and intensely competitive. Gore-Ewing probably had the edge, but deemed it politic to let his boss win most of the races.

The chalet they hired was fully serviced, but the staff had been dismissed for the evening, having served up a traditional Swiss supper of cheese fondue and *rösti*. Morand and Gore-Ewing then repaired to the hot tub on the terrace, with views overlooking the slopes and the main resort. They took a bottle of champagne in an ice bucket with them. Both wore swimsuits. They weren't German, after all.

The conversation was relaxed, beginning with a review

of the day's skiing, and gradually drifting towards matters of business.

'Do you think he'll come?' asked Gore-Ewing.

'*Bien sûr*,' Morand replied. 'Switzerland is safe territory for them. The Little Tsar even keeps his second family here, and his riches of course. He used to visit regularly before the unfortunate Ukraine business.'

No sooner had he spoken than a tall man appeared on the terrace, limped over to the hot tub, dropped his towel on the decking and climbed in naked. His emaciated frame was in stark contrast to the two Eurocrats, whose figures were verging on obese thanks to Brussels's world-renowned cuisine.

'You English and you French are such prudes,' the new arrival ventured in perfect cut-glass English.

'I'm not English, I'm French,' insisted Gore-Ewing.

'And I'm not French, I'm Belgian,' said the Commission president.

Tarakan laughed and accentuated his own upper-class British accent still further.

'We are none of us quite what we seem.'

He reached for the champagne with his three-fingered hand, exposing the deep, pitted scar etched into his shoulder, and drank deeply from the bottle, before adding:

'But we are all European, that's for sure. Sandwiched between the Asiatic Mongol hordes, and the equally barbaric Americans. That is what binds us together, and that is what motivates our quest.'

They sat in silence, drinking and taking in the stunning view.

'Did you invite Clem?' Tarakan asked.

'Of course,' Morand replied. 'But he couldn't get away. The whole Breturn thing is keeping him busy. I'll brief him in person, either in Brussels or London.'

'OK. How are the Breturn negotiations going?'

Gore-Ewing replied:

'The British officials are being their usual bloody difficult selves. They hate having to deal with me, and are constantly trying to backtrack on areas we've already agreed on.'

Morand nodded in agreement, and then added:

'But Clem needs this. He's staked his whole political future on Breturn. He might not be here, but he's still one of us.'

'What about Trident?' Tarakan asked.

Again, it was Morand who answered:

'Clem now sees that it has to be part of the deal. It's not truly independent in any event – they can't use it without the American's permission. In future it'll be our permission they need.'

The bald head nodded and Tarakan fixed Morand with his heterochromatic gaze.

'And MI6? The Admiral?'

Aware of the deep animosity between Tarakan and his British counterpart, Morand paused before replying.

'Clem hates the Admiral almost as much as we do. He might have proved impossible to remove, if it hadn't been for the botched operations in Belgium. Now Clem thinks the Admiral is tired of fighting against the tide, and thinks we may be able to buy him off with a seat in their ridiculous House of Lords.

Tarakan nodded his satisfaction.

'Whatever happens, we have to separate the British

from the Americans, and shatter the Five Eyes anglophone alliance. We either need them back in Europe, weakened and subservient, or we need them isolated and powerless. In the process we neutralise Trident, and I can finally get even with the man who caused me to be sent to the gulag, and did this to me.'

With his good left hand he touched the deep gouge on his right shoulder, and the striped scars across his chest.

Having outlined his strategy, and delivered his orders, Tarakan raised his right arm and snapped his remaining fingers.

The hulking figure of the Chechen Dudayev emerged from the chalet, carrying an ice bucket with a bottle of Stolichnaya Elit vodka and a tray of shot glasses. Dudayev poured a large measure for each of them, and Tarakan raised his glass.

'A toast. To Yvette, a wonderful woman who lost sight of the cause, and sadly had to pay the price.'

Morand and Gore-Ewing exchanged glances, and raised their own glasses. The implied threat was obvious to them both.

CHAPTER 52

KREMLIN, MOSCOW

When Tarakan was summoned to the Kremlin he mentally ran through the list of topics the president would expect him to report on. The FSB, and under them the SVR and the GRU, were running a wide range of espionage and hybrid warfare operations designed to destabilise democracies across the world.

On reflection the FSB chief decided that he was likely to be quizzed about one country in particular. The Little Tsar was fixated with the European nation that had, throughout history, consistently opposed Russian expansionism.

As it was a Friday Tarakan had arrived at the Lubyanka in casual civilian clothes – urban camouflage combat trousers, a khaki T-shirt, a scuffed black leather jacket and paratrooper boots. He decided not to change, but before heading to the underground carpark he donned a dark blue Lenin cap and a pair of cheap unbranded reflector sunglasses.

He also decided to drive the short distance to the Kremlin in his ancient Soviet-era Lada, avoiding the "Zil

Lane" reserved for senior members of the government and the securocracy. Where others flaunted their wealth and power, he preferred to disguise his.

The spy chief arrived at the main entrance to the Kremlin. A sergeant from the FSB Border Guards came marching out to send this nondescript man in the decrepit car on his way. He strode up and aggressively knocked on the glass with his gloved hand. Only when Tarakan manually wound down the window and removed his shades, revealing his different-coloured eyes and missing fingers, did the flustered guard snap to attention and wave him through.

As Tarakan emerged from the car an aide de camp in the immaculate uniform of the Presidential Guard came hurrying out and threw him an impeccable salute. The ADC led him through a series of vast marbled halls with enormous chandeliers, until they finally reached the anteroom to the president's office.

Guarding the doors were two especially tall soldiers, in the ceremonial uniforms of Imperial Russia. Unlike many short leaders, this vertically-challenged president made a point of always being seen with soaring ceilings, full-height doors and exceptionally tall guards. That way everybody felt small.

As Tarakan was shown in he saw the president seated at the far end of a long conference table – a habit he had adopted during the pandemic. Known for his swagger when walking, the Little Tsar was the only man Tarakan knew who could strut sitting down.

The president gestured for Tarakan to take a seat at the other end of the table.

'Give me your report,' he demanded coldly.

Tarakan looked down the table at the distant figure, and then, for once, he was the one who averted his gaze. He ran through a list of combat operations in Africa and the Middle East being undertaken by the remnants of the Wagner Group, and the newly-formed Africa Corps.

He then moved on to the hybrid warfare campaigns being conducted in Europe. These were designed to destabilise the newer democracies in the old Soviet sphere, and promote populist politicians and parties in the more established Western nations.

'And the British?' the President demanded.

Tarakan was waiting for this question, and had saved the best for last.

'As I told you at the dacha, *Sobstvennik*, we have penetrated the British political establishment at the very highest level. What's more, we now have control over whether their attempts to re-join the European Union succeed or fail. If they were to succeed, part of the price would be their giving up control of Trident. So, as you instructed, they are either isolated, or neutered. Either way we win.'

The president nodded.

'And your opposite number? The one who bested you before. The one who had you removed, disgraced and consigned to the gulag?'

Tarakan weighed up his words carefully.

'The Admiral. He is losing his touch, and his reason. We have tortured and killed his agents, which he takes personally. Our agent-in-place at the pinnacle of the British political establishment will either retire him, or prosecute him for his bungled operations in Brussels. MI6, our enemy for more than a century, will shortly cease to exist.'

The president nodded, and his heavily Botoxed face made an attempt at a smile.

CHAPTER 53

EUROPEAN QUARTER, BRUSSELS

Now that the Breturn Bill had passed all of its House of Commons stages, unamended and on schedule, negotiations between the EU and the UK were ramped up.

Day-to-day negotiations had been left in the hands of officials, but at this crucial half-way stage it was decided that discussions should be escalated. Commission President Philippe Morand invited British premier Clem Clark over to Brussels for face-to-face talks.

Clark was due to attend an emergency NATO summit to discuss the dramatic increase in Russian military convoys traversing the Suwalki Gap. This narrow, one-hundred-mile-long corridor separates the Russian exclave of Kaliningrad from Belarus, and is the only land border connecting Lithuania, and the other Baltic states, to Poland and the rest of NATO. As such it represents a potential flashpoint in the growing tensions between the two blocs.

After the traditional "grip and grin" in front of the large Brussels press corps, Clem Clark and his team expected to be shown up to the Commission president's seventh-floor office suite, or to a conference room.

Instead, the UK PM was ushered alone into a small lift that descended to the basement. From there he and Morand entered the suspended bug-proof Perspex bubble, which contained nothing other than a clear plastic table and chairs, all of which were stuck to the floor. There was nowhere for any listening devices to be secreted.

Now that they were alone Philippe Morand hugged Clem Clark and gave him a continental greeting, consisting of three kisses on alternate cheeks.

'How are you, my old friend? We have both come a long way since Oxford.'

Clem Clark nodded in agreement.

'I'm well, thank you. We've come a very long way, and none of us would have expected it then. And these talks are important – to myself personally, and to the country I lead.'

Morand was not yet quite ready to discuss Breturn.

'We missed you in Switzerland. What a tragedy about Yvette. We need to take care, or we could suffer the same fate.'

'Yes, a real tragedy. I'm struggling to come to terms with it, between you and me. I'm haunted by the thought that I might, however indirectly, have been responsible for the death of such a beautiful person. And yes, if he could order her death, after all they shared, he wouldn't hesitate to do the same for us.'

'Indeed. OK, to business. You are probably wondering why we're meeting here, alone, in this plastic bubble, rather than my offices?'

'Yes, it did strike me as odd. Not exactly protocol.'

'We could not have a proper discussion in my offices.

Because they have been bugged. By one of my own staff. On the orders of your MI6.'

Clark seemed genuinely shocked.

'What? That bloody Admiral. Don't worry, I'll have a word with him.'

'And then there was the very unfortunate incident on Belgian soil, which resulted in the death of two of your spies?'

The British PM pushed back this time.

'We both know who was behind that incident. He even sent his pet Chechen to finish the job.'

'Yes, but it would not have happened – it could not have happened – if your Secret Intelligence Service hadn't been spying on us, your supposed allies.'

Clark shrugged.

'As I said, I'll have a word with him.'

'More than a word. The Admiral must be sacked, and MI6 wound up. He is out of control, and Vauxhall Cross is now a rogue operation. We both know that.'

Clem Clark considered arguing, but instead nodded his reluctant agreement.

'We have a security and intelligence review already underway, and you have my word that MI6 will be absorbed into MI5, and effectively neutered. Is that it? Can we talk about the Breturn negotiations now?'

'There is one more thing. As we both know France has withdrawn from NATO's command structure again, and with America now entirely in the control of an isolationist president, Europe has no nuclear deterrent. Are these rumours true about the Trident missile test failing?'

Clark resorted to the agreed lines:

'It was a one-off. It was event specific. We're confident we've identified the problem, and that next week's test will be successful.'

'That is good to hear. Because if Breturn is to become a reality we will obviously need the UK to join the new European Defence Community. And we will need your Trident fleet to come under its command.'

The British PM was clearly disturbed by this demand.

'I'm really not sure if I can deliver that. We've spent tens of billions of pounds on the Trident project, and we're struggling to wrest control of it away from the Americans.'

'I am sorry, *mon ami*, but this is non-negotiable. If we are to bail you out of the political and economic mess you find yourselves in, you must deliver the Admiral's head on a plate, and control of Trident must be handed over. Otherwise, Brexit really will mean Brexit. You will be completely alone, a small island stuck between two giant continents, neither of which will want anything to do with you.'

The British prime minister realised that he had little choice. Having started down the road towards re-joining the EU, he could not now admit failure. The markets would crucify him, and so would the electorate. For the second time, he nodded his reluctant agreement.

Philippe Morand adopted a friendlier tone.

'Now that she is gone there are only the four of us left. And we both know who is in charge of this particular quad.'

Clem Clark threw up his hands in exasperation.

'Of course, it's always been about him, right from the beginning. But she was the glue that held our little group together, and now she's gone I'm not sure my heart's in it anymore.'

The commissioner reverted to his negotiator persona.

'America has turned its back on you, and on Europe. The only way we can survive as a continent is to make proper peace with Russia and reunite Greater Europe. Then at least we will have a chance to compete with China, economically and militarily. The Russians are Europeans, just like you British are Europeans, even if you do not always realise it. We both know that. We have known that since our Oxford days. You and I are in a unique position to re-unite our great continent, to make it whole, to make it strong, and to bring peace to the West once again.'

Clark again nodded his reluctant agreement, not wanting to give verbal confirmation, even in a bug-proof bubble.

The two men shook hands, and embraced. Continental style.

CHAPTER 54

HOUSE OF LORDS, WESTMINSTER

The minister Baron Beaufort of Pimlico had never been fully accepted by the House of Lords.

Nobody likes a traitor, and his decision to jump ship and desert the Tories in favour of Labour was almost universally regarded as a cynical career move. On those occasions where he had appeared in the Chamber to speak in debates or answer oral questions, his reception had always been cool.

Now was his big moment, opening the debate for the government's flagship Breturn Bill at second reading. He had received two briefings ahead of the debate. His private office, the government whips in the Lords and his special adviser had spent hours honing a speech designed to persuade their lordships not to try to impede the progress of the Bill.

There was a degree of nervousness on the government side, because no indication that the Labour Party was considering Breturn had appeared in the manifesto. This meant that the Bill was not entitled to the protection afforded by the arcane, but well established, Salisbury convention.

Early that morning Beaufort had also had a meeting with the Admiral and Frobisher. They had discussed the timing of their attempt to scupper the project to re-join the EU. They only had one torpedo, and it had to be fired at precisely the right moment.

The Admiral had wanted to consult some of his friends and former comrades who had been elevated to the House of Lords. He also wished to consult like-minded and powerful interests in the City of London. The results of both meetings had been inconclusive. There was never a perfect time for a coup d'état, or indeed for a coup de main.

As a result, when Beaufort entered the packed chamber he had no definitive orders. Therefore, as well as having a copy of his official speech in a red ministerial folder in his hands, he also had a hastily-sketched-out bullet-point alternative in his jacket pocket. Also in his pocket was a sealed envelope addressed to the government chief whip, Lord Anstruther.

As Beaufort took his seat on the government front bench one of his ministerial colleagues was answering a routine question on Marine Conservation Areas. Beaufort hoped that she would string out her answer for as long as possible, because Frobisher had yet to arrive in the Strangers' Gallery to signal the Admiral's final instructions.

As his ministerial colleague wound up her answer, and the noble lord who had raised the issue of the Marine Conservation Areas inveighed against the government's failure to fully respect nature, Beaufort was feeling uncharacteristically nervous.

All too soon the Lord Speaker rose from the woolsack and intoned.

'The European Union (Application for Readmission) Bill, Second Reading, Minister the Lord Beaufort of Pimlico.'

Beaufort rose, placed the folder containing his official speech on the despatch box, and glanced around the chamber, before once again looking up at the Strangers' Gallery in search of Frobisher. There was no sign of him. Disappointed, he opened the red folder containing the official speech, and began to read it out, slowly and unenthusiastically.

'My Lords, I would like to begin by pointing out that this Bill has had safe and speedy passage through the elected chamber. Although the British people narrowly voted in favour of leaving the EU in a referendum in 2016, this government, my government, was elected earlier this year with a massive majority. It therefore feels entitled to make the judgement that Brexit has been a disastrous mistake, politically and economically, and that it has a duty to reverse it.'

Murmurs of dissent were now swelling to a crescendo, and the Lord Speaker rose to restore order.

'Honourable peers must remember themselves. The nation is watching. The noble minister must be heard.'

As Beaufort stood up to resume his speech, he caught sight of Frobisher arriving, and managing to squeeze his ample figure into a seat in the front row of the packed Strangers' Gallery. Beaufort paused, and looked enquiringly up at him. Frobisher slowly drew his hand across his neck in a throat-slitting gesture. The instruction was clear: kill the Bill.

A huge weight was immediately lifted from Beaufort's shoulders. He closed the folder on his official brief with a snap, and reached into his inside his pocket for the alternative. Not that he really needed it. He knew exactly what he wanted to say.

'Noble lords, you will have heard my opening remarks, and you will have concluded that I am about to urge you to give this Bill a Second Reading. You would be entitled to expect that. I am, after all, a government minister, and I am charged with steering this Bill through your Lordships' House.'

More groans from assembled peers.

'However,' he paused for dramatic effect, 'however, in arriving at that conclusion you would be entirely mistaken. To my mind this Bill is badly conceived, poorly drafted, constitutionally unsound and unfit for purpose. This Bill was rammed through the other place, without proper debate, by sheer force of numbers. This Bill is an offence against democracy. It sullies the reputation of Parliament, and would bring shame on us all if passed. We are the land of Richard the Lionheart, whose mounted statue stands outside this House, and we are the land of Winston Churchill, whose statue overlooks us from Parliament Square. This is not a land of traitors, this is not the land of Quisling or Pétain, this is a land of proud, independent heroes, warriors willing to fight and die for freedom. Not only do I not commend this Bill to this House, I urge every peer who respects democracy, and who values the history of this great nation, to take this opportunity to decisively vote it down. And having urged you to do so, I hereby resign as a government minister with immediate effect.'

Uproar ensued. The Press Gallery woke from its torpor and began feverishly writing and tapping. The government chief whip, Lord Anstruther, had been pulling at Beaufort's coat tails, trying to make him sit down. Beaufort turned and contemptuously brushed his hand off. He removed the letter of resignation from his inside pocket, and thrust it into Anstruther's hands.

The former minister the Lord Beaufort of Pimlico then walked from the chamber, to the deafening cheers of the Conservative and crossbench peers.

*

Three hours later, at a hastily-convened press conference in Downing Street, the government announced that the Breturn Bill had been "paused".

The political blogs crashed under the weight of traffic, the newspaper front pages were ripped up and reset, and the government desperately searched for representatives willing to tour the studios to try to explain this inexplicable and unprecedented development.

Beaufort, meanwhile, was on his way to Hanslope Park.

CHAPTER 55

CHEQUERS, BUCKINGHAMSHIRE

Like many prime ministers before him Clem Clark liked to spend weekends in the tranquillity and security of Chequers.

He had invited the Admiral down for Sunday lunch, making sure that none of the other guests would irritate the ageing and cantankerous spy chief. Those invited consisted exclusively of serving or retired senior officers of the three armed forces, in whose company the former naval officer would feel at ease.

After a long and convivial lunch, the prime minister suggested to the Admiral that they go for a walk. The other guests, taking the hint, made their excuses and departed.

Knowing that the Admiral was not one for small talk, Clem Clark waited only until they were out of earshot of the big house to broach the subject that had prompted the invitation to lunch.

'I suppose, if you were still a serving officer, you would have passed mandatory retirement age by now?'

'Yes, I would, Prime Minister, but I'm steering a desk, not a warship.'

'Even so, you must feel the urge to take things a bit easier from time to time? Suppose I found you a seat in the Lords, where your decades of experience could be put to good use, and you could continue to serve your country?'

Having been forewarned by the Tory MP Geoff Simmonds about the submission from the National Security Adviser recommending a MI5-MI6 merger, the Admiral was anticipating this offer. He knew that Clem Clark saw him as the biggest obstacle to the merger and was intent on removing him. He was also aware that if he rejected the offer the PM was likely to threaten him with an official inquiry into the Brussels debacle that had led to the deaths of Taylor and Samantha.

He decided to play for time.

'Of course, Prime Minister, none of us can go on for ever, and times are most certainly changing. Perhaps my era, with its focus on human intelligence, has had its day. Let me think about it. Give me a month.'

'My dear fellow, of course. After all your years of service – in and out of uniform – that's the very least you're entitled to.'

The Admiral was secretly delighted. He now knew he had a month to perfect the plan he had been developing for weeks. He was convinced that it was the only way to ensure the survival of the service that he led and loved, and which the nation needed to guarantee its security against the predations of the CRINK axis.

CHAPTER 56

HANSLOPE, BUCKINGHAMSHIRE

Situated in the heart of rural Buckinghamshire, Hanslope Park is one of the most secure locations in the UK.

During the second world war it was a mere adjunct to Bletchley Park, situated just three miles away. Now it serves as a vital outstation for MI6, harbouring its paper and digital records, and facilitating secure communications for secret agents around the globe.

Vital though these logistical support elements are, Hanslope Park is about more than just admin and communications. Within its 300-acre site it has firing ranges, shell buildings to train recruits in urban warfare scenarios, forests to practise escape and evasion, labs for developing lethal gadgets, and basement cells for teaching resistance to interrogation. It also contains gyms where instructors teach close quarters combat.

Beaufort already had a good grounding in unarmed combat, after his many years of martial arts training. He also had a high level of fitness, at least compared with the average civilian. None of this counted for much when he was faced with the intensive training course that had been devised for him.

Having arrived late at night in one of the Firm's Range Rovers, Beaufort was walked through the rigorous security protocols. These were overseen by the Ministry of Defence Police, a specialist armed unit charged with defending the nation's vital military infrastructure.

After a short and restless night's sleep, Beaufort was given breakfast and issued with an army tracksuit, before being taken to an indoor firing range. There, an armourer from the Parachute Regiment was waiting to teach him how to draw, aim and fire a handgun. It had been decided he should focus on handguns, rather than shoulder-held, longer-range weapons.

The range varied from five to 25 metres, beyond which a handgun is generally reckoned to be ineffective. The guns he was issued with varied from session to session: from the Sig Sauer favoured by the US army, to the Grach used by the Russian *spetsnaz* – special forces – and the near ubiquitous Glock 17, standard issue for all British military and police forces.

To begin with Beaufort's performance was highly erratic, but after a week he could routinely draw, aim and fire at speed, successfully placing several rounds within the main body mass of full-size cardboard silhouette targets of a charging soldier.

Having achieved an adequate level of proficiency with a range of handguns, Beaufort was then handed over to a Royal Marine physical training instructor, who began work on his fitness and agility. This aspect of the training involved long morning runs around the perimeter of Hanslope Park, increasingly difficult assault courses and a lot of gym work.

After two weeks of intense training, akin to the "beasting" inflicted on potential recruits to the Royal Marines, Beaufort had lost seven kilos, and felt leaner, fitter and sharper.

He was now ready for the most important part of his training. Unarmed combat.

*

The Royal Marine fitness instructor had warned Beaufort that he was about to enter the hardest part of the course.

Having been through several weeks of intense training for six to eight hours a day at the hands of instructors from the Parachute Regiment and the Royal Marines, Beaufort wondered what could possibly be in store for him. These were two of the fittest and most aggressive units in the British armed forces, so he assumed he would now be handed over to special forces – SAS, or possibly SBS.

Having had a light breakfast, he arrived at the gym 15 minutes early to go through the warm-up routine his Royal Marine instructor had taught him. He had just finished a block of 20 push-ups, and was catching his breath, when a familiar voice said:

'Hello Damian, long time.'

Beaufort leaped to his feet and turned around to be confronted with Sabina, dressed in a dark, loose-fitting track suit emblazoned with the Royal Military Police logo.

'Jesus, Sabina, what the hell are you doing here?'

'I've been sent to complete your training. Forget all that macho crap the Paras and the Marines have been teaching you. And forget about having a weapon, nine times out of ten there simply won't be one to hand. Besides, you don't need one. Everything you need to kill you carry with you at all times.'

'But you were private security? You sorted out the drunks at my general election party.'

Sabina laughed.

'We all rotate in and out of the private sector and government service, as circumstances require. The Admiral asked me to keep a discreet eye on you, way back then. I'm pleased you never noticed. In fact I owe you an apology. It was me who arrived late at the dojo, and distracted you, and got you knocked out. I wanted to see first-hand how good you were. Not that you should have allowed yourself to be distracted – your opponent wasn't. Now, I have a week to teach you how to kill. And remember what I said about the Marines and Paras – the female is always the deadlier of the species.'

'I kind of knew that already. OK. Teach me how to kill.'

'First off, your weapons. Yes, you have your fists, but I'm sure you know the bones in the hands break easily, and knuckles are far more delicate than people think. If you're going to use your hands, use the ridge, or the heel, or failing that the back of the hand. Like the guy who laid you out.'

Beaufort flinched at the memory.

'Yes, that's what they teach us in karate. We usually only punch to the body, where there's cushioning over the bone structure.'

'Good. Moving on, you have your elbows. Very hard, pointed, and you can get great leverage if you use them properly. Moving down, your knees – same as elbows, hard bone, and lots of leverage. Finally, your feet. They can impact with great speed and power, but again the bones are delicate, so make sure you have the right footwear if you're going to use them.

Second, tactics. In martial arts you're banned from causing permanent damage. And any street fights you might have witnessed or been caught up in, unless they're gang related, are usually largely performative. Big round-house swings with the fists, or kicking out, usually at thin air.'

'Yes, I've seen a few of those, but always managed to talk my way out of situations like that. If a martial artist gets involved in a street fight, the courts take a dim view.'

'Right. So there are two secrets to effective close-quarters combat. Number one, you need to stun, distract or disable your opponent before you deliver a knock-out or killer strike. A kick or knee to the groin will usually do the trick, if it's a male opponent. It won't kill anybody, but it will slow them down, and certainly ruin their love life. Kneecaps, on the other hand, work for both sexes. They are best taken off from the inside – they pop off like a Pringles' lid if you get the angle right. Agonising and disabling at the same time.'

'And the second secret?'

'All the fatally vulnerable points on the human body are within ten centimetres of the median line'. She moved forward to demonstrate. 'Starting at the top, working down.'

Sabina reached out with both hands and tapped Beaufort's temples.

'This is the pterion, the thinnest part of the skull. It's where four skull bones intersect. Hit either temple with the back of your hand, your elbow or a single knuckle strike and it will either induce instant unconsciousness or death.

It doesn't even require much force.'

Beaufort nodded, rubbing his temples in reaction to her touch.

'Next, the nasal apex – the base of the nose. Punch an opponent on the bridge of the nose in a boxing match or bar brawl and it will induce bleeding and eye watering, yes, but not much else. Push upwards at the base of the nose with the palm of your hand and it'll drive bone and cartilage splinters into the brain. Instant death.'

Beaufort reflexively touched the base of his nose.

'Moving down again. The throat. Aim for the laryngeal prominence – Adam's apple to you. Ridge hand strike, or elbow. Crush the windpipe, and death will follow, very quickly. Not much good if you want to interrogate them, as the buggers won't be able to breathe, never mind speak, but it does the job.'

Beaufort swallowed, and gingerly massaged his Adam's apple.

'Is that it?'

'One more. But I'm not sure you have the strength, or the skills.'

'What is it?'

'The heart, just off to the left of the breastbone. This time you use a punch, but a short, straight-armed punch, using rotation of the fist and retraction of the opposite hip to provide the power. If you get it right, you drive bone splinters through the heart, and maybe also collapse the aortic arteries or rupture the aortic valve as a bonus. But maybe leave that one to the experts.'

Beaufort mentally filed that move away, along with the other lethal options.

*

Over the next seven days Beaufort sweated and strained, either hitting life-size dummies and punchbags, or trying to land a punch, strike or kick on the lightning-fast Sabina. He ended every session exhausted, and soaked in sweat. She never seemed to perspire, and almost invariably remained untouched and unmarked.

In time Beaufort's performance improved, his punches and strikes developed more snap, and his kicks more penetration. He also got better at warding off Sabina's counter-strikes, which she invariably pulled at the last minute to avoid injuring him.

On the final day of their scheduled training week, Sabina smiled broadly, and nodded her approval.

'You're ready – or as ready as you'll ever be. Dinner in the officers' mess tonight. And I have a surprise guest for you.'

*

Throughout his stay at Hanslope Park Beaufort had been eating in the course-attendees mess, along with the directing staff who had been training him. This time he was told to put on a suit and tie and report to the officers' mess for pre-dinner drinks at 7.30pm.

Drinks were served in the book-lined library, with a roaring fire providing a focal point for the small group who had gathered there. There were half a dozen men and two women in their twenties, who Beaufort took to be MI6 operatives undergoing either initial training or a refresher course.

Sabina looked stunning in her formal scarlet and black mess-kit, displaying a small array of medals. She was talking to a short, dumpy man in civilian clothes. Even with his back to him, Beaufort recognised the distinctive outline of Frobisher.

'Ah, Beaufort, good to see you, and all in one piece as well,' was the MI6 man's jovial greeting.

'No thanks to her,' Beaufort replied. 'She half kills me on a daily basis!'

'Pleased to hear it,' Frobisher replied. 'Where you're going there'll be people trying really hard to kill you, very much for real.'

*

Dinner in the main dining room took place under the disapproving gaze of generations of Hanslopes, Watts and Heskeths – in portrait form – whose families lorded it over their guests for generations.

The commanding officer of Hanslope Park was Sir Ronald Maitland, a major general from the Irish Guards. He had seen action in Iraq and Afghanistan, and done a stint as commanding officer of the SAS, based at Stirling Lines in Herefordshire.

The general tapped his glass for attention and got to his feet.

'This is an informal occasion, so no speeches, and first names only. We all know that while we may not technically be at war, our enemies, the CRINK states, never cease to try and attack our interests, and to undermine our way of life. So enjoy your evening, but don't overdo it – and remember there are ladies present.'

The general looked at the two female trainees, and then at Sabina, who had to restrain herself from rolling her eyes. She had seen, heard and done as much as any man in the room, and his condescension riled her.

The old general sat back down, as the guests gently tapped the table in muted approval of his words.

Frobisher was seated at the head of the table, at the far end from the general. He had Beaufort to his right, and Sabina to his left. Keeping his voice low he said to Beaufort:

'I have to get back tonight, but I wanted to come in person to tell you that we may be about to get a chance to have a crack at Tarakan. As you know on the odd occasion that he does leave Russia it's nearly always to go to Tazmenistan. He's inherited his mother's farmhouse about 30 kilometres outside of Dustana, and we believe he regards it as a bolthole, a safe haven in case of regime change in Moscow.'

Beaufort interrupted.

'But how do we know when he actually makes one of these rare visits?'

'Usually, we don't. However – and you won't have heard this being holed-up here – the president of Tazmenistan has just died, quite suddenly, of a brain aneurism. He's been smoking those filthy Russian cigarettes for years, and now they've done for him. The funeral is next week. His son will take over, of course, to provide continuity, but Tarakan won't miss this opportunity to pay his respects, and to reinforce his Tazmen credentials.'

Beaufort nodded, and then asked:

'How do I get an invitation? I'm no longer a government minister.'

'Don't worry about that. The oligarch Abdullaev is

attending, and we've told him to add you to his party. That'll get you in reasonable proximity to Tarakan. The Admiral believes he won't pass up the opportunity to meet you face to face. As far as we can establish you're his only living relative.'

*

Beaufort had not drunk alcohol for weeks, and even the modest amount he had drunk over dinner affected his balance, and his judgement.

All the time they had been training one on one, Beaufort had struggled to banish the vision of a naked Sabina from his mind. As he shakily ascended the quarter-turn staircase, lined with more family portraits, Sabina put her arm around his waist to steady him.

When they reached the upper corridor, with bedrooms off either side, she paused outside her own room, reached up to kiss him goodnight, and then changed her mind.

Instead, she opened the door, took him by the hand, and led him into her room. She shut and locked the door, steered him towards the bed, and pushed him onto his back. Seemingly entirely unaffected by the alcohol, she deftly undressed him, until he was naked on the bed, and hardly able to believe his luck.

Sabina slipped off her shoes, slowly discarded her skirt, and then her pants, but kept her stockings, blouse and mess jacket on. Climbing onto the bed she grasped his rampant erection, mounted him, and began to slowly ride him. Beaufort reached up and unbuttoned her mess jacket, and then her blouse. She was not wearing a bra, and having freed her breasts, he began to gently massage her nipples, eliciting a low moan of encouragement.

As with their training, Sabina took the lead, dictating the pace of their love-making. Using her internal muscles she maintained a firm grip on the base of his penis, delaying his orgasm until she had reached her own.

Having climaxed, she relaxed her muscles, reached behind, and cupped his balls. The effect on Beaufort was immediate, and explosive.

Afterwards he lay still, drained, and relieved not to have repeated the abject failure of their first sexual encounter.

Sabina, lying beside him, steadied her breathing before saying:

'I am really sorry about your mother – and about Samantha. Did you love her?'

'My mother or Samantha?'

'Either. Both.'

'Yes, I guess so. I never really got the chance to love my mother as a person, she wasn't around enough, and she didn't show enough of herself to me. But I loved her as a mother, of course I did.'

'And Samantha?'

'I think so. We'd become close, and were getting closer all the time. She wasn't sentimental – she was tough, and funny, and alive. Until she wasn't any more.'

'I'm sorry,' she said again.

They slept, but woke up to make love again in the small hours.

Before the other guests got up for breakfast, she sent him back to his room.

Appearances had to be maintained, even in this house that existed to teach death.

CHAPTER 57

PACIFIC AND SOUTH ATLANTIC OCEANS

The last, and embarrassingly unsuccessful, Trident test had been closely monitored by the Americans, the Russians and the Chinese.

It was essential that the second test launch succeed, and that an element of uncertainty be maintained by varying both the launch area and the designated target zone. As a precaution the launch and hoped-for splashdown would not be broadcast live, but pre-recorded for the BBC News at Ten.

The failed test had a scheduled flight path that would have taken the Trident D5 missile across the Royal Australian Air Force Woomera Range Complex, flying from west to east from the Indian Ocean to the Pacific Ocean. This time the planned trajectory would be from east to west: the missile would be launched from the 11,000-metres-deep Mariana Trench in the Pacific Ocean, travel across the Woomera range and land near the British garrison island of Ascension.

The dud missile had been fired from HMS Vanguard, the "boomer" fleet's flagship. The boat assigned for the second test launch was HMS Vengeance, the newest of the Vanguard class, captained by Commander Venning.

In the intervening three months the launch codes had been rewritten, tested, and retested. Artificial Intelligence had been deployed to identify flaws in the software, and several minor glitches ironed out. British owned and operated Tyche satellites would track the missile's progress, and guide it to its target.

For this second crucial test launch the Admiralty had insisted on deploying a rear admiral on board the boat to oversee all procedures. Admiral Haslam was a veteran of the original Polaris nuclear submarine fleet, with nearly 40 years' service in the Royal Navy.

The small fleet of ships deployed around Ascension Island to monitor the splashdown and retrieve any debris included the aircraft carrier HMS Prince of Wales, the flagship of the Royal Navy. So important was this operation judged to be that she had been diverted from a round-the-world goodwill tour in order to secure the target zone.

The prime minister had also prevailed on the chief scientific officer and his specialist coders to spend six weeks away from their families, enduring the discomforts of submarine life, so they could be on hand in the case of any last-minute glitches.

Nothing could be allowed to go wrong this time.

*

The nerves on the bridge and throughout the boat were palpable as the countdown began.

The two keys were inserted and turned, and the launch button for tube number one pressed. As with the previous test launch, there was a thump and a shudder throughout the submarine, as compressed air launched the missile and thrust it clear of the sea surface. In light of the previous failure, the sense of anxiety did not dissipate following this indication of a successful initial launch.

The executive officer raised the optronic mast and scanned the horizon. When he turned to look at the commander there was a broad smile on his face. The missile was streaking up into the heavens: the boost-phase rockets had successfully kicked in.

Twenty-two minutes later, having passed through the Woomera test range precisely on schedule, the D5 missile splashed down in the South Atlantic, and disintegrated. Merlin helicopters from HMS Prince of Wales pinpointed the area of impact, and rigid inflatable boats manned by Royal Marines were deployed to locate and recover the floating debris.

*

The Northwood command centre resembled the NASA control room after a successful moon landing. Senior officers shook hands exuberantly, and junior ranks exchanged jubilant high fives.

*

Beneath the Cabinet Office in COBRA the prime minister, secretary of state for defence, foreign secretary and top brass from all three services exchanged congratulatory handshakes.

Clem Clark made for the door, and then, changing his mind, turned around to say a few words.

'Colleagues, we are back in business. Nobody, but nobody, can now threaten this country with impunity. And nobody can tell us who to strike, or when. We have taken back control of our nuclear deterrent. We are a truly independent nation once again.'

The PM left the room to applause, and took the underground tunnel to return to Number Ten.

A celebratory whisky beckoned.

CHAPTER 58

DUSTANA, TAZMENISTAN

The funeral of the late Tazmen president was attended by many heads of state and heads of government.

Although he had become increasingly autocratic in his old age, President Barakat had led his country to independence after the break-up of the Soviet Union, and succeeded in reclaiming at least a proportion of the territory seized by the Ujikistanis in the early years, so he was loved by his people.

The president had also successfully straddled the ever-widening divide between the West and the CRINK axis. His sheer physical presence, his facility for languages, and his subtle mind, had enabled him to avoid being sucked into the increasingly bitter struggle for world domination between the two opposing power blocs.

The president's son had gone through a playboy phase in his youth, but a short officer training course at Sandhurst, an MBA at Harvard and a stint at the Moscow Diplomatic Academy had matured him, and prepared him for his future role. He had graduated from these prestigious institutions better equipped to navigate his country's path between the rival ambitions of the world's two big rival power blocs, having seen and studied them at first hand.

As the Admiral and Frobisher had anticipated, Tarakan could not resist the chance to return to the land of his birth, and begin the process of luring the new president into his orbit. At the funeral, which took place with full military honours on the Avenue of the Martyrs, a hillside high above Dustana, Tarakan sat discreetly at the back of the main stand that accommodated all the top visiting dignitaries.

Beaufort was seated with Abdullaev, the oligarch, in a lower stand some distance from the elaborate bronze casket and hastily constructed mausoleum. He thought he could just about make out Tarakan at the back of the main stand, but as the Russian wore a black fedora hat to cover his bald head it was hard to be sure. Until the hulking shape of Dudayev lumbered over to whisper a message into his master's ear.

Faisal, the fixer who had helped Beaufort set up the honeytraps during the APPG trip, had been ordered to find out where Tarakan was staying and deliver a message. Most of the VIPs were staying in the five-star Four Seasons or Ritz-Carlton hotels, but Tarakan had chosen an obscure *caravanserai* in the old walled city.

Faisal left a note written in Tazmen with the receptionist. It was short, and to the point.

'Your son would like to meet you. Leave a message with your hotel receptionist. I will collect it.'

*

Tarakan had survived all these years by dint of his caution. He rarely left Russia, and when he did so he always had the formidable, and ultra-loyal, Dudayev with him.

But despite his innate caution, and his awareness of Beaufort's multiple roles, Tarakan could not resist the chance to meet his son. He felt safe in the land of his birth, visiting his "home from home".

After some thought, he penned a reply, in English.

'Come to the Sultan Hammam in the old city at eight this evening. Alone.'

Faisal collected the note, and delivered it to Beaufort shortly after 6.30pm. There was no time for him to consult Vauxhall Cross, or to make any security arrangements, just as Tarakan had calculated.

*

Beaufort had been in saunas in London before, but he had no idea what to expect from a traditional Turkish hammam.

Faisal told him to dress simply, leave his watch and phone in the hotel room safe, and take only a small amount of cash. Although lockers were provided for clothes and valuables, there were too many duplicate keys in circulation for them to be secure.

The fixer accompanied him to reception, spoke to the elderly woman behind the counter, paid the entrance fee and left. Beaufort thought about asking him to stay, but concluded that the diminutive fixer would have been no help in a fight, and was probably not completely trustworthy in any event.

An elderly male assistant in loose-fitting white cotton *salvar* trousers, white tunic top and flip-flops led him to the male changing rooms. Both sexes used the hammam, but they were strictly segregated, and the changing room contained only a handful of mainly elderly male customers.

Beaufort undressed, wrapped a threadbare white towel around his waist, hung his clothes on a peg, and placed his few belongings in a numbered locker. He secured the key to his wrist with the rubber band attached for that purpose, but concluded that it was too small to double up as a viable weapon.

The heat was extreme, even in the changing rooms, and the smell of sulphur permeated every room. The elderly assistant led him down a brick-lined corridor with a curved roof. In the alcoves either side naked men were being massaged by muscled male masseurs. A few were being flogged with twigs, to their obvious enjoyment.

Beaufort was led to a small plunge pool filled with icy cold water. He placed his towel on a white plastic garden chair, and climbed down the steps into the icy water. He gasped at the cold and felt his testicles flee upwards into the safety of his stomach.

After no more than a minute, which felt much longer, the assistant gestured for Beaufort to get out. He did so, quickly and gratefully, and, having retrieved his towel, was led through to a high-domed area that housed the main spring-fed hot pool. A dozen men, alone or in pairs, languished on the ledge running around the edge of the pool. Those in pairs were speaking softly in what sounded like a mixture of Tazmen and Russian.

Beaufort placed his towel on another white plastic garden chair and used the tiled steps to enter the hot, inviting water. He located the ledge, and leaned back, spreading his arms along the tiled poolside.

As his eyes adjusted to the gloom and the steam, Beaufort realised there were a series of alcoves cut into the ancient walls around the pool. Some were unoccupied, some were occupied by pairs, and one had a single occupant. The alcoves were heavily clouded with steam, fed from grills set into the floor.

After a few minutes Beaufort's testicles decided it was safe to return to their natural location. He began to relax, before remembering what he was doing in this particular establishment.

It was at that point he realised that the single figure in the alcove almost immediately opposite was staring at him. He returned the stare, and the figure gestured for the Englishman to join him. Beaufort emerged from the pool naked, but picked up his towel and wound it around his waist before obeying the summons.

The man seated in the alcove was extraordinary. In the gloom Beaufort could just make out the two heterochromatic eyes, green on the left and brown on the right. He knew that Tarakan was bald, but now realised that he was completely hairless, on his head and body. His skeletal frame bore the scars of several deep knife slashes across his chest and back, and he had a cratered stab wound in his right shoulder.

In addition to the scars, Tarakan's body was covered in tattoos. Not the artistic swirls beloved of the young generation of Westerners, but the crude etchings of the gulag tattooist. There were a mixture of Orthodox crosses and gang symbols, interspersed with slogans in Cyrillic script. On the side of his neck was the trademark tattoo that had given him his nom de guerre.

The cockroach. The creature that even radiation cannot kill.

Seeing Beaufort's hesitation Tarakan laughed, and invited him to enter the alcove fully.

'Come in. Sit. Don't stand on ceremony. You are, after all, only half-English. Embrace your Tazmen side.'

To Beaufort's surprise Tarakan still spoke with the accent of an Oxford-educated Englishman. The voice and the laugh were both incongruously deep and mellifluous for such an emaciated body, and they echoed around the small alcove.

Awkwardly Beaufort sat down opposite Tarakan, positioning his towel to protect his backside from the heat of the sodden but scalding wooden bench.

'I haven't come to talk.'

'Of course you have. I'm your father. And you're curious to know how much of me is in you.'

'Very little. Or just enough, I guess. You know I've come to kill you.'

Tarakan laughed again.

'I know that you have come to try. Is there anything you would like to ask, before you try to kill me?'

'Did you have my mother murdered?'

'Yes, but with great regret. I loved her in our Oxford days, and Dudayev tells me that she still loved me, or so she claimed on her deathbed. But she was dying anyway, and I had to protect my secrets.'

'And did you kill Samantha?'

'Yes, I had her killed. She was an enemy agent. She knew the game, and she knew the risks.'

'And what about the snooker balls? Was that really necessary?'

Tarakan hesitated before replying, sensing Beaufort's suppressed fury.

'I regret that. But I had to send a signal to your boss, the Admiral. I had to warn him off. And besides, Dudayev must be allowed his little pleasures.'

On cue the steam curtain parted and a giant figure lumbered into the alcove, stooping at the entrance, and positioning himself halfway between Beaufort and Tarakan. He wore the same *salvar* and flip-flops as the elderly attendant who had ushered Beaufort into the hammam, but his chest was bare. His red beard matched the matted red hair on his immense chest.

Tarakan rose and spoke again, his voice echoing off the alcove's curved ceiling.

'So, you've met your father, and you've learned the truth about the fate of your mother, and of your lover. I'm afraid you'll have to settle for that. I'm glad that we've met, and talked, because I suspect we will not meet again.'

He moved towards the archway exit and slipped away, careful to keep the imposing figure of the Chechen between himself and Beaufort.

Beaufort stood up. He could have tried to follow Tarakan, or he could have tried to run. But he knew that if he showed his back to the Chechen his fate would be sealed. Besides, the thought occurred to him that if he could not exact revenge on his father, perhaps he could do so on his instrument, the man who had performed both killings to order.

Seeing the uncertainty on Beaufort's face Dudayev grinned widely, showing his two gold front teeth. He flexed his rippling pectoral muscles, and stepped forward. Beaufort took half a step back and assumed a fighting stance, with most of his weight on his back foot. But he knew he was at a disadvantage in this confined space, given the size and strength of his opponent.

The Chechen lunged forward in an attempt to grab Beaufort's throat with his two massive hands. Then, at the last moment, he hesitated. What was it his boss had said to him when they had first discussed the tall, slim Englishman?

'Do not touch him, not now, not ever.'

Dudayev shook the memory of the words from his head and started to move forward again, this time determined to snap Beaufort's neck, or seize him in a bear hug and squeeze the breath and the life out of him.

Then he hesitated again.

Standing in the entrance to the alcove was a woman. Not just any woman, but a slim, beautiful, young woman. She was wrapped in a towel, like almost everybody else in the hammam. Then she reached up and untied the knot that held it in place, and let the towel fall to the floor.

Dudayev stood stock still, his eyes feasting on the beauty of the naked female body just feet away from him.

Realising that Sabina had provided him with an opportunity, Beaufort lunged towards the Chechen. He unleashed a ferocious *gyaku-zuki* reverse punch with his right hand, rotating his fist mid-strike, and snapping his left arm and his left hip back to add to the force that his rage and fear had already imparted to the blow, and uttering an explosive *kiai* battle cry that cut through the steamy atmosphere and echoed around the hammam.

At that range, against a static target, Beaufort could not fail to land a telling blow. His punch smashed into Dudayev's ribcage five centimetres to the left of his breastbone, where the right aortic artery left the heart, and where the ribcage was not protected by the giant's bulging pectoral muscles.

The bones splintered and were driven into his heart, the aortic valve ruptured, and the Chechen sank slowly to his knees, blood pouring from his mouth and nose. A red veil descended over his eyes, and the blood from his mouth streamed down and stained his red beard a deep crimson. He fell forwards, his face smashing into the tiled floor.

Beaufort looked across at Sabina.

'Am I pleased to see you.'

His towel had fallen to the floor as he had surged forward to strike Dudayev, and she glanced down at his naked form. Having taken a life for the first time, he found he was strangely aroused.

'I can see that. Anyway, I thought I told you to leave that particular strike to the experts?'

Beaufort grabbed his towel to hide his tumescence.

'Well, it worked, didn't it? Anyway, thanks. Without your little. . .distraction, he wouldn't have stood still long enough for me to take him out.'

Sabina shrugged.

'Hey, it's not the first time I've struck a man dumb. Come on. There's a staff entrance at the back. We can grab some clothes on the way out. Faisal has got a car outside.'

'Where are we going?'

'To the Turkish border. The car has diplomatic plates, so we should be able to get through unhindered, especially if we leave right now. Say goodbye to the land of your ancestors. I don't think you'll be coming back any time soon.'

'What about Tarakan?'

'Well, I guess he lives to kill another day.'

CHAPTER 59

NINE ELMS, LONDON

The old American Embassy in Grosvenor Square had become impossible to defend, from protestors, terrorists and tourists. The new embassy in Nine Elms was designed and built as a fortress, surrounded by a moat and guarded by armed "leathernecks" from the US Marine Corps.

The CIA station in the embassy, situated in the multi-storey basement, is a fortress within a fortress. The whole subterranean floor is surrounded by an impenetrable Faraday cage. Access is policed by armed CIA agents from the innocuously-titled Directorate of Support. Technically civilians, they are in reality a paramilitary force, and armed when inside the embassy compound.

When the CIA station chief requested a meeting, the Admiral decided to walk the short distance from Vauxhall Cross to Nine Elms. He was met by a CIA senior agent, who helped him bypass the normally stringent security procedures. From the atrium reception area they entered a lift that only went down, and which personnel needed a special pass to activate.

The station chief's office was large and well furnished. It did not have any windows, unlike the Admiral's office with its panoramic views across the Thames. Instead, there were screens on each wall made to emulate windows, showing CCTV feeds of all aspects of the embassy's surroundings.

The position of US ambassador to the UK has always been a much prized posting, usually given to a businessman who helped fund the incumbent President's campaign. The CIA station chief post, on the other hand, is very much reserved for a career spook.

Brendan Brewster III had joined the agency fresh from the Green Berets, and his service record was a roll-call of the world's trouble spots. He was a bowtie-wearing Anglophile, having attended Oxford as a Rhodes Scholar, and his family could trace their roots back to the Mayflower.

Brewster got up from behind his desk and came round to greet the Admiral.

'Good of you to come, Admiral. Interesting times.'

'Indeed they are – very much in the Chinese curse sense. How are you getting on with your new president?'

'Just fine. He may worry our liberal elites, but he scares the crap out of the CRINKs. As you know he loves the royals for family reasons. Apart from that, though, the only Brit institutions he really admires are the SAS and you, the SIS. Anyway, what's keeping you awake at night?'

'The usual – the Middle East, Ukraine, Taiwan. And, of course, our new government. And most particularly our new prime minister.'

'Yes, I was going to ask you about him. How are you going to handle him? I hear he wants to get rid of you, and wind up the Firm?'

'Apparently so. But I can't let that happen.'

Brewster half-smiled.

'So, who will rid us of this turbulent politician?'

'I'm working on a plan. He's offered me a peerage to go quietly. I hinted at assent, but asked for a month to think about it. But I'm going nowhere. He is. And with luck the Russians will do the job for us. Or at least it'll look like they have.'

Brewster chuckled.

'Spare me the details, but I knew I could rely on you, the most perfidious of all Albions. May the Five Eyes be with you!'

They stood and shook hands, like the gentlemen they were not.

CHAPTER 60

TRAVELLERS CLUB, PALL MALL

Considering the massive majority they had achieved at the last general election, the Labour government's collapse in the opinion polls was unprecedented.

Clem Clark was not liked or trusted by the British people, and his declared intention of re-joining the European Union without a referendum was not as popular as Bill Blythe and Rory Cochrane had predicted.

Normally the official opposition, in the form of the Conservative Party, would have been the principal beneficiary of the government's unpopularity. However, their spell of over a decade in power, and their failure to tackle the ever-growing migration crisis, meant it was the insurgent Revival Party that raced ahead in the polls, winning by-election after by-election. The party's leader, Claude Weber, encapsulated and articulated the British people's growing dissatisfaction with the established political parties.

The clubbable Weber was a member of Frobisher's club, the Travellers. One evening they found themselves two urinals apart in the club's ornate and cartoon-bedecked toilets.

Frobisher was not in the habit of striking up conversations in such situations, but Weber had no such inhibitions. It was an open secret in the club that Frobisher was something more than a dry statistician, and Weber decided to seize the moment as he relieved himself of several pints of best British ale.

His opening gambit was predictably direct.

'We should have a chat, you and me. My enemy's enemy is my friend, and all that.'

Frobisher, acutely embarrassed at being ambushed in the toilets, felt his own stream drying up. He decided to cut his losses and zipped up prior to departing, without answering.

'We're not that different, you and I,' was Weber's follow-up. 'We both hate the EU, and we both think Clem is riding roughshod over our constitution.'

By this stage Frobisher was at the suite of marble sinks washing his hands. Weber took the sink next to him and began his own superficial ablutions. He decided to try a third time.

'I know you work for the Admiral, and I know we're of one mind on this issue. We should meet.'

Frobisher considered for a moment before replying.

'Not here. I'll be in touch.'

CHAPTER 61

COLCHESTER, ESSEX

They met at the Colchester service station, which was on the way to Claude Weber's Suffolk coastal constituency.

Because Weber was instantly recognisable to most of the British public, the meeting was due to take place in the back of one of the Firm's fake London black cabs. This did not stand out in the car park, Essex being very much the habitat of choice for the London cabby.

The Admiral and Frobisher were sat on the bench seat facing the front of the cab. The service driver had been instructed to make himself scarce for the duration of the meeting.

Weber's driver, who doubled as his bodyguard, cruised round the car park in his large Jaguar saloon until he spotted the correct black cab. He pulled in two bays down, and Weber made his way swiftly to the taxi, not wishing to be recognised. He hurried over and tapped on the window. Frobisher opened the door and the Revival Party leader climbed in, pulled down the jump seat and sat down.

The Admiral tried hard to hide his distaste for this

populist rabble-rouser, whose breath smelt of cigarettes and beer even this early in the morning.

He leaned forward and shook hands, and Frobisher followed suit.

'You wanted to meet?' Frobisher ventured.

Weber settled back in the jump seat and began his trademark rant.

'Yes. Breturn cannot be allowed to happen. This government has no mandate for it. It is unconstitutional and anti-democratic, and the demonstrations against it are getting larger every week...' The Admiral leaned forward to intervene. 'Let me finish. If they're going to behave unconstitutionally, so can we. I have over 200,000 members, and many of them are ex-forces. I also have the support of a phalanx of retired generals, air vice marshals, and admirals – people like yourself.'

This time the Admiral did intervene.

'So what exactly are we talking about here?'

Weber threw his hands up in frustration.

'I would have thought that was blindingly obvious. A coup. To take back control. Leave the king on the throne of course, but install me as his emergency prime minister.'

'And if Clem doesn't go quietly?' Frobisher asked.

'If Clem won't go quietly, then – what is it you spooks say? – he'll have to be terminated with extreme prejudice.'

The Admiral and Frobisher exchanged surprised looks. It was Frobisher who replied.

'We hear what you say. We'll be in touch.'

Claude Weber beamed. They shook hands again, and he left the cab and hurriedly re-entered his Jaguar.

'Sound and vision?' the Admiral asked.

'Of course,' was Frobisher's laconic reply.
The Admiral considered for a moment.
'We can call it the black cab coup.'
They both laughed.

CHAPTER 62

VAUXHALL CROSS, LONDON

Following Beaufort's failure to kill Tarakan, and with the clock ticking on the month's grace Clem Clark had given the Admiral, the MI6 chief called a meeting in the clear Perspex bubble in the basement of Vauxhall Cross. It was the equivalent of that used by Morand in the Berlaymont.

There was no formal agenda. No notes were to be taken. No teas or coffees, no drinks, no refreshments of any kind were to be served. This was a business meeting, and if there had been an agenda, there would only have been one item on it. The removal of Prime Minister Clem Clark.

Without preamble the Admiral turned to Beaufort.

'You were unlucky in Dustana. You got closer to Tarakan than any of us have for years. But like his namesake, he survived. We did, however, manage to get an up-to-date photograph of him as he fled across the border. Oh, and well done for killing that thug Dudayev. I'm glad that the Hanslope training was put to good use, and that Sabina was on hand to help.'

Beaufort nodded, accepting the praise, but clearly still

frustrated that his father had escaped unscathed.

Still primarily addressing Beaufort, the Admiral continued:

'I met the CIA station chief last week. He used the old Henry II line – 'who will rid me of this turbulent priest'. And then Frobisher and I met that oleaginous populist toad Weber, fittingly in a black cab. The idiot actually mooted a military coup and hinted strongly that we might have to assassinate Clem Clark. We have it on tape.'

Beaufort decided it was time to ask the obvious question.

'Where are you going with this, sir?'

The Admiral trained his spiky eyebrows on the younger man.

'I would have thought that was obvious. And I can say it within these Perspex walls: we're going to have to kill the PM.'

Beaufort had been half-expecting this to be the focus of the meeting, but was nevertheless shocked to hear the Admiral express it in such bald terms.

'But surely, sir, that's unprecedented? It must be way beyond our remit, and perhaps beyond our capabilities?'

Frobisher decided to respond.

'Not really, Beaufort. When the Firm found proof to back up our suspicions that Wilson was a Soviet asset, and when he demonstrated his true loyalties by refusing to help the Americans in Vietnam, we blackmailed him into resigning. If he hadn't gone quietly, we would have exposed him, or even killed him. Historically, other awkward prime ministers have been removed. John Bellingham assassinated Spencer Percival within the precincts of the Palace of Westminster. Bellingham had just returned from Russia, where he was commissioned by Tsar Alexander I to enlist the support of Percival in repelling Napoleon's invasion. Percival refused, Bellingham shot him, and his direct descendant now sits in the Lords.'

The Admiral chimed in.

'And then, of course, more recently there was the lettuce lady – though the least said about her the better! We don't make a habit of it, Beaufort, but where a PM represents a clear and present danger to the state, we have to act, and they have to go.'

Beaufort was still unconvinced.

'And are we sure, sir, that Clem Clark really is a danger to the state?'

The Admiral was running out of patience.

'Of course he bloody well is! He's been a Russian asset since his Oxford days. He wants to take us back into the European Union, without a confirmatory referendum, and as part of the deal he would hand over control of Trident to the European Defence Community. And, I would remind you, he wants to wind up MI6. He's given me one month to agree to go quietly, and we only have a few days left. We need to act quickly, and we need to act decisively.'

Beaufort shrugged his assent and asked.

'But how, sir? Clem has a close protection team with him at all times.'

'Not at all times,' Frobisher replied. 'Like Spencer Percival, he's at his most vulnerable in Parliament. He and his protection team think it's a safe environment, and we can use that.'

The Admiral's patience was now exhausted.

'Just tell him the plan, for the love of God.'

Frobisher did just that.

'OK, here's what we're going to do. As I say, Parliament is a weak point. Once somebody has been vetted and gets a permanent photo-ID pass, they can move around the Palace pretty much at will. And, as with any other building, the cleaners are a point of vulnerability – they're never noticed, and they have freedom to roam.'

'So you're going to get a cleaner to shoot Clem?' Beaufort asked.

Frobisher snorted.

'Of course not. But we have identified an older Chagossian woman, Aurelie Barcoult, who is livid with Clem for selling out her island home to the Mauritians. Her son is in prison in Port Louis for agitating for Chagossian independence. She is nearing retirement age anyway, and we can offer to help get him out of prison, plus a great deal of money to get the rest of her family over here.'

Beaufort was still unconvinced.

'But what precisely are you going to be asking this old cleaner woman to do?'

'We have "obtained" a portion of the Novichok used in the Salisbury poisonings from Porton Down. We're going to supply the cleaner with a small quantity in a nail varnish bottle. She will paint it on the brass corner bindings of the despatch box.'

'Isn't that dangerous. Couldn't it poison just about anybody?' Beaufort asked.

Frobisher responded confidently.

'We don't think so. We've studied Clem's performances in the House. Most ministers grasp the near corners of the despatch box for support, he's the only one who leans across and points at the leader of the opposition. And while his right hand is jabbing at her, his left hand grabs hold of the far-left corner of the box, or vice versa. We only need her to paint a small quantity on there, and if he touches it, he'll be dead in minutes.'

Beaufort had one last effort at objecting.

'Hold on just a minute. There would be a massive outcry, and a police and parliamentary inquiry. Won't the finger be pointed at us?'

The Admiral smiled.

'Of course we've thought of that. If necessary we can leak the tape of Weber plotting a coup and talking about Clem's assassination – it has the big advantage of being genuine, and it would stand up to forensic analysis. But the FSB are the obvious candidates as scapegoats. After all, it's their bespoke poison, developed over many years at their labs in Shikhany. As a clincher, it will be Tarakan himself who hands the poison over to the cleaner. Or at least that's how it will appear.'

At the mention of his father's name, Beaufort became more interested.

'And how are you going to get Tarakan to do that? Or how are you going to get it to appear that he has done it?'

The Admiral laughed, relieved that he had caught Beaufort's full attention, and that he was now sufficiently intrigued to want to know more about the plot.

'Simple. You will become your father. I am afraid we may have to shave your head, but a bit of posture training, a few cosmetic wrinkles, coloured contact lenses for your eyes, and a temporary tattoo should do the trick. When the cleaner is traced – and she will be traced – the only thing she'll remember are the different-coloured eyes, the bald head and the tattoo. Even the cash we'll be giving her was "confiscated" from the slush fund of an FSB agent we caught. Tarakan will get the blame, the Little Tsar will go berserk at this unauthorised hit, and we might finally see the back of him once and for all. Two birds, one stone.'

As Frobisher and Beaufort stood up to leave the latter asked:

'But sir, if Clem Clark goes, who will take over?'

The Admiral laughed once again.

'Have you read House of Cards?'

Beaufort responded enthusiastically.

'Of course, sir, everybody has. Brilliant book.'

'And what was Francis Urquhart before he manoeuvred himself into becoming prime minister?'

Realisation dawned on Beaufort's face.

'The chief whip.'

CHAPTER 63

DOWNING STREET, WHITEHALL

The Admiral had been granted very few one-to-one meetings with the prime minister. That was one of his biggest problems with the Labour government, from his point of view. The PM continued to admire Dame Sheila Norris, and to trust Box, whereas he disliked the Admiral and distrusted the Firm.

Three weeks after their talk in the grounds of Chequers, Clem Clark invited the Admiral to Number Ten. He was shown straight through to the White Drawing Room.

Clem was all bonhomie.

'Ah Admiral, good to see you. Sherry? Whisky? Perhaps a tot of rum?'

It occurred to the Admiral that the PM was either bending over backwards to be hospitable, or mocking his naval background.

'Thank you, Prime Minister. Whisky will do very well.'

The Admiral sat on the sofa and Clem Clark poured two whiskies, handing one to the spy chief. Having taken a short sip, the PM cut to the chase.

'Well, Admiral. You asked for a month to consider my proposition, and we're nearly four weeks on. What is your thinking? About the peerage?'

The Admiral took a sip of his own whisky, buying time, and building up the tension.

'Well Prime Minister, if the deal is still on the table, I'll take it. I will retire and take the title of Lord Carr of Dartmouth, where I graduated from the Royal Naval College. I recommend you appoint my deputy Frobisher as interim chief. He'll oversee the transition.'

'Splendid,' the Prime Minister enthused. 'I'll clear your elevation with the Palace today, and make a statement to the House tomorrow. And of course we can forget all about that unfortunate business in Brussels.'

The Admiral nodded, rose, and shook the hand of the man he intended to have killed.

CHAPTER 64

CRAWLEY, WEST SUSSEX

The elderly and ailing Chagossian Aurelie Barcoult lived in a small council flat in a tower block in Crawley. Much of the UK's small Chagossian community had gravitated there because of its proximity to Gatwick Airport. Most of them hoped to return to their homeland one day.

Beaufort was dropped off a discreet distance away by one of MI6's fleet of black cabs. He was wearing the nondescript dark clothing favoured by Tarakan, and a navy-blue Lenin cap.

He had managed to avoid having to shave his head. Instead, the make-up artists who had aged him had provided a prosthetic bald cap. He had non-prescription tinted contact lenses in, to emulate his father's different-coloured eyes, and a temporary tattoo of a cockroach crawling up the left side of his neck. He affected the limp his father walked with, and carried a cheap canvass satchel over his shoulder.

As a precaution against the lethal poison he was carrying Beaufort wore rubber surgical gloves, beneath thick black leather ones. The gloves also hid the fact that, unlike

Tarakan, he had a full complement of fingers.

He pressed the bell for the cleaner's flat, and affected a faint Russian accent when a voice over the intercom asked his identity. He used Tarakan's old trade name of Ivan Ivanov and, since she was expecting him, she buzzed him in. He made no effort to avoid the CCTV cameras in the hallway, and took the urine-smelling lift to the 12th floor.

The woman's flat was tiny, but warm and neat. A prominent cross and a cheap print depicting Jesus feeding the five thousand proclaimed her faith.

'Come in,' she said to Beaufort, in a heavy Creole accent. 'Shall I call you Ivan? Would you like tea?'

Beaufort removed his Lenin cap, revealing his prosthetic bald head. Aurelie noticed this first, and then her gaze was drawn to the cockroach tattoo.

'Yes, call me that, but no tea.'

Beaufort delved into his satchel.

'Here is the bottle. Handle it with great care, and always wear rubber gloves when you do. Also wear a mask too, just as an extra precaution. Here is a pack of medical-grade Covid masks you can use.'

'Yes, we always wear gloves at work. And I sometimes wear a mask on public transport, and at work too, if there's Covid or flu going around.'

Beaufort moved a step closer, and locked his gaze on the Chagossian woman. He noted with satisfaction that she flinched at the sight of his artificially heterochromatic eyes.

'When you clean the Commons Chamber, are you alone?'

'No, it's a big area. My friend Jenna and I do it together. She's from Barbados. We take one side of the Chamber each.'

'OK, make sure that you do the government side, to the left as you face the Speaker's chair. When your friend isn't looking, brush the lacquer from the bottle onto the brass corner fittings on the far side of the despatch box – the large wooden box. Be sure – it must be the far side only.'

Beaufort took out his mobile and showed her a photograph of the Commons Chamber, and then a close-up of the despatch box, pointing out the brass corner fittings.

'OK I understand. What do I do with the bottle after that?'

'Reseal it carefully, and after your shift ends put it in the rubbish bin by the statues of the Burghers of Calais in Victoria Tower Gardens. Do you know where I mean?'

'Oh yes, I walk past it often. In summer we sometimes have our sandwiches there. What will it do to this man Clark? Will it kill him?'

'No, but it will make him ill, so he has to resign. Then your islands can be saved from the Mauritians.'

The elderly Chagossian seemed reassured by this answer.

'OK. And the money. I need it so I can bring my family over to the UK. Or I wouldn't do this thing.'

Beaufort handed over a thick brown envelope. It contained cash MI6 had confiscated from an FSB agent who had been caught trying to bribe a security guard at Hanslope Park.

'Here is £25,000, in British money. If you succeed, there will be the same again. My government, which is very powerful, will get your son out of the Mauritian prison, and your family will be able to come over here and look after you. You can retire and spend your final days with them.'

Aurelie Barcoult seemed pleased at this prospect. She

nodded, took the cash and placed it under the cushion of her battered armchair. She then put on a pair of rubber washing up gloves, took the nail varnish bottle, and slipped it into a zip-up plastic make-up bag.

'One more thing. Give me your mobile phone, please.'

The elderly woman looked around, and then remembered it was in her pocket. She handed it over. There was no pin code.

Beaufort added the name 'Ivan' to her contact list, and keyed in the number of a phone they had confiscated from the same Russian agent they had taken the money from.

'When it is done, just message me the one word – Hallelujah – then delete the message.'

'How do I delete a message?'

Beaufort showed her how to delete a message, and then decided to try and reassure her before leaving.

'Don't worry. Clem Clark is a wicked man. God will forgive you.'

She shrugged, only partially convinced, and showed him to the door.

Beaufort felt a pang of guilt at having deceived the old woman, but he was sure that his father would have been impressed by the impersonation of him.

As he waited in the dim hallway for the foul-smelling lift to arrive he decided that he wanted to be far away when the Admiral's plan came into fruition. Perhaps the West Indies, a world away from leaden London skies, hopefully with Sabina at his side.

He had fulfilled his mission, and now it was up to others to make sure that his efforts had not been in vain.

CHAPTER 65

HOUSE OF COMMONS, LONDON

Early the following morning Aurelie Barcoult clocked on as usual. She met up with her friend Jenna, and together they made their way to the Commons Chamber.

'Why you wearing that mask?' Jenna asked.

'I've had a bit of a cold. Don't want to catch anything worse, or spread it around.'

Jenna grimaced sympathetically, and took her vacuum cleaner to start cleaning the back row of the opposition benches.

Aurelie began polishing the enormous Clerk's Table with a yellow duster, careful to avoid moving the stacked leather tomes on parliamentary procedure that took up much of the surface.

She then moved on to the despatch box. Checking that Jenna's back was turned, she extracted the plastic make-up bag from the pocket of her tabard, and gingerly took out the bottle of nail varnish.

With nervous shaking hands, sheathed in a pair of surgical gloves underneath her usual Marigolds, Aurelie twisted open the top of the container. With the small brush attached to the bottle cap she daubed the viscous liquid over the brass fittings on both of the far corners of the despatch box.

At that point the supervisor came in and her clumsy gloved hands almost dropped the bottle. She hastily re-fixed the lid and stuffed it back into the big front pocket of her tabard, and began vigorously polishing the side of the despatch box, before moving back to the Clerks' table.

'Come on girls,' the cockney supervisor called out, 'get a wiggle on. We don't have time to sit around on our arses – not like these MPs!'

Both women laughed, and continued with their normal chores.

CHAPTER 66

VICTORIA TOWER GARDENS, WESTMINSTER

After the end of her shift, instead of exiting via the subterranean passage to Westminster tube station, Aurelie Barcoult headed south, towards the more distant Pimlico station. She nodded to the two policemen guarding Black Rod's entrance, and then, as she passed the entrance to Victoria Tower Gardens, turned left and entered the park.

As instructed, she located the Westminster City Council litterbin positioned just past the statue of the Burghers of Calais. Looking around to make sure she was unobserved, she reached into her tabard pocket, pulled out the plastic make-up bag containing the nail varnish bottle filled with deadly poison, and dropped it into the bin.

She then took out her ancient mobile and sent a text message to the strange looking bald man who called himself Ivan.

'Hallelujah', she sent. She tried to delete the message, but failed.

*

Heading for his favourite bench overlooking the Thames, Mac the homeless veteran paused to root through the litter bin. Finding the makeup bag, he opened it and discovered the bottle of nail varnish. Holding it up to the light he saw that it still had some lacquer in it.

Pleased, he stuffed it in to one of the bags on his trolley. It would make a nice present for Sharon, the middle-aged bag-lady he had been gently courting for several weeks.

*

Bryant, the MI6 chauffeur, arrived half an hour later in the Firm's Jaguar, and parked in the Abingdon Street car park. As instructed he headed for the litter bin by the statue. He lifted off the top, and pulled out the black branded Westminster City Council rubbish bag.

He tied the top of the bag and stuffed it in to the large sports holdall he was carrying for that purpose. Then he hurried back to the car, remotely opened the boot and loaded the sports bag inside.

He did not know what was supposed to have been in the bag. And he certainly did not know that it was no longer there.

CHAPTER 67

HOUSE OF COMMONS, LONDON

Later that morning the Commons annunciator screens flashed up.

'Statement: Prime Minister. Future of the Intelligence Services.'

As it was a Tuesday the statement would be at 12.30pm, following scheduled Transport Oral Questions.

Frobisher watched the proceedings on the Parliament Channel in a meeting room at Vauxhall Cross. The Admiral had managed to obtain a ticket for a seat in the Speaker's Gallery reserved for visiting dignitaries and VIPs.

Both of them watched carefully, willing the Transport Secretary, a young woman with prematurely grey hair, not to lean across or grasp the far corners of the despatch box. Fortunately proceedings were routine and calm, with no histrionics on either side of the House.

Ahead of the PM's statement the Chamber filled up, as did the Press Gallery. There had been no pre-briefing, but members of the lobby knew that something momentous was about to be announced. The PM rarely made oral statements in the House, and when he did, they usually followed PMQs on a Wednesday.

The transport secretary shuffled down the government front bench and the prime minister took her place.

The Speaker announced: 'Statement – the prime minister'.

Clem Clark rose from the Treasury bench and placed his red leather briefing folder, embossed with his title and the royal coat of arms, on the despatch box.

'With permission, Mr Speaker, I would like to make a statement on the rationalisation of our security and intelligence services. For more than a century there has been an unhealthy rivalry between MI5, the Security Service, and MI6, the Secret Intelligence Service. Over those years there have been endless territorial disputes, and a distressing lack of collaboration and coordination between these two services. Moreover, the costs of running two such organisations in parallel have been prohibitive. We therefore intend to merge MI5 and MI6.'

There was a collective gasp of astonishment around the Commons Chamber, and a flurry of activity in the Press Gallery as newsrooms were alerted.

At that point the leader of the opposition, Chloe Baverstock, half-rose and placed her right hand on the opposition despatch box, indicating her desire to intervene. Although it was unusual to accept an intervention that early in a statement the prime minister, in a confident and benevolent mood, resumed his seat, signalling that he was giving way.

'The prime minister, as ever, is not being straight with the British people. Isn't this, in reality, a takeover rather than a merger? Is this not a power grab by the prime minister's old university friend, Dame Sheila Norris of MI5? Will not the end result be a diminution of our ability to garner international intelligence? And will not this inevitably bring about a reduction in our capability to project our influence around the world, and defend ourselves against the ever-growing threat of the CRINK axis?'

Clem Clark rose in relaxed fashion and gripped the near side of the despatch box before replying.

'The Right Honourable Lady is entirely mistaken, as she so often is. This merger will enhance our capabilities, and reducing overheads will allow us to devote more resources to the front line. Moreover, the chief of MI6, Admiral Sir Richard Carr, is in full agreement with this proposal.'

The leader of the opposition again indicated her desire to intervene, to the sound of impatient groans from the government backbenches. Nonchalantly, the prime minister sat down once again.

'It is interesting that the Right Honourable Gentleman the Prime Minister should say that. Because this morning I received a letter from the Admiral, stating very clearly that he vehemently opposes this plan, and regards these proposals as being highly detrimental to our national security.'

Chloe Baverstock theatrically waved the letter, and resumed her seat.

MPs gasped at this stunning revelation, and the Press Gallery was in turmoil. Many MPs and journalists looked up at the Speaker's Gallery, where the Admiral had been spotted and recognised. He sat gazing impassively at the proceedings.

The prime minister, now visibly angry, stood up once again, determined to proceed with his statement, and not take any further interventions. In his fury he leaned across the despatch box, gripping the far corners with both hands, and then raised his right hand to jab his forefinger at the leader of the opposition.

'The Right Honourable Lady, with frankly astonishing naivety, has allowed herself to be drawn into the very factional fighting I referred to earlier. She does not have the vision to perceive that this initiative will enhance our national security. And if the chief of MI6,' he glared furiously up at the Admiral, 'cannot recognise that, then he will have to leave his post, sooner rather than later.'

The House erupted in 'hear hears' from the government benches, and cries of 'shame' from the opposition benches.

The Admiral remained impassive.

Clem Clark returned to his script, now moderating his tone.

'These proposals will not affect GCHQ, which has time and again proved its world-leading capabilities, and is in no need of reform...'

Then he seemed to lose his thread, and his speech started to become rambling, with the words emerging in random order.

'The descendants of the World War Two code-breakers at Bletchley Park carry that mantle forwards with pride, and set an example....an example...upholding the great traditions...Alan Turing...genius...'

The leader of the opposition looked amused, then confused, and then concerned. The chief whip and other cabinet ministers on the front bench exchanged worried glances.

The health secretary, sitting two down from the prime

minister, poured a glass of water from the carafe on the clerks' table and placed it in front of him. The PM grabbed the glass and gulped down the contents.

At first it seemed as though the water had restored him. He rallied, looked down, found his place in the prepared script, and loosened his grip on the despatch box in order to use his hands to emphasise his points.

'As I was saying, these proposals have met with almost universal approval within the intelligence community....'

Then, quite suddenly, he grasped his chest, and his handsome face spasmed uncontrollably. Clawing at the despatch box he held himself upright for another few seconds. His grotesquely protruding eyes rolled upwards, and locked with those of the MI6 Chief.

The eyes of the Admiral expressed not concern, not sympathy, but satisfaction. They were as cold as the gun barrels on an Arctic-bound warship.

In what looked like slow motion, as his colleagues reached out to try to support him, Clem Clark slid down onto the thick red line that ran the length of the Chamber's green carpet.

For all of two seconds there was silence. Only the prime minister's desperate gasps for air could be heard.

Then pandemonium erupted. In the Commons Chamber. In the Press Gallery. In the Strangers' Gallery. But not in the Speaker's Gallery.

The Speaker recovered from his shock to rise to his feet and roar:

'This sitting is suspended! Clear the galleries! Clear the Chamber!'

The Serjeant at Arms rushed from his miniature

transverse pew and started shepherding reluctant gawping MPs out of the Chamber.

Two of their number stayed behind. One was a still-practising GP, and the other a retired cardiologist. They moved the PM onto his back on the Treasury bench, and took it in turns to perform vigorous cardiac massage.

Five minutes later an ambulance screamed into New Palace Yard, and two paramedics rushed into the Commons Chamber. They took over the CPR, but it was soon clear that they were going through the motions.

Clem Clark's shirt was ripped open, and defibrillator pads affixed to his chest. Three times they shocked him, but although his limbs spasmed, his heart remained resolutely still.

*

Parliament, like most ancient institutions, has its history and its traditions. Being a royal palace, nobody is allowed to die within its precincts.

The convention is that anybody who does actually die on the premises is taken by ambulance the short journey across Westminster Bridge to Guy's & St Thomas' Hospital. There they are pronounced dead on arrival.

That was the case with Clem Clark. In reality, he had been dead for almost an hour. One might say he died the moment he offered the Admiral a Faustian pact.

EPILOGUE

The Breturn project died along with Clem Clark.

A massive investigation into his death was launched, led by the Metropolitan Police.

*

The cleaner Aurelie Barcoult was quickly identified as the prime suspect.

She was initially charged with murder. She turned King's evidence, and pleaded guilty to manslaughter. In her evidence she maintained that 'the bald man with the tattoo and the strange coloured eyes' had assured her the substance she smeared on the despatch box would only make the prime minister ill, not kill him.

*

A public inquiry was set up. It reviewed all of the evidence, including that thrown up by the police investigation, and eventually concluded that rogue elements within the Russian FSB were the source of the Novichok, and therefore almost certainly responsible for the assassination of Clem Clark.

Since the publication of the recent photograph of Tarakan leaving Tazmenistan matched Aurelie Barcoult's description of the man who had supplied her with the Novichok, suspicion fell directly on him.

Twenty-five FSB agents operating under diplomatic cover in Russia's London embassy were expelled, and the

Russian ambassador was summoned to King Charles Street for an unprecedented dressing down.

*

Bert Withers, Clem Clark's chief whip, took over as prime minister, having assured the Parliamentary Labour Party that he had never been in favour of the Breturn project.

*

Dame Sheila Norris resigned as soon as the findings of the inquiry into Clem Clark's death were published. MI5 had been heavily criticised for its failure to detect and foil the plot.

She was not made a Baroness, as several of her predecessors had been.

*

Edward Gore-Ewing, his Breturn dream shattered, resigned from the EU civil service, and spent his remaining days brooding in his wife's chateau. He drank himself to death on French Cognac.

*

Commission President Philippe Morand served out his full term, but never recovered his credibility, having staked so much of his reputation on the Breturn project.

*

Jennifer Bishop left Number 10 and took over the running of Beaufort Public Affairs. She changed the name to Bishop Public Affairs. The company prospered under her astute management.

*

Tarakan fled to his bolthole in Tajikistan, but was declared persona non grata by the new young president.

He was extradited to Russia, where he was locked up in the basement of the Lubyanka. He was tortured with great diligence and little mercy.

Despite the ferocity of the torture, and the desperation of the torturers to produce results, he never confessed to the assassination that he had not in fact commissioned.

Despite everything, as ever, he survived.

The Little Tsar sent him for his second stint in the gulag.

*

The itinerant veteran Mac and his girlfriend Sharon died of Novichok poisoning.

*

Admiral Sir Richard Carr received his peerage, and stayed on as chief of MI6.

Frobisher thrived under his patronage.

*

Sabina went to Israel, to study Krav Maga, the mixed martial art favoured by Mossad.

POST EPILOGUE

SIX MONTHS LATER

When Frobisher received the urgent summons, he hurried up the stairs to the seventh floor. He rushed into Ms Danso's office – looking at her and raising a quizzical eyebrow. She shrugged and rolled her eyes, before gesturing for him to go straight into the Admiral's office.

The chief stood staring through the window at the Palace of Westminster across the river. As soon as he heard Frobisher enter his office he turned and shouted:

'Where the hell is Beaufort?'

'We're not sure, sir, he took himself off just before Clem's, um, untimely death. Said he needed a break, and a change of scene.'

'Well bloody well find him and get him back here. We have a situation, and we need that bastard to sort it out.'

Frobisher nodded and beat a hasty retreat.

Here we go again, he thought.